WELCOME
TO
WITCHLANDIA

Welcome to Witchlandia

Steven Popkes

Book View Café

Also by Steven Popkes

Caliban Landing

Slow Lightning

Cover design by viknCharlie
Cover illustration © 2019 by Wendy Zimmerman
Published by Book View Café Publishing Cooperative
P.O. Box 1624, Cedar Crest, NM 87008-1624www.bookviewcafe.com

ISBN: 978-1-61138-821-3

As with all things, for Wendy and Ben.

Table of Contents

Copenhagen, 1926

The sun glared off the snow, shining the early November light into the room as if from a mirror.

Niels Bohr noticed when he walked into the light he felt noticeably warmer than when he walked into its shadow.

Werner Heisenberg stared outside the window without moving.

"You are taking it too hard," Niels said.

Werner waved his hand in the air, the smoke from his cigarette making spiral figures. "Schrödinger's 'visualization is not quite right'—he is correct in that, certainly. His visualization is crap."

"Werner," said Niels gently. "He has shown his wave equation and your matrix mechanics are equivalent."

"Crap."

"Did you read Von Neumann's paper?"

"Yes," Werner said shortly.

"He shows that both sets of equations can be shown to be equivalent in Hilbert space. Is that crap?"

Werner remained silent for a moment. "There is a fundamental problem. A presumption that there is *anything* there at all until it is measured."

"Yes. Even Erwin admits that."

"Then, we cannot know that which cannot be measured!"

"Yes." Niels thought for a moment. "But there is opportunity there."

Werner looked away from the window. "What do you mean?"

"It is true that we cannot know that which cannot be measured," said Niels casually. "But the corollary is also true: we *can* know that which *can* be measured."

Werner looked blank. "Yes."

"We can measure the speed of light to be a constant and the lensing of light in a gravitational field. Thereby, we can know relativity. We can measure the interference pattern of light and the activity of electrons. Therefore, we can know quantum mechanics."

"We can't know everything. Not everything can be measured."

Niels nodded. "I know. But let us remain with those things that can be measured."

"All right."

"Quantum mechanics and relativity are two independent views of how the world behaves. How we observe the universe determines what we will observe."

"Of course."

"There is an apparent contradiction between quantum mechanics and relativity. I am not saying this contradiction will stand, but it does stand now. There could, therefore, be other views of world behavior equally rigorous and compelling but with equally strong apparent contradiction as there is between relativity and quantum mechanics. A verifiable observation contradicting both quantum mechanics and relativity would require its own different view of the universe."

Werner stared at him. "What are you talking about?"

Niels paused for a moment and knocked the ash from his cigarette. "I must tell you about my mother."

Part 1: Katelin and David, 1994

Chapter 1.1: Katelin

"Katelin, there's a party over on the ball field tonight. Want to come?"

I shook my head, not looking up. "I have to study."

Sandy sat on my bed next to my desk. In our dorm room that was about the only place she could have faced me.

"Come on. It's Friday."

"And I have a forensics test on Monday. So what?"

She gave me *that look*. "And I'm writing a paper on live electron microscopy of tardigrades. So what? It's no sin to have fun."

Blonde, blue-eyed, quick as a jackdaw and curved to kill, Sandy didn't have much free time. She was one of those women who breeze through life. She worked hard enough to wreck the curve for the rest of us and then quit and had fun with her time. Me, I have to study to get my grades. I'm a hundred pounds soaking wet and need to work out to have a chest at all. Which I do—I want to be a cop and muscle mass counts for a lot when you're as small as I am. I liked Sandy all right—she was nice enough, kept her half of the room uncluttered. She was finishing her Ph.D. in physics improving electron microscopy for the world so we were never in the same classes. Why she decided to live in an undergraduate dorm I'll never understand. When we became roomies I figured she would be living the quiet life. She had a good head for math and liked to help me shop for clothes I didn't think I needed.

I looked back at her. I could see the evening spread out in front of me. Sandy would shortly be joined by her two girlfriends. They would spend the next three hours talking while sporadically getting ready. About nine, they'd leave and I'd get a blessed three or four hours of solitude until she returned, somewhere between tipsy and outright drunk. If she returned alone, and I was awake, she'd want to talk about the party. If I was asleep, she'd bump through the drawers getting ready for bed, giggling to herself and thoroughly waking me up. If she didn't come back alone, I'd go down the hall to the Resident Assistant and bunk out on the floor for the night. If Sandy didn't come home I'd go looking for her.

Better to declare defeat early and leave the field to the victor.

"I'll study at the library. Catch you later."

"Oh, come on, Katelin. Live a little."

I didn't answer. I put on my slicks, threw my notes and the textbook into my backpack, grabbed my stick—a beautiful Bianchi I had bought just last year—and started to head out the door when I remembered I'd forgotten my beeper. Columbia's not a big town. The Police Department isn't big enough to have its own staff of divers, boat captains and pilots. So, they take on flyers like me. It's similar to volunteer fire departments, except for the part about the fire.

"Go on," she said waving her hands. "Off to Witchlandia with you, then."

Witchlandia: Sandy's term for any place I went outside of her interest. Coined the day she met me since I am, by popular definition, a witch. Not that any sort of witch exists. Or could exist, since there is no magic but only as yet undiscovered physics. Not that—but never mind.

I stopped by the RA's room and claimed the floor study area so I'd have homesteading rights when I got back. Then I ran down the stairs muttering to myself. When I decided Sandy and I were the least difficult combination out of the choices handed me, I hadn't counted on so many *interruptions*.

I consoled myself. I could use the flying time, anyway.

Dobbs Hall is one of only two tall dorms on campus, and because Tabitha Purlin threw herself off the eighth floor balcony in 1992, the balconies were fenced over. I couldn't get outside until I'd gone all the way to the ground floor. I could have insisted on a roof access. Paranormals have odd rights. We have our own little clauses carved out of the Civil Rights and Americans for Disability acts. Comes from being useful, I suppose.

It gave me time to get my temper in check. Sandy was a good roommate in most ways. Like everybody else, she had her idiosyncrasies. I did, too. I strapped my helmet on.

The weather had turned cool an hour before but now it was downright chilly. I could feel it right through my slicks. The thin spandex wasn't much insulation. It was early March. I could smell impending spring in the air but it was going to have to fight through the mud to make it.

A stick isn't like a bicycle—there isn't much air resistance if you're properly trained. Once you wrap yourself in the bubble—or the envelope or the field; we use a lot of different terms for it—the air is still. Practically speaking there was no reason for wearing slicks at all. I could fly just as well in an overcoat—minus the weight issues, of course.

But bicycle tights look way cooler than galoshes when you're flying over people's heads. Besides, slicks are about the only thing my physique looks good in.

I settled into the seat—took a moment to admire the paint job. The summer before I'd started college I'd blown a month's worth of minimum wage on those golden flecks swimming in shocked violet. I checked the instruments and pulled the cover off the pitot tube in the front point—just long enough to stick out of the bubble. Got myself in the right frame of mind. I hovered about a foot off the ground to get settled, rose at an even hundred feet a minute and took off across campus, as pure of thought and bereft of machinery as Peter Pan.

Chapter 1.2: David

I was lying in bed staring at the ceiling. Misty made pictures out of the ceiling paint trying to make me laugh. Some of them were pretty good. Not bad for a delusion. Carl rapped on the door.

"David. You naked?"

"You wish."

He came in and sat down in the only chair in the room. "You should be so lucky."

I chuckled.

He didn't notice and looked uncomfortable. He was quiet for a minute. "You can stay here for as long as you want—"

I grimaced. I could guess what was coming.

"—but it's been a week."

"You've gotten some calls, I take it."

Carl cocked his head to one side. "You could say that."

"Who's called?"

He ticked them off on his fingers. "Conductor Senbein has graduated from threatening dismemberment if you don't let him immediately submit you to the Washington University Young Artists Piano Concerto Competition to eternal banishment if you don't at least return his calls. Meister

Eisenhart has expressed grave disappointment that after all his years as your teacher you could treat him this way."

"What about my dad?"

Carl shook his head. "He probably hasn't heard."

I nodded. My father was a fisherman out of Gloucester. He was likely far out in the Atlantic hunting swordfish.

"So," Carl said. "What happened?"

I didn't say anything. The room grew thick with awkward silence. "You know what happened," I said finally. "I finished the audition and Senbein called me back to have dinner with him. He told me he wanted submit me and I excused myself and left the building. I called you—it's not like I know anybody else in this state."

"That's what you did. But that's not what *happened*."

I knew what he meant. "I stopped breathing."

"Eh?"

"It *felt* like I stopped breathing." I looked at him. He was waiting for me. "I've been playing since I was four—since I went to the hospital. And always when I went to the well—"

"The well?"

I stared at him. "You must know what I mean. The place it all comes from. Whatever it is that turns a bunch of chords into music. The water. The air. The *oxygen* of the music."

"I know what you mean."

I looked away. "It wasn't there. Then, while I was playing for Senbein, it went away completely. When he said he wanted to submit me all I could see was concert after recital after concert where I felt like I was choking. I left."

Carl didn't say anything for a moment. "You do know that everybody has bad days. Sometimes the inspiration just isn't there."

"Why play, then?"

"To get paid, mostly." He chuckled. "Even when it's merely a mechanical exercise. You've been playing in contests for years. Surely, it was like that sometimes."

I shook my head.

"It's a rare gift to have uninterrupted passion for so long." Carl sighed. "But now it's time to grow up. You'll have good days and bad days. The show must go on."

"Maybe I should be a fisherman like Dad. He could probably use the help."

"Your father would skin me alive if I sent you back to the boat."

"That's because I'm not very good at it."

"No, it's because you're meant for different things. It's a sin to squander your gifts."

"Some gift."

"Yeah," said Carl sadly. "Some gift." He slapped both hands on his knees. "Well, then. The band is doing a mixer out on the ball field tonight. Big bonfire. Lots of girls. Want to come?"

The room seemed suddenly small and claustrophobic. I shrugged.

Carl sighed. He stood up and scratched his ear. "I grew up with Guillermo. I cosigned the note when he bought his boat. I've known you since you were born. I helped out when you went to the hospital. So I'm glad you came here. I'm happy to help." He stopped for a moment. "So listen to me about this. You don't get off this easy. You have something in you any one of us would kill for and that takes away your right to waste it. That's the way to end up a bitter old music teacher at a half-wit college who gets off playing in a nostalgia band."

"That doesn't sound so bad."

"The glamour fades after a while." He slapped my foot. "You know where the ball field is. Come if you want to."

I wandered downstairs after he'd gone. I saw he'd left the Liszt transcription of Beethoven's seventh symphony out near the piano—something he'd introduced me to years ago. I must have been nine when I first attempted it.

"Nice try," I said.

I was staring off the edge of the piano, past the Statue of Liberty lamp resting on the lid, through the window into the gathering darkness. I remembered he'd gotten it when we had all vacationed down at Coney Island.

I sat down at the piano and drew my fingers across the keys, gently, feeling the smoothness of the ivory. I didn't like Columbia. I didn't like Missouri. I didn't like Carl's house or the pollen-scented breezes. Not that I had anything against Carl—he'd taken me in when I needed him.

I leaned against the keyboard.

Misty turned the head of the lamp towards me.

"It's too pretty a night," she said. "Let's go out. It'll be fun."

"Hush," I said. I fiddled with the keyboard. The price of psychosis is inane chatter from inanimate objects.

"Come *on*, David. It'll be *fun*." She put on her deep sultry voice.

I put my hand over the lamp stand to shut her up. Lady Liberty grew a triple D cup size with hard little nipples. Startled, I let go. She was eyeing me lasciviously with a big silver-plated grin.

"Stop that."

Lady Liberty deflated like an old balloon. Then the lamp turned to me and winked. "Better?"

"Okay," I said. I grabbed my coat. A symbolic gesture of defeat as the heavy black buttons gave her something of mine to talk through should she be so inclined. She gets cranky when she's thinks she's been left at home alone. As if I could. I should write a book on the care and feeding of schizophrenic delusions. I looked at the buttons. "But don't make me crazy or I'll throw you in the river." The buttons smiled back.

"You're already crazy."

"Crazier."

But I liked that coat. It was a really nice black overcoat made from wool. Not so heavy it felt like wearing armor, but not so light you forgot it was there. A dress coat under which I wore my jeans and T-shirt. Deceit is part of appearance, I guess.

Then down the stairs and across the grass into the gentle air. Misty was right. It *was* a beautiful night.

Chapter 1.3: Katelin

Practice makes perfect, I said to myself as I came in a good thirty feet over the top of the library. I held it still in mid-air—*precision*, Sam had told me. The regulations say within fifty feet but don't settle for that. The stick had all the required aircraft instruments but I didn't consult them. I wanted to be able to hold it by sheer will. It's an important skill for a couple of reasons. The first is obvious. If you don't know where you are you could be history already. This is true for any aircraft. Besides, when you're flying around buildings, you don't have time to fly by the instruments.

The second is unique to witchflying—all right, I'll use the term. It's the only good one around. I could call it "psychokinetic object self-motivation" but I'd gag first. Witchflying is all about *psychology*. Human beings know they can't fly so they can't. But deep in their hind brains we're not so convinced that *other* things can't fly. And if other things can fly, why not a stick? Why not a stick under my control? It's like that old story about the high jumper not being able to jump his own height. But then, he thinks, if I can't jump my own height, why can't I jump *one inch over* my own height?

Even with that little self-conceit, if your mind isn't right, it's not going to work at all. It wasn't enough to know the instruments said your stick was five hundred feet in the air; you had to know your stick was five hundred feet in the air since it was your knowledge that was *keeping* your stick five hundred feet in the air. Remember, like every other civilized act, we're using brains evolved to throw rocks and gather berries, organs never intended for advanced math or levitation. The brain is built to use sight, balance and tactile information to track what's going on. Witchflying isn't any different than the uneven parallel bars or swinging on a trapeze. You have to know where you are.

I knew I'd never be more than a visual pilot—a really *good* visual pilot, but eyes only nonetheless. That's the limit of my ambition. There are perhaps five thousand people in the world that can lift themselves an inch off the ground on anything at all—broom, vacuum cleaner, Bianchi. Of that, maybe a couple hundred are really good pilots—I'm trying to be number 201. Of those, there are three who have the genius to witchfly on instruments. There used to be four, but last winter my old teacher, Sam Kozak, got lost in a snowstorm and pancaked on Mount Washington while looking for two kids who wandered off the trail. Pilots track their own.

I let myself down slowly until my feet were about six inches off the deck. Then, I pulled back the stick and set the tail down and stepped off. Sam would have been proud.

"Nicely done," came a voice in the shadows.

I twitched but didn't move more than that. "Are you stalking me, Arnie?"

Arnie laughed and came out into the light. "I suppose now you're going to tell my wife."

Arnie is built like a sideways brick wall. He's a security guard at the library and my jiu-jitsu teacher. He's about the nicest person on the planet you don't want to piss off. As far as I was concerned, he and his wife Mattie walk on water.

I pulled a towel out of the storage compartment under the seat and wiped down.

"Looks like you had a good workout."

"Slow flight is like a brisk walk. Fast is like a good run. Aerobatics hits you like wind sprints. Hovering, though. That's like doing isometrics. It's not really aerobic."

He looked down into the book compartment. "Forensics? Are you going to be a policeman, now?"

"Changed my major last year."

"You do keep your secrets, don't you? Just like your father. How is the Honorable?"

"Fine," I said shortly. "Legislature's in session and he's in Jeff City so life is good." I put the towel back and closed the compartment.

"I used to be a cop back in the day," Arnie said idly.

"I know."

"I'm still a volunteer EMT, you know. That's an honorable profession."

"I know."

"Tell me you're not studying to be a cop on *my* account."

"I'm not," I said.

"How come, then?"

"I met these pilots when I was up in New Hampshire at Sam's advanced clinic a year ago." I spoke reluctantly—I hadn't told anybody I'd changed majors. That was between me and my advisor. Dad didn't care as long as my grades were good and I didn't get in trouble. He didn't want the political liability. My older brothers didn't take much of an interest in me. Patrick was busy trying to shape his state rep's office into a run for the governor, and if it didn't shriek money or land trust, Matthew wouldn't notice it.

"Yes?"

"They're a team," I said quickly. "Left seat handles direction and forward velocity and right seat handles lift and altitude. But sometimes, they split off—they have this stick that can break apart into two solo units so they can come at a target from two different directions."

"Witchflyers, then."

"Oh, yeah. For the Philadelphia Police Department. Between the buildings, over the roofs at ninety knots and as silent as owls. I saw them practicing in the MOA over the White Mountains. They do surveillance and pursuit—it is the hardest, most challenging flying I've ever *seen!* I decided that's what I want to do."

"But you have to get a degree in enforcement."

"Right."

"Much is explained, then. You're here almost every Friday night." Arnie leaned against one of the cornices at the edge of the library roof.

"Forensics is pretty hard."

Arnie shrugged. "Even so, you're here every night you're not working at home in the dorm. You ought to get out some."

"You *have* been stalking me."

"Just observant. Not so many witches flying around in bicycle slicks that I can't pick you out. Since I met you I look up at the sky lot more. I heard there's a party on the ball field tonight."

When somebody sticks their nose into my business I'm usually right there to cheerfully tear it out by the roots. But I'd been in Arnie's class since I was a freshman. I knew his wife. I knew his daughter. I even knew he was just trying to look out for me.

"Arnie—" I tried—I really tried—to keep the growl out of my voice. I started, but he waved it away.

"Come on. Anita's downstairs. Mattie doesn't get off until ten and I don't get off until midnight." He shrugged. "You know Anita. She's going to sneak over there one way or the other. If she goes with you she won't get into trouble."

I hesitated. I'm not a complete stick in the mud. Even I like to dance once in a while. And Anita was fun as only a fifteen-year-old girl can be with someone who could still remember what it was like to be such a girl. Besides, I knew these parties. The drinking was sporadic until the proctors left at eleven. After that it got serious. Anita would be home and safe by then.

"Mulholland Smog is playing." Arnie grinned at me.

I liked Mulholland Smog. Sure, all of them were older than God and they played a mix of rock and blues older than they were. But they were really good at it. Last time they played this rocked-up version of "Crossroads" that could have brought the dead to life, dancing. "She'll want a pizza."

Arnie ponied up thirty dollars without a word.

I took the money. "Arnie, you have bought your daughter a good time."

Chapter 1.4: David

Misty would have known where the party was even if I hadn't. But she had her own route to follow. We went past Stewart Hall where she took me up to see the rattlesnakes. Misty wanted me to open the cases but I declined. I don't know when I heard about Stewart Hall's little zoo, but I must have heard about it at some point since Misty seemed to know all about it.

Then, we wandered over behind the biology building. Nobody was there so I just walked in and wandered through the greenhouses. It was safe enough, I suppose. All of the dangerous areas were marked with biohazard signs. In the horticulture section, one class had been making miniature ivy bonsais complete with tiny clay people. Misty got two of them in a fight but I straightened them out.

Out of the greenhouses, past the physics building to the experimental corn plots. I stood there and watched and, for once, Misty shut up. There is something strange and spooky about a cornfield. The way the stalks stand there, the tops fluttering over in the wind, the stalks straight up and ramrod stiff and the leaves rattling against one another like mechanical hands.

Behind the veterinary school and along the creek in the dark. I smelled the bonfire before I saw it licking the sky over the trees. I stumbled out of the woods into the ball field.

"Could we have wandered in the woods some more?" I muttered. "I didn't get enough poison ivy on me."

"Crybaby," Misty said. "You're here, aren't you?"

Carl's band had already set up but no one was on the stage. I saw Carl talking with some students in the crowd. I just stood in the shadow of the trees for a bit while I brushed the leaves from my coat.

"I don't like this coat on you," she said, opening the front. The three black buttons frowned at me. "It makes you look too self-contained."

"Never mind my wardrobe." I went out into the crowd to shut her up.

Carl and the rest of the band were getting on the stage. They started out with "Traveling Roadside Blues" so I knew the direction they were going tonight.

I crept up through the crowd so I could watch them.

Tony on piano and trumpet, Carl on bass, Emilio on guitar and sax, Narunha on drums. The wonderful secret about blues—rock, too, I suppose—is that you can do *anything* if it sounds good and keeps the beat. You've got a fair amount of leeway when you're playing Bach or Beethoven to lengthen the time to be more expressive or shorten it for emphasis. Every conductor does it. But in blues, that beat is coming in 4, 3, 2, 1, *now*. And if you're not on it to the millisecond, everybody in the world is going to know. Blues is musically simple. There's nowhere to hide.

I watched Carl and I envied him. Is this how you do it? Carl was rocking slow now, with "Little Queen of Spades," Emilio's gravelly voice dragging over the notes. Absolutely trivial compared with Carl playing the Kirchner cello concerto last year with the Saint Louis Symphony. I don't think I was the first to leap to my feet after he was done but I'm pretty sure I wasn't much past the tenth. *He* knew where the well was. *He* knew how to breathe.

Is it variety that does it? I've been playing the classical canons for years. I started competing when I was ten. Maybe I was burnt out. Middle-age fatigue coming early.

After "Queen," Emilio ripped into "Crossroads" and I realized they were going to do the Robert Johnson songbook. Carl and I had played Johnson together when he was still back in Gloucester. I looked at him and he was watching me. He motioned me to come up. Tony grinned and slid over and picked up another guitar.

I sat in front of the piano, frozen for a moment.

Misty winked the console at me. "Show them what you can do."

I slipped into the rhythm, backing up Emilio as he sailed away on the chorus, felt my way into the chords. I looked out into the crowd, misstepped, caught myself. Wondered what the hell I was doing here.

I saw this boy, say fifteen years old, dancing with a young girl. Could be fourteen. Just bouncing with the beat. What had I been doing when I was fifteen? I was living with Carl and studying with Meister Eisenhart. Carl didn't leave until I went to Paris. I didn't remember ever going out and just dancing.

So, I watched them, bounced on the keyboard right along with them. Carl and Emilio came in together with some sweet harmony. They stopped playing so I picked up Carl's part. Tony started clapping which left a hole where the rhythm guitar used to be. I picked up some of it. Narunha picked up the rest. That boy and his date were going *nuts*.

Then, came the chorus and Emilio nodded to me so I took it and it was just me and Narunha. I kept up the bass and rhythm with my left hand and let my right hand do what it wanted. The audience picked up Tony's clapping and we kept that going through two choruses. Then, first Carl took the bass back and Tony the rhythm. I took the chorus way, way up the keys and then brought it down to the bottom just in time for Emilio and Carl to pick up the vocal line. That's the way we took it home.

I leaned back, my fingers tingling. The crowd roared back. Carl grinned at me. I thought the boy and his date were going to make their hands bleed.

I'd found the well again.

Carl gave me a questioning look.

"How about 'Hellhound on My Trail'?"

"Sounds good to me."

He and I started the boogie together. I remembered like it was yesterday, like I was ten again:

And the days keeps on worryin' me
There's a hellhound on my trail
Hellhound on my trail
Hellhound on my trail

I looked over to the boy and his date but they had moved over to the coolers and were talking to this amazing blonde woman. Sister? Friend? I had no idea. She looked up and gave me this wicked smile. She left the boy and his date and sauntered over towards the stage. I almost lost my fingering. She had eyes you could drown in and if her face hadn't already been enough to launch a thousand ships the rest of her would have made up the difference.

We finished "Hellhound" and Emilio began "Kind Hearted Woman Blues." And just as quick as it came, the breath went away. I could keep the time and the notes but it felt no better than shoveling dirt. I motioned to Tony and slid back over so Tony could pick it up.

I slipped off the stage and she was waiting for me. "Hi," I said over the music. "I'm—"

"I know who you are," she said and gave me a slow glance over the rim of her cup. "You're David Sabado."

I nodded, stammering. "And you are?"

"Sandy Kohl," she said in a low voice. Dancing slowly, she drew me away from the stage.

Chapter 1.5: Katelin

Mattie got off shift at ten. Arnie didn't get off until midnight. The plan was for me to take Anita to the party, then walk over to the hospital to meet Mattie when she got off work.

I changed out of my slicks and put on a sweatshirt. We had pizza at Shakespeare's where she told me about this cute boy, Shawn, she was interested in at school, whether or not she was too old for rubber wrist bands and if she should get her tongue pierced. My matronly job was to feed her and take her dancing while keeping her out of trouble. I didn't expect any trouble since, unlike some girls her age, Anita actually looked fifteen. Nobody in their right or unperverted mind would be interested in her. I was there to account for anybody left over.

We walked up Ninth Street College Avenue and past the old gym to get to the ball field. The band was just finishing setting up the instruments when we got there so we just milled around. Anita looked for people she knew but didn't see any. This was an older crowd. Sometimes, I think the reason Anita likes me is I don't look that much older than she does.

The band went up on stage. I felt a little nervous. All the way over I'd been talking about Mulholland Smog. But the Smog can be heaven or hell. One night, they can shake the stage with some terrific blues or rip up the floor with rock and roll. Other nights, they'll play these ancient songbooks for bands known only to historians of trivia. One time they spent an entire fall afternoon playing the complete repertoire of Earth Opera and Giant Crab. They had to do both; the combined repertoire was too small for one set.

Tonight I could tell from the first chord we were in good hands.

Then, they brought up this big guy in a long black coat. He must have been six two. He had big shoulders and a block and tackle head. He had the biggest hands I'd ever seen. He sat at the piano like he didn't know what it was. The light fell on his face and his dark eyes seemed to glow.

Anita was dancing by this time so I joined in. The big guy started playing and it was like the whole band picked it up a notch just on account of him. Anita and I really threw ourselves into it. I looked up and he was watching me. *He's playing right to me.* And the band cranked it up again. *Anita's glowing. I'm sweating like a pig. And he's* still *watching me.*

So I danced back right at him. I have to say he looked pretty good. I don't normally think much about men but I realized I was thinking about him. I could get used to him.

The song ended and the band rolled right into another one but I was thirsty. Anita wanted an ice cream so we went over to the coolers. Sandy was there.

"Do you know who that is?"

"No," said Anita from my elbow.

"That handsome man is David Sabado. He's from Boston. I heard him play for the Washington University Chorale last Christmas. He's really, really good."

She grinned past me up to the stage. I looked back and he wasn't looking at me anymore. He was handing off the piano back.

"He's ferocious." Anita was still breathing hard from dancing.

"I hope so," said Sandy and glided away from us.

Like a barracuda sliding noiselessly over the reef, Sandy slipped around people she didn't know and gracefully avoided entanglements with those she did. Sandy could charm the fangs off a rattlesnake if she wanted to. I admired her the same way I would admire a tiger stalking a gazelle. Sandy drew David off into the darkness as I watched, standing with Anita.

I felt a little bereft for a moment. Then, I shook my head. Anita was right here. David wasn't much more than a pretty face with magic musical fingers. I'd never see him again.

Anita and I stayed for another hour. By then it was close to ten. We walked back across campus and I delivered her to Mattie.

After that I felt at loose ends. I rode my stick back to the library roof to brood. Brooding is good for a twenty-year-old girl. Cleans out the soul.

But Arnie was waiting for me. Seems Mattie didn't like the way I looked and decided Arnie should look after me.

Which is how I ended up over at Terry's little apartment on Paquin Street about one in the morning.

Arnie ran the jiu-jitsu class, but Terry had started it years ago and given up control of it to Arnie since Arnie was a second dan black belt and Terry only had a brown. But then

Joe came to the university from Okinawa with a third and outranked the both of them. This is how a little self-defense class with barely nine students can have three teachers. Go figure.

Now, the four of us were sitting in the little terrace behind Terry's apartment. The terrace was surrounded on three sides by this ornamental brick wall. It was still cold but we were stubborn. If it took sitting in the cold to bring on summer, we were willing to make the sacrifice. They were drinking beers. I stayed with Coca-Cola. The FAA takes a dim view of drunken pilots. It's one of the few things that can cost you your license.

After about three beers, Joe said, "A new bartender at the Boone Tavern asked me if I could break boards."

"Yeah," said Arnie. "I get that, too."

Terry nodded. "I used to break two-by-fours."

"I can do that," agreed Arnie.

"Ever do bricks?" Joe looked around the terrace.

"Sometimes." Terry finished his beer and popped another one.

Arnie reached down and brought up a loose brick. He stared at it a moment. "I bet I can break this brick."

"Okay," said Terry. "I'll bet you a beer."

Arnie took the brick and put it on the top of the terrace wall. Everyone fell into a respectful hush. Arnie concentrated on the brick for perhaps a minute, then, with a sudden yell, brought his hand down on it. Arnie held up his hand and stared at it.

"Son of a bitch," he said, looking at the brick and then back at his hand. The brick was unscathed.

"Let me try," Terry said.

About ten minutes later, all three of them stood next to the table with their right hands in the same bucket of ice, each

32

muttering to the other. Arnie's hand was only dislocated but Joe's was broken. Terry said he wasn't sure but thought he'd be able to tell better when the swelling stopped.

"What the hell's that thing made of?" Joe shook his head.

I picked up the brick and threw it against the wall with all my strength. The brick was unscathed.

"I don't know. Think any of you could break that brick with your head?" I felt disgusted with the three of them.

"I believe I can drive," Terry said a low voice. "It might be a good thing for the three of us to go over to the ER."

Arnie nodded. "It's a good thing Mattie's off now."

I left them working out the logistics. I was angry at all of them. I was angry at David Sabado for going off with Sandy and angry at Sandy for pursuing him. I was angry at myself for being angry. Jesus, things sucked right then.

Witchlandia: my warm and cozy little corner of the world.

Chapter 1.6: David

When a woman wants you it's a gift, I thought drunkenly as we danced. Any woman. But when this woman wants you, it's a miracle. Men display, deceive and preen, but it's the women who choose.

Sandy pushed her head off my shoulder and looked me straight in the eyes. I felt as if I had been bludgeoned, tongue-tied and drooling. If she were to push against me, I would fall. She wanted me. I was certain. She would stop dancing with me any minute and leave me cold. I was certain.

She pulled me over to the coolers and grabbed two Cokes and poured out half of each. From her purse she took a flask and refilled the bottles. Sandy handed me one bottle and took a drink from the other. She looked up at me and smiled gaily. "Let's go for a walk."

We necked in the woods leaning against a grand and ancient oak. Walked behind the stadium and then hid in the bushes on the bluff over the creek where we nearly managed to pull off everything but our pants. Sandy held me off, grinning. "Impatient boy." She pulled her shirt back on, twirled her bra in the air and threw it down into the water.

I was past caring. I would have followed her anywhere. Done anything. Her skin tasted of talcum and sweat. Her eyes glittered. Her skin was soft and fluid to the touch, warm, mercuric. We drained our Cokes together.

"Time to go home," she said, suddenly rising.

I was stricken. Was she going to leave me now?

Instead, she reached down and hauled me to my feet. "Don't think you're getting off that easily. You're coming with me."

The two of us leaned against the elevator walls and each other on the way up to her floor. I cupped my hand around her breast and she nestled her head against my shoulder.

It took both of us to navigate the hall to her room. She giggled as we entered the room and fell on her bed. Again we nestled together. The room was quiet. All I could hear was her breathing. The sound deepened.

I realized: *she's passed out.*

"Take her anyway," Misty said.

Misty so startled me I almost fell out of the bed. I rolled off the bed onto my knees, staring at Sandy.

"Come on," Misty wheedled. "It's not like she didn't want you. It'll be interesting."

I shook my head and the room spun. There was a sour taste in my mouth. I didn't know exactly where I was right then but I knew I needed to find a bathroom quick. I guessed at the door and ran through. There was a toilet at the far end. I had barely enough time to raise the lid and bury my head inside before everything I had drank or eaten in the last twelve hours came pouring out.

Afterwards, I leaned my head against the porcelain rim and just lay there. When I thought I could, I staggered to my feet and looked around. The bathroom was shared, apparently, between two dorm rooms. I cleaned up after myself, washed my face and rinsed my mouth out. I looked in the mirror. I hadn't stained my clothes anywhere too obviously. Even so, I could still smell myself.

Nothing kills romance like puking in the middle of the night.

I crept silently back into Sandy's room. She was still asleep. I stood over her, watching her breathe. She really was beautiful—it hadn't been a product of my drunken imagination. But now, unconscious, she was no longer so compelling.

I pulled my clothes together and found my shoes. Dressed, I stood again over her.

I didn't think about doing anything while Sandy was unconscious. But I *did* think about waking her up or at least waiting until she woke up on her own. After all, she was beautiful and I was male.

Misty didn't say anything.

No, I decided. I would remain uncompelled.

"Noble," Misty said. "Very noble." Pause. "Pussy."

Of course, I thought, wearily.

I quietly left the dorm room and walked down the hall towards the elevator. But I was still unsteady on my feet. I sat down and rested in the floor's common room.

"What does it say about you that you won't take free sex from a beautiful woman?" Misty said from the piano on the other side of the room. She made the keys ripple like water in a breeze.

"Stop it," I said wearily.

"Of course, you were more than willing while she was awake."

"I was drunk."

"Do you need an excuse? You know, it's more than likely she'll wake up just as interested as she was when she fell asleep. She hasn't woken yet. You could still go back. No one would ever be the wiser."

"Go back smelling of vomit and whisky? No thanks."

"So are you concerned about your appearance or worried about your performance?"

Suddenly angry, I ran over and raised my fist. I was going to strike the piano. Either the wood or my hands would break. Either way, I would be free.

When did I start to think of the piano as my master?

I slid onto the bench and leaned against the lintel. I rested my hands on the cool ivory. What was I going to do?

Live. Breathe. Get through the day. But I wanted something *more*.

I could almost hear Carl's voice: "You're not a kid any longer."

I shrugged, sullen as an eight-year-old.

Well, then, I said to myself. *Didn't I feel* something *tonight? Well, then. It's not completely lost, is it?*

Maybe not, I thought. I straightened up and rested my hands on the keyboard. Maybe I could recapture it. I tried the Mussorgsky Promenade—softly. It was still late. I was the only soul awake on the floor.

Nothing.

"Okay," I said to myself. *Clair de Lune*—like Philippe Entremont used to play it, that deft touch that so drew me to the piece. A glimmer but nothing more. One after another, I tried pieces I'd always loved. Pieces I'd struggled with just to feel them spin out from under my fingers. Where once they felt like fire, now they were barely glowing, all of them.

I stopped. Maybe there was nothing left.

"Excuse me?" came a voice from the hall.

I looked over and saw the kid I'd been playing to that night. *Curious*, I thought. *What's a boy too young to shave doing here?*

"You left the dance with my roommate," he said in a low fierce voice. "Is she all right?"

Roommate? I looked at the boy and my mind danced a quick jig of reorientation: that was no boy.

"Oh," I stammered. "She's fine. She's asleep. I'm David."

She nodded. "David Sabado. Piano prodigy. I heard. I'm Katelin. Sandy's roommate." She looked at me for a moment. "Wait here." She disappeared for a moment.

I looked at my hands. Maybe it would remain intermittent. Growing ever more rare until one day I would realize it was gone forever. Wonderful. Puke in the middle of the night instead of having the most beautiful woman I'd ever seen and fail at music. Both in the same night.

She returned. For a moment, she watched me. "I guess you're harmless."

"Completely." *You'll never know how much*, I thought bitterly.

Chapter 1.7: Katelin

I stalked halfway across campus before I calmed down. *Why are you so upset?* I kept asking myself. *Three guys get together. They maim themselves. Where's the surprise?*

Face it, I told myself. *You're not angry at any of them.*

You're so smart; who am I angry at? I asked myself. When you're having a conversation with yourself, you may as well take the opportunity to actually find something out.

You're pissed Sandy got there first.

I stopped dead in the quadrangle. "*What?*"

The sound of my own voice startled me. I looked around. There was nobody nearby to hear.

I thought about David playing the piano. Sure enough, I was actually *interested* in him. Fancy that.

I shrugged. It's not like I actually had a clue as to what kind of person he was. I thought he looked good. He played well. He watched me while I danced. Not much to go on. It must not take much to get me interested if I was so inclined. Not that I was so inclined very often. Not in years, as a matter of fact. Not since high school.

Subdued, I walked the rest of the way to the dorm.

Coming out on our floor, I heard the sound of a piano. Great. He's serenading her. Just what I need.

But he was playing by himself, rolling through one snatch of music after another. He looked bad, too. Not hung over—though you could see that in his face. He had that sallow look people with a little pigment get when they're sick or they don't get out much. A sort of grimness around the jaw and lips. I wondered if he had a Spanish family. Sabado sounded Spanish. But this was more than the after-effects of alcohol; he looked haunted.

What had happened to Sandy?

"Excuse me?" I asked. Then, I told him to stay put. Sandy was snoring. She'd wake up cheery and smiling, I supposed. She always did after she took somebody home.

I returned to the common room, told him he was off the hook. I was going to tell him to either go back to Sandy's room or get the hell out of here. There was no need for strange men to be on the floor. But I thought better of it.

We looked at each other for a moment. He still looked good to me but Sandy had got there first and I wouldn't try to pick up the pieces later—I had a little pride, after all. But I didn't want him to leave just yet.

"I really liked the way you played tonight," I said. Lame. Very lame.

He nodded.

"I can't play anything." *Shut up. Just shut up.*

He looked up at that. "You just never learned."

"I'm about as tone deaf as they come. I'd never be able to learn it." I didn't know what I was saying—*just leave*, I told myself. *You're embarrassing yourself.*

"Anybody can play the piano."

"Yeah. Right. Anybody can get up on that stage and do what you did."

He shrugged. "I didn't say that. That takes a long time and a little talent. But anybody can play the piano and make music. That's nothing special."

"All right," I said, irritated. I'll call your little game. "Show me," I said.

He looked startled, then scooted over. "Okay."

I leaned my stick against the wall and came over, a little smug to see him surprised and then a little scared that he had agreed.

He thought for a minute. "Did you ever hear the theme from the Ninth Symphony?" He hummed a little of it.

"Maybe," I said guardedly.

"It's easy. A child of three could figure this out."

He picked up my right hand—instant *shock* and for a moment I couldn't breathe. I had expected his hand to be weak, somehow. Loose. Flabby. Like he'd never worked a day in his life. Instead, it was thin and strong and utterly controlled. He placed my hand on the piano with a gentler touch than I could have imagined. Heck, for a second I think I would have let him put it on a hot stove.

"Here," he said. "E-E-F-G-G-F-E-D-C-C-D-E-E-D-D." For each note he named, he pushed a finger down to make the sound. What do you know? I was playing music.

"So, this is all there is to know about playing the piano?"

He grinned at me and chuckled. "Mostly. And a lot of practice."

I liked that grin. I liked the way his hand felt.

I pulled my hand away. *Don't get attached,* I told myself. "Your folks must be proud."

He fiddled on the keys for a moment and looked up at me sideways. "You should know."

"Beg pardon?"

He nodded next to the piano. "I know a stick when I see one. You're a witch. Can't be more unique and special than that."

"You don't know anything about it."

David shrugged. "Fair enough."

Something in the way he just let it go pissed me off, as if it was okay to poke at me and then walk away. Like half the people I've ever met. Like my brothers. Like my father. Like Sandy. "My dad ran for governor in 1984."

He stopped playing for a moment. "Governor?"

"Yeah. Representative democracy. Separation of powers. We're giving it a try now that they've worked the bugs out of it back east." I caught his eye. He was looking at me now. *Really* looking. "I was ten years old. He was dragging me all over the state—my brothers were older and campaigning on their own for him. But nothing makes photo opportunities like a little girl. In fact, his *handlers* thought that I was too old. They thought it was fortunate that I was small for my age and dressed me like I was six."

"Sounds like…"

"Oh, it was *fun*. People like to *kiss* little kids. Especially, kids of politicians. I was coached, trained and ordered to stand still and *smile* when they did it. Reporters asked me what I thought of my father running for such a big office. I had three or four responses for that, all written out and memorized." I let my voice drop to a whisper. "But I had a secret. I could ride my bike down the street and lift it up a whole foot in the air before it came down. I could keep it there, too. I tried it every chance I could get and one day a reporter saw it." I leaned towards him. "You see, we're not entirely enlightened out here. I mean the aptitude tests are voluntary, and a whole lot of people don't let their children take them. After all, the Baptists and Church of Christ people aren't so keen on witches. Not so sure we really should be covered by the Civil Rights Act or if the government should be even testing for it. After all, they teach evolution in schools, right? Who's to say what those aptitude tests are *really* testing for. It cost Dad the primary. It almost cost him his seat in the Senate, but he rallied. After all, it's an American ideal that I be treated just as if I was as good as everybody else."

David was silent for a moment. "I was just returning the compliment."

"What do you mean?"

He gave me a long sad look. "You said something nice to me and I was saying something nice back to you. Something folks from back east like to do."

"Witch is not a nice word."

"I'm from Gloucester."

I stared at him. "What does that mean?"

He gave me a look I couldn't interpret. "It's about eight minutes from Salem."

Light dawned. The Salem Conclave. "I get it." Crap. I'd ripped into him for no reason at all. *Great, Katelin.*

"Yeah. They practice for the games right over the harbor."

"I know." It made me remember flying with Sam over the water. Sam had been from up there, too. "I'm sorry."

He looked at me and it was gone. He'd just let it go. He wasn't angry at me or hurt—it was as if in the great scheme of things my blowing up at him was not so big.

Usually, when I burnt a bridge there wasn't much left but a greasy streak floating on the water. Not having charred embers to rely on was a new experience and I wasn't sure what to do next. "You might have seen me flying, then. I've been to the Conclave. Once, anyway."

"Maybe," he said at last. "I left Gloucester twelve years ago. You would have been six?"

"Twelve years ago I would have been eight. But I was out there just last year."

He turned back to the piano.

It was a little thread of connection but I wanted to keep it going. "How old were you when you started piano?"

He chuckled like I'd said something funny. "They had a piano in McLean's."

"McLean's in Belmont?"

"The same."

Even I had heard of McLean Mental Hospital—Boor and Miegle did most of their work there. "You're a paranormal? What kind? What were your scores?"

"Witch? Me?" He laughed out loud. "No. I'm just a run of the mill psychotic."

He used the word as if he were talking about a tomato or an onion. "Excuse me?"

He played a series of descending chords I recognized. "Rhapsody in Blue," I said. "My dad played that on the stereo when I was a kid."

He nodded. "When I was seven, I had imaginary playmates."

"Don't most kids?"

"Mine wanted me to burn down the house next door." He made a chord that sounded so sad it could make you weep. "So they sent me to the hospital. I was an inpatient there for three years. Outpatient for another four. Gerald wanted to blow things up. Amanda liked fire. Donald kept telling me to steal things."

"You don't act crazy."

"I'm a very well-adjusted psychotic." He slipped into that long soft section in the middle of the Rhapsody, that part that feels like you've been wrapped in a blanket. "Turned out I was actually gifted. Came as a surprise to my folks—Mom's a nurse. Dad's a fisherman. But they made sure I had teachers in Gloucester. Finally, Carl heard me play—he used to live up there. He's known Dad since before there were boats. He put me in touch with Meister Eisenhart and I moved to Boston. Then, I studied in France." He saw my blank stare. "Carl Spotts? Bass player for Mulholland Smog? Teaches cello in the school of music?"

"How did he end up here?"

"I have no idea. It happened while I was in Paris. How about you? What are you doing here?"

"I'm from Jefferson City. Columbia is practically my home town."

He glanced up at me. "What's keeping you here?" He nodded at the stick. "You could likely study anywhere. It's not that common a talent."

"Neither is playing the piano," I said hotly.

He stopped and looked at me curiously. "I just complimented you again and you got angry."

"No, I didn't."

"Ah, I see." He didn't say anything for a moment but just kept playing Gershwin.

After a while, I calmed down. I felt stupid about getting mad—he hadn't actually said anything wrong. There was just something about him that got under my skin.

He kept playing Gershwin and I sat next to him and listened. It came to me his playing stood in for his apology even though he didn't really have anything to apologize for. It felt cozy. After a few minutes, it felt too cozy.

"Well, it's been a night," I said. "I'd better get on to bed."

I stood up and he looked up at me, suddenly sad. I remembered he'd just been sleeping with my roommate and got pissed off all over again. How many women were enough for him?

"You'd better go. There shouldn't be any strange men in the dorm this time of night."

He started to speak but then nodded. "Good night."

I stood in front of my door and watched as he got on the elevator. If he was gone, there was no reason not to sleep in my own bed.

Sandy was sitting up when I came in. "I saw you out there. Did you like him?"

I stared at her. Was I the only woman in this entire damned dorm that thought about something other than sex? "Should I have brought him back for you?"

Sandy shook her head. "No. It would have been nice, but I passed out. Of course, if *you* like him—"

"Not at all. You can have him."

She lay back in her bed. "I don't think he really fancied me or he would have stayed. It would have been nice to have a little piece of him. But that's the way things go, sometimes."

"A piece of him?"

She turned on her side. "That's the interesting thing about men. When you have sex with them you own a little piece of their heart afterwards. A small bit that they can never give to anyone else ever again."

"What a twisted idea!"

"Isn't it?" She clapped her hands. "I got it from this evangelist that tried to convert me years ago. Just think: Someday, when David Sabado is playing in some great concert hall, he'll think about our one night and the mixture of regret and sadness and joy will just come pouring out." She sat up. "At least, it would have if we hadn't drunk so much."

"So his heart is intact."

"Well, *I* didn't break it, anyway. The most we did was make out a little. Maybe *you* did something to him."

"Not likely."

"You talked to him longer than I did."

"Too long, I think."

She pointed towards the door at the other end of the room. "And *I* think he puked in the bathroom. I haven't had the courage to look."

Did it make any difference to me that they hadn't actually had sex? That he had left? I had no idea.

I didn't say anything. I just turned off the light. Whatever mystery awaited us in the bathroom could keep waiting until morning.

Chapter 1.8: David

Of course she was angry with me. She had every right to be. She thought I had just had sex with her roommate and now I was coming on to her.

Did it actually matter that I hadn't done anything with Sandy? I had in fact wanted to, for a while at least. My reasons for leaving while Sandy was still asleep were obscure to me, much less anybody else. It wasn't as if my body wasn't ready to go for it. It wasn't as if Sandy wasn't about as beautiful a woman as I would ever be likely to meet. Even so, the idea gave me a queasy feeling—I felt compelled by that beauty. Still, Sandy had been willing—enthusiastic, even. I could have woken her up or waited.

I had a sudden image from high school biology: the decapitated praying mantis mindlessly humping as the female chowed down on his head. Was I *afraid* of Sandy?

Maybe, I thought while I waited for the elevator to reach the ground floor. Maybe the compulsion of physical beauty was something I didn't want. And where did Katelin come into this? I felt stricken by her poor opinion of me at the same time I felt relieved to be away from Sandy.

I had mistaken her for a *boy!* I rubbed my forehead.

"Maybe you're gay," suggested Misty from the elevator switchboard. "Not that I would care, you understand."

"I'm not gay." How could I have mistaken her for a boy? She was *obviously* a woman.

"Of course, you would say that if you were in denial," Misty said.

"I'm not gay."

"Is it that important one way or the other?"

I didn't answer.

As I left the dorm I was as angry and cramped as an old man.

The weather had changed outside. It had warmed and the air had grown close and thick—clammy, almost. There was no wind. It felt as if a fat man had sat down on the town.

I looked around. It was a little past midnight, now. Should I go back to Carl's? Back to the party?

To hell with all of it. I picked a direction at random and started walking. I'd end up somewhere or I wouldn't.

Past the lights. Past the unlit stadium. Past what looked like an inflated balloon over a swimming pool. Past a square building wreathed in suspicious steam. Up the hill and past the shopping centers until I reached the clear outskirts of Columbia. The road divided. Up to now, the road had run north to south but now an east/west decision had to be made. The sky was gray, low oppressive clouds hung overhead. I chose west: in the direction of the setting sun, California and Japan. Maybe if I hurried I'd get there by morning.

"Not likely," sniffed Misty.

"You have no faith."

A cool wind started to blow from behind me.

"Being gay might have its comforts. Especially if you're attracted to women."

"Will you *shut up* about that?" I said savagely. "I can't be gay. I like Katelin."

Misty thought for a moment. "Of course, if you *were* gay and you met a girl you liked, your subconscious might trick you into thinking she was a boy."

I barely heard her. I liked that girl. I liked her when I saw her dancing—boy or girl, there was something about her that attracted me. Something beyond hormones and a cute figure.

What? I thought. *Do you like a girl* because *you don't think she's pretty? Now* there's *a secret you'd have to take to the grave. If it were true.*

"She looks pretty good, actually, David," Misty interrupted. "For a girl, I mean."

She did, didn't she? With that huge smile erupting out of those thin, pursed lips and the eyes that locked on you like laser sights one moment and then melted into sharp amusement the next. I remembered the way she felt when I took her hand. A forgiving hand, maybe. Certainly a trusting hand. I remembered the way she smelled.

"Oh, God." I stopped in the middle of the road. Columbia was barely a glow behind me. I could hardly see the road. In the distance around me there were a few distant mercury lights signifying farms but nothing else.

"I like her," I said dully. "And I already screwed it up."

The clouds above me rumbled. Slowly, inevitably, it began to rain.

Chapter 1.9: Katelin

I hadn't been to bed more than twenty minutes when my beeper went off. I sat up suddenly, an alarm-driven reflex. I turned off the alarm and the beeping continued. I picked up the phone.

"Hello?" I said thickly.

Still beeping.

Finally, it penetrated that I had to pick up my beeper. I found it still in the storage compartment of my stick. I turned it off and looked at the readout: they could use a flyer. I called the police department and found out why: a semi had run off the I-70 Bridge. The officer on duty told me to go directly to the site. Sheriff DeWitt would be waiting.

I went in the bathroom and washed my face. I looked around. If David had been sick in here, he had cleaned things up. My respect for him went up a couple of notches.

I grabbed a Starbucks out of the fridge and chugged it down as I got dressed. I needed to be awake.

I was a fully licensed VFR pilot: fixed wing and rotary, ultralight and self-propelled—those were the actual terms, lame as they may be. They came under part 91, part 103 and part 103A of the regulations. My stick was a fully certificated flight vehicle. When I flew it, I could fly it as a self-propelled part 103A aircraft—what I had been doing most of the night— which allowed me to fly below normal airspace boundaries and within municipalities. Something similar to the dispensation granted to police helicopters. I could fly it part 103, ultralight, which allowed me limited access to normal airspace—though that didn't apply here since ultralights were not allowed to fly at night. Or I could fly it part 91, which granted me full access to the airspace but meant I had to maintain above a specific altitude, keep up a certain speed and fly with lights. I hated flying with lights; they stuck out of the envelope and caused a lot of drag. It made flying six times harder than flying without them.

But I needed to get over to the bridge quickly and I didn't want to take a chance on braining myself on some tower I didn't see. Besides, they might have a helicopter at the site and nobody sees anything at night without lights. I didn't want to be diced into chutney.

I pulled out my headset and plugged in, quickly tested out my transceiver. Then, downstairs to the landing and outside. Great. It was raining. I looked down and then up, listened to the automated weather briefing. The ceiling was three thousand feet but I wouldn't get that high. I muttered a quick curse about Tabitha Purlin, settled my fanny in the seat and took off. I made a quick climb to just below pattern altitude for Columbia Regional, then called in and gave them my particulars. They were pretty understanding—I figured DeWitt must have greased the wheels ahead of time—and in a few seconds I was following a vector over Columbia at twelve hundred feet, lights deployed and breathing hard. I figured this was the equivalent of a two-mile run. I could run two miles in my sleep. That was my story and I was sticking to it.

Ten minutes later, I could see the bridge. The police had spotlights up and that gave me enough light to work with. I gave Columbia Regional a kiss goodnight and switched to the police band as I descended. DeWitt was waiting by the phone. I landed next to his cruiser. Arnie was with him, his hand in a plastic cast.

The three of us went to the edge of the roadway. The semi had broken through the guardrail and made a straight run down the embankment into the water. I could see it half submerged in the water about sixty feet below us.

"We figure he drove it down after he lost control or the whole rig would have tumbled." DeWitt pointed at the sides. "I have two divers to go down there and get him out, if he's still alive. But the climb down is dangerous and the currents are tough. I don't want to risk it in the dark if he's dead. Can you fly over there and see if he's worth it?"

"Give me a minute." I walked up along the bridge for a bit, trying to see if I could manage to get down there without getting disoriented. Flying here, in the dark and the rain, had been pretty strenuous. But I'd had the lights of the city and the highway as well as the spotlights on the bridge to guide me.

But here those same lights washed out any contrast and the brown muddy water was the same color as the mud-splashed truck. I couldn't look up at the bridge to get my bearings; I'd be blinded by the spotlights. DeWitt wasn't kidding about the current. Some of the river was lit by the spotlights and every now and then, you could see a whirlpool boil up and shake the truck. The spring rains from up north were still working their way downstream. I could be hovering just a couple of feet over the water and get caught by an uprooted tree. But the rain was steady and clear. There was no real mist to make things too vague to see.

"What do you think, Katelin?" Arnie said from behind me.

"I think it's dicey." I leaned over and looked down. Dark as a dungeon, way under the bridge.

"Then don't do it," Arnie said promptly. "Tell DeWitt to hell with it. You know that man is dead."

"There's a chance he might be alive."

"Katelin, there's no chance," Arnie said slowly. "You need to understand this. You're going to fly down there and find that man is dead—probably be a pretty gruesome sight, too. And then, you'll have to fly yourself back up here."

I stared at him. "You're trying to tell me this is what it's like to be a cop."

He nodded. "Most of the time you're going through the motions trying to save a lost cause. This is one of those times. If you go down there, you have to understand the situation."

I nodded and turned back to the railing. It came clear to me what Arnie was talking about. There were rewards that came from being a police officer. But they were bright little flashes in a big landscape. A lot of the time it would be dull and mostly thankless. Sometimes it would be dangerous *and* dull. Ninety-nine times out of a hundred, the result would be a foregone conclusion.

I didn't know the trucker. But maybe he had family. Even if he'd lost control, he still tried to ride that thing down into the water. He didn't just give up and let it tumble. He deserved some kind of a chance. Morning was hours away. If he was still alive, he could be long dead by then. Somebody had to do something and right here and right now I was the person to do it. Maybe that was what it meant to be a cop.

I went back to DeWitt's cruiser.

"Well?" he asked.

"I need you to point the spotlights directly on the cab from the middle of the bridge. So I can fly down there with all the light at my back. Can you do that?"

DeWitt looked at the bridge a moment. "Yeah. Give me fifteen minutes."

Arnie got me a snack and some coffee. I wolfed down both of them. I knew the coffee was hot and the sandwich was dry but that's about all the taste I got from them.

Then, twenty minutes after I'd gotten here, I took off.

I slipped between the girders of the bridge and out into the darkness, keeping my eyes fixed on the cab of the truck. It was the only real point of reference I had. I had planned my route to run far out over the river and then back to the cab to avoid any part of the bridge supports. If I hit one of them, I'd lose my concentration and gravity would take over.

When I was fifteen feet or so above the cab, say twenty feet over the water, I leveled off and approached along with the current. The obvious way to check on the driver would be to ease down in front of the cab in a hover and look in the window. But I didn't like the odds. If I messed up, or the truck shifted, I'd only be a couple of feet over the water and that was too close for comfort. Instead, I came in over the cab and pushed on it with my foot. It seemed more or less solid so I eased down to the side door. The river pushed itself along the middle of the window. I'd hoped I could kick it open and squat down or maybe lie on the cab and look over. But now I could see if the window was suddenly opened, the river would pour in. It might or might not fill the cab, but it would bring the awful force of the river to bear on the cab and I didn't want to take the chance it would shift the truck.

I moved over to the high side and caught a flash from the spotlight full in the face. For a moment, I was lost. I had no idea what was up or down—I fell and caught myself on the airhorn. Somehow, I held on to the stick. I looked back into the shadows until my eyes adjusted back and then brought the stick up again. It had to be a hover approach. There was no other way. I brought myself above the cab again and backed out in front.

The light at this angle only shone part way into the cab. My own shadow got in the way. I pulled my flashlight out of my pocket and lowered myself until I was hovering a foot over the boiling water. If something happened now it would be nasty.

I brought the light up slowly, keeping my concentration on where I was. *Precision*, I thought. *Sam? Is this precise enough?*

The driver had been crumpled against the wheel and part of the dash. It looked in the shadows that he had been torn into pieces. I didn't dwell on that. I let my mind take the picture and store it somewhere. The driver was dead. I'd think about it later.

I rose over the truck and then backed out of the light so I could look around without getting blinded. Altitude was what I needed now. *This is like Everest*, I thought. When you get there you've only gone halfway.

But as I gained altitude I began to breathe easier. From above, the outline of the bridge was clearly illuminated by the glare back from the river and the truck. The lights of stalled cars on both sides of the highway helped. I threaded my way back through the girders and eased down to the road. Arnie was there in a moment, helping me down. I felt as if I'd run all the way to Saint Louis.

DeWitt was there a moment later. "Do I send down a crew?"

I shook my head. Arnie gave me another sandwich. This time I could taste it. Tuna salad. Normally, I don't like tuna but this tasted wonderful.

"He's dead. He must have died when the truck hit the water."

DeWitt nodded. "I thought so. How about staying here for a while?"

"Have a heart, Connor. She's all in," Arnie laid a blanket over me but I was sweating from the exertion. I shrugged it off.

DeWitt shrugged. "Just asking. The river has been rising all day and it's going to rise some more tomorrow. I was just hoping she might to stay and help at first light. "

"Right now, she's going home with me." Arnie stood up and helped me stand up. "She's going to get some sleep and a nice breakfast. And tomorrow when it's light out and the weather's good and she's inclined, she might do you a favor."

DeWitt shrugged and waved us away. I followed Arnie to his car. He made sure I was seated and then leaned in. "Mattie would have my skin for a doormat if I let you go home like this. You save my ass and let me boss you around just this once, okay?"

I smiled at him. "Just this once."

Chapter 1.10: David

The rain didn't let up. After an hour, the wool coat gave up any pretense of water resistance and became a great, heavy sponge. My shirt and jeans were soaked not from the rain but by the continuous streams of water that seeped through the coat. I found out what wool smells like when it's thoroughly soaked.

My pant legs slapped wetly against one another, the coat flapped in the wind. My feet splashed through the sheet of water on the road. I felt like a wet, pissed off one-man band.

If I could have figured out somebody else to blame, I would have indulged myself in some heartfelt vitriol. As it was, I just silently steamed—literally—in the dark.

"Did *I* tell you to take a walk?" Misty complained. "No. We could have turned and gone back—there was a perfectly serviceable Starbucks in the shopping center just before we started this death march to the *end of the world!*"

I didn't say anything. I didn't think I could stand her more than another half hour but I gritted my teeth and made ready to try.

"All of this dreary, wasted effort because you upset some *girl?* Come *on.* So you're all afraid she won't *like* you? Here's a news flash, piano boy: *lots* of people don't like you. Sometimes, even the people who do like you have their doubts. There is Senbein who thinks you're an unreliable prick. There's Meister Eisenhart who is desperately trying to cover his ass since he's made no secret that you're the best student he's ever had. Carl is wondering if he spent all those years helping you along just to see you self-indulgently *destroy* yourself because you can't always feel the great power of music flooding through you."

"Shut up, Misty."

The rain opened up with a roar. Solid sheets of it pouring down. Nets of lightning spun across the sky—flashbulb bursts that strobed the world and blinded me. But, nothing could drown Misty out.

"There are people, like that first row violinist, Murdock, for example, who envy you your talent—currently being squandered in a rainstorm in the middle of Godforsaken Missouri, in case you haven't noticed—and would pay for *tickets* to watch you go down in flames. I bet even *Sandy* is trying to remember what the hell she ever saw in you."

"Shut *up*, Misty."

I looked around. The wind blew up the leaves so they looked pale and dead. The wind tugged at me. I held the coat shut. Heavy as hell. Heavy as sin.

"You're throwing away everything we worked on for the last seventeen years and *I* should shut up? Just because you're upset that some flat as a pancake boy-wannabe justifiably thinks you're jumping every slut that comes your way you think *I* should be the one to shut up? Get a grip, little boy. Wake up and smell the riverbed."

"Get the fuck out of my head!" I screamed at the sky, the woods, the rain.

"I'm here to stay, buddy boy."

The rain eased a bit. The road forward at least was downhill. There were some lights shining over the ridge. Maybe I could find a phone.

Water always runs downstream, I thought. The road hugged the side of the hill as it wound down and the water ran across the hill, over the road, and down the other side. It brought all manner of mud and gravel with it. My sneakers had been soaking before this. Now they had rocks in them, too.

Amanda had been the first. She was the one who persuaded me that setting the Christmas tree on fire on New Year's Day would be a good celebration. My parents thought it was just boyish excitement. Then, Gerald convinced me the only way to see what was coming out of the end of a Roman candle was to light it and stare down the tube. Gerald and Amanda and I figured out how to break into the hospital kitchen. Then, Donald spoke up for the first time to tell me the best way to use a knife.

Misty had beckoned me to the piano while the stitches in my wrists were still fresh and sore. It was Misty who helped me get rid of the rest as long as I kept *her* a secret. Which was kind of like an exorcism except without the fun of rotating heads and projectile vomiting. She'd been with me ever since.

This whole trek was stupid. I laughed a little in the rain. Maybe the light was a bar. I could get some guy in a red shirt with a pickup to take me back to Columbia.

Or, I thought, *maybe there's a new life under that light. It's the Emerald City—or somebody I could care about, anyway.* Something spectacular that would make everything clear. Something amazing.

The road leveled out and I walked around the curve into the thriving village of McBane—well documented by the city limits sign. Two houses, one trailer on stilts and a tiny ripoff grocerette in a green cinderblock building. Bait and beer sold here. When it was open. The light from a reddish street lamp shone down. The transformer on the same pole crackled and the air was laced with the faint smell of ozone.

I sat down on the bench in front of the store. The rain let up to a drizzle and the clouds rose up so they no longer looked like they were scraping the trees. The only sound was the hum from the light, the snap of the transformer and a rushing sound I guessed was the river.

There was no phone. I'd either have to hike back or knock on the door of one of these houses. Or the trailer.

At least I couldn't smell myself anymore.

"Okay," Misty said. "What are you going to do now? Maybe you can *conjure* up a taxi like your little witch friend."

I tried to ignore her. But she kept chattering at me.

"Maybe you're not even much of a pianist. Maybe all those people were *pretending* to enjoy it. After all, if you can't enjoy it yourself, *somebody* ought to get something out of it."

There was another, brighter and more distant glow in the direction of the river.

What the hell, I thought. I started walking towards it.

"Great. What rough beast its hour come round at last is slouching towards the river to drown."

You know, I thought. *Maybe Misty was right. Maybe I had this all wrong. So I didn't get the rush I used to get when I played. I could still hear it. I could still play it—play it damned well, too. There was some pleasure in that. Nothing was perfect. It wasn't like I would never feel anything about music ever again. There was no perfect darkness any more than there was perfect light.*

The lightning and thunder stopped but the rain still came down. All I could hear was the rain.

The road curved to the right deep into the trees but there was a trail that led up a rise. I could now hear the river from the other side. I started walking up the trail.

Carl seemed to have a good life. So it was a little smaller than I had wanted. He had a house. He had a job. He had a good time with his band. Carl obviously enjoyed his life. He didn't mind it. Why should I?

The edge of the bluff was bare and the edge was darkness. The light was below at the edge of the water shining over nothing more than a dock. I could feel the river, smell it. "Oh, yeah. *Carl* is so great. Maybe *he* would have actually been able to get it up for Sandy."

"Shut *up!*"

"Make me, fat boy."

"That's *it.*"

I reached over my left shoulder, just like I had for Amanda and Gerald, just like I had for Donald, just like Misty had instructed me, and grabbed her by the neck. I pulled her across. She felt light. Flimsy. I threw her to the ground.

She fell in a heap, too weak to stand on her own.

"No," she wailed. "You weren't supposed to do it to *me!*"

I knelt next to her and grabbed her by the throat with my left hand. "Go away," I said quietly. "I abjure thee."

"It doesn't mean anything," she snarled at me. "I'm not some demon. I'm not some evil spirit. You can't exorcise *me.* It's just psychiatric crap I fed you to get rid of *them.*"

"I consign you to the Hell from whence you came."

"You can't get rid of me!"

I kissed the thumb of my right hand and held her tight as I brought it to her forehead. She screamed and her skin smoked and caught fire.

Then, she was gone. My hands were holding empty rain.

She was gone. Just like Amanda. Just like Gerald. Just like Donald.

"Hallucinatory psychiatric crap that works," I said to the air. I didn't call her. I didn't want her to come back.

I could see up the river from here. There was something going on upstream at the bridge. I recognized the sheen of police lights—I'd seen them shine off the Tobin Bridge down in Boston when they were searching the water. Sometimes I'd read the next day it was a body or a smuggler's boat. But a lot of the time I never learned anything more than I saw in the lights. Somebody was searching for something.

I stared down at the black river. *Maybe that's all there is. Is that so terrible? You pick a place to be,* I told myself. *Playing concerts. Teaching music. A place to live. As permanent as this river,* I thought. *As strong as the earth I'm standing on.*

I looked around. Could I go back, now? Had this all been an exercise to get rid of Misty?

I heard an odd sound and looked back upstream towards the bridge. Like a wave curling over, the bluff caved in and the fall raced down towards me. Before I could move, the ground I stood on rolled forward and I was flung into the darkness until I hit the water.

I was under in a moment, the coat heavy as lead.

The coat dragged me down. *Off! Get it off. Kick to the surface. Come on. It's just a couple of feet.*

The water felt so cold it burned down my chest and my legs. I felt a cramp start in my leg but let go. I managed to break the surface and choke down a breath when the water spun and dragged me down again.

Don't panic. Don't panic! It's a whirlpool. They must come off the banks. It's no worse than the ocean off the back of Dad's boat.

68

Just swim for the surface so you don't get dragged down too far. Hold on.

I felt a cough spasm in my chest. I couldn't swim. I yanked off my shoes.

Come on. Hold it a little more. The surface has got to be only a bit further.

I broke the surface again. My legs felt heavy and I was having trouble breathing.

A log smacked my head. I grabbed it and held on.

A few seconds later, I felt silt suck down my right foot. I slid off. The water was still here. I pulled myself up on the muddy bank.

On my hands and knees I looked around. I couldn't see the bridge anymore. Not even a shimmer of light above the trees. My right foot throbbed and I sat down on gravel—a road? I was shivering. It had to be near dawn. I'd never wanted to see the sun as much in my entire life.

Sure enough, I looked in the east and saw a gathering light. The clouds were dissipating. I lay down on the gravel, suddenly sleepy.

I fell asleep there, cold and wet next to the river, alone for the first time in years.

Chapter 1.11: Katelin

I'm one of those people who always wakes up at the same time regardless of when I go to sleep. So, at 5:30 a.m. I woke up on a sofa. For a moment, I thought I was still dreaming. I looked around the pine walls. *So this is Witchlandia,* I thought. *Not bad. Not bad at all.*

Then I remembered: I was sleeping on the sofa at Arnie's. I didn't remember falling asleep. The last thing I could recall was staring out the window as Arnie drove west over the I-70 bridge towards his Wooldridge farm. I don't think I made it to the exit. Arnie must have carried me inside. Or maybe Mattie. I wasn't so conceited I didn't think I was tiny. I got off the sofa and went into the kitchen.

The house was quiet in that early morning way when the world only exists surrounding the kitchen. The only sounds were the house, breathing in and out. Ticking sometimes. Cracking, as the earth roused and shook itself. It was warm outside. I set up the coffee maker, put on my jacket and went out and sat on the porch swing to wait for it.

The rain had cleared and it seemed that the dawn had dipped the world in golden honey. Every surface glinted yellow and wet. The house was on a little hill and looked down on Arnie's furrowed fields. The winter wheat was an impossible green. The sky an unlikely blue. It irritated me. As if the stormy death of last night was meaningless. Hadn't happened. Without form and void. Thinking about the dead trucker made me think about Sandy last night. And David.

Mattie came out a few minutes later and handed me a cup and a plate with some raisin toast on it.

She sat down on the chair next to the swing. Mattie was a big woman and the chair creaked. "I'm letting Arnold sleep in. You should, too. On a Saturday, Anita gets up when she wants to."

I nodded and we sat in a companionable silence for a while. "Pretty," I said. It was in point of fact beautiful.

Mattie nodded. "Arnold says farming is the best life there is if you don't have to make a living at it." She sipped her coffee. "Arnold told me what happened last night. I called DeWitt and when he decided to change ears, as I had burnt that one right off, he said to tell you the divers managed to get to the truck a little after first light. The driver was dead just as you said."

"That's what I told him last night."

"So DeWitt said."

I drank my coffee and didn't say anything.

Mattie looked at me. "There wasn't anything you could do."

"I know that."

"Your mood on this fine morning has nothing to do with the trucker last night?"

"Some," I admitted. "But not as much as I wish it did. Does that make me cold and heartless?"

"You'd feel better about yourself if you were crying and carrying on?"

"Maybe. He was dead, after all. It seems like I should have more of a reaction than just getting pissed off."

"People are different," she said. "I see lots of things at the hospital. Arnold, too. Unspeakable things. I come home short-tempered, then, and bake up six or seven pies."

I smiled into my coffee.

She watched the crows hovering over the winter wheat. "So what's bothering you then?"

I shrugged and didn't answer.

Mattie shook his head. "You know, one time or another you might let something kind of slip out and see what happens. Just for fun. I might die of shock."

"It's not important."

"*That* tone I know. I have a daughter, you remember. That sounds like a problem with a boy."

David as a *boy*? It's kind of hard to maintain that sort of image when they're sleeping with your roommate. Or, I corrected myself, *not* sleeping with your roommate. If Sandy could be believed.

"It's complicated."

She laughed. "Knowing you, I expect it is."

"What's *that* supposed to mean?"

She leaned forward towards me. "I grew up with your father, you know. But I didn't get to know *you* until you came into Arnold's class. Now, why do you think that is?"

"I have no idea."

"Because you keep to yourself. Peter Loquess was born a politician to the bone. Patrick is just like him and Matthew's eye is never far from a dollar. Your mother, bless her, just didn't *last* long enough to change any of them. Don't get me wrong. Peter did right by Arnold and there are far worse scoundrels could be in office than either him or Patrick. And

Matthew is about as straight a businessman as you could expect to find anywhere. But even so, a person raised in a family like that learns to protect themselves or they don't last long. That little fiasco on the primary trail was only the expression of something that had been going on before you were born." She pointed at me. "You are *always* protecting yourself tooth and toenail. That'll serve you well up to a point. But it'd be tough to be your boyfriend."

"I hate that word."

"Anita does, too." She sat back and laughed quietly. "She says I'm old-fashioned. So does Arnold. I expect I am." She looked at me. "Tell me God's own truth. Is there *any* joy in your life?"

"What do you mean?"

"You work hard and I respect that. But I do not see that you take any chance to enjoy yourself on the way. Even when you fly—and what a blessing *that* must be—your mouth is set and your heart grim. Do you think we're put on this earth to *practice?*"

"I do okay. I don't need anything."

"I think otherwise." Mattie looked back over the straight, green rows. "I've been married twenty-five years. Do you know what Arnold does for *me?*"

"What?"

"When I come home and bake those pies, burned as they get sometimes, he eats every one of them with a smile. After a while, I get so I can smile back and things get better." She looked back to me. "That's worth a lot."

I didn't say anything. I finished the toast and the coffee. "I have to get back."

"Burning daylight, aren't we?" Mattie stood up and took the cup and plate from me. "Your stick is in the hall closet. If you could, DeWitt wanted you to fly back over McBane. Seems Dawson's Bluff fell in the river last night. Nobody's been reported lost and all the houses are intact. But he thought you might take a look."

I nodded. "It's on the way."

The sky was clear as I took off east towards the big, muddy river. The Missouri is always a flat brown in spring; water boiling up with trees or broken bits of wood floating past. Once when I was a kid in Jeff City I saw a house float by serenely under the Highway 63 Bridge.

I flew among the hawks and vultures, catching the updrafts as the day warmed up. The flat plain unrolled under me. I could see the curves of the river and the green of the new crops and the spring leaves on the trees. I couldn't remember the last time I actually *saw* things when I flew. Mattie was right. This *was* a blessing—even if we might not mean the same thing with the word. And I had taken it for granted.

So I took my time rolling over the river. I paced the vultures as I came down the river valley. I looked for fish jumping. I watched the deer coming to the water's edge, the wood ducks and geese.

I thought about what Mattie had said. Was there any joy in my life? I did work hard. I *liked* working hard. But joy?

I watched the light strengthen on the land, to slowly change from a feather touch to a steady grasp. *Feel it,* I thought. *Just a little bit. Just a touch.* And for a moment, I felt like singing.

Maybe there was more. More than just working for the sake of satisfaction. More than moments. I thought of Mattie and Arnie. And I thought of David. Someone like him. Maybe.

When I saw Dawson's Bluff I descended to the height of the bank. The bluff had carved off a couple of hundred feet, a great stinking pile of mud staining the water. There was a breakwater just above the boat landing. Below that, I saw someone sprawled on the gravel road.

I came in and landed next to him. He was face down in the dirt, in a wet T-shirt and jeans, bareheaded and barefoot. I didn't want him to be dead, whoever it was. I'd seen enough of that.

I reached under his jaw and felt of his pulse: strong but a little slow. I tapped him on the shoulder.

"Sir? Excuse me? Can you wake up?"

He stirred and coughed, then rolled on his back.

I stepped back. It was David Sabado.

Chapter 1.12: David

I opened my eyes and saw the sky and Katelin. I guessed I was alive but I felt like hell. For a moment, I thought I was going to throw up but my stomach thought better of it.

"Katelin?" I asked. I really, really hoped it was her name and I wasn't foggy from last night. Sandy? *Sandy*. Katelin was her roommate. Good.

"What are you doing here? How drunk *were* you last night?"

I shook my head and sat up. The world spun a little but stayed mostly where it was. "I wasn't drunk." I stopped for a second. "Well, not then, anyway. I just went for a walk."

"From the dorm?"

I nodded. Rolling over to my knees occupied my attention. *Knees are good*, I thought.

"David, it's sixteen miles from Columbia."

"I remember it took a while."

"Why?"

I slowly pushed myself up. Full height. A triumph of the will. I would have given anything right then for an easy chair and a cup of coffee. "It seemed the thing to do at the time. Then, I was standing on this hill looking at the river. The bluff shook me off into the water. I made it here." I looked upstream. "There was a boat ramp? I could have crawled up the damned boat ramp instead of the mud?" I shook my head and laughed.

Katelin looked up at me. She smiled. "You're lucky to be alive."

"I am," I said, still grinning. My face was tight. It felt good. "I am at that."

"Where's your coat?"

"New Orleans, I think. Along with my shoes."

"I'm sure they never made it past Jefferson City. Why didn't you walk over to the store? There's got to be somebody there by now."

"Store?" I looked up the road. Perhaps a hundred yards away there was a small wisp of smoke over the trees. "I thought it was a bait shop. Wasn't it closed?"

"That's McBane. This is Easely. You must have floated a mile or so."

"That far?"

"The current's six miles an hour on a calm day. Covers ground pretty quick."

She helped me to walk down the road. The gravel was sharp and hurt my feet. I followed her inside the store and picked out overalls, a shirt and a pair of sandals. Katelin told the man behind the counter what had happened and he agreed to let me pay later as my wallet was on its way to New Orleans, too. Or at least Jefferson City.

I couldn't keep from grinning. It was like I could hear for the first time. The fan in the window had a Verdi-like rhythmic clanking. I swear there was a bird outside singing

Dvorak. The cash register had a Fats Waller beat when it closed.

Katelin waited for me while I changed in the bathroom. The wet things I threw in the trash. I grabbed a brownie and two cups of coffee on the way outside and handed her the brownie as I sat next to her on the bench. My head was stuffy and my feet hurt but my hands were okay. It was important that my hands were okay.

She took the brownie, broke off half and gave it back to me, then took her cup of coffee.

It came to me as we sat on that bench in the warm sun that I had been thinking about it all wrong. Sure, it was fine that I felt great stuff when I played—I never wanted to give that up. I was right to think of it as breathing.

But if that were all there was, there would be no difference between playing in a concert hall or a closet. When I played for anyone else, *I* was there for *them*. *They* were there for *me*. It had to be something we did together. That's what I had been missing since it all began at McLean's. All those years of lessons and performances.

I listened to the birds, the river and the air conditioner. There was a rhythm there. A beat. I could hear the song underneath. I could play it right now. I could play all night for Carl's audience. Or for Eisenhart. Or for Senbein. The well was inexhaustible because I didn't have to do it alone.

I looked over to Katelin. She was watching the birds.

I could play for you.

"I didn't do anything with Sandy," I said out loud.

"I know. She told me." Katelin tilted her head and watched me for a moment. "You look different."

"Near-death experience, maybe?" I smiled at her. "Could change a man's attitude."

She stared at me searchingly. "Maybe."

I stared back. She looked different as well. Happier, maybe. I wondered why.

"So," Katelin said, turning away. "I've got my cell. Want me to call a cab?"

"I think I'll walk."

"Are you sure? It's sixteen miles. 'Near-death experience,' remember?"

"I walked down here, didn't I? I'm not so frail."

She didn't say anything for a moment. "I'll walk with you for a while."

I nodded. "And then you'll fly off on your broomstick?"

"Yup."

Katelin looked small and tough and warm. I thought of her flying over the trees in the sunlight. It was a point of view I'd never considered. The damp world seemed bright with possibility. "I'd like the company."

She stood up and hoisted her stick over her shoulder.

"This place isn't so bad," I said as we started walking.

She grinned at me. "Welcome to Witchlandia."

And we were off.

Part 2: Katelin, 1999

Chapter 2.1: Monday, October 18

I woke to a buzzer. For a long time I just ignored it. It didn't go away. Sleepily, I rolled away from it. My head spun and for a moment I thought I was going to be violently ill—but my stomach just lurched and relaxed, grumbling. My head pounded and the inside of my mouth made my think of a factory pig farm.

More buzzing.

I thought about sitting up but didn't actually attempt it.

It's not my pager.

What the hell *did I do last night?* I panicked and turned to look at the bed. It was blissfully empty. *Relax. Okay, then.* I tried to piece together the previous night. Out at the Sevens with some witches in town for Conclave—a lifter from Somalia and a flyer from the Ukraine. I didn't remember their names. Then we had rolled over to some nameless dive in Somerville. Obviously I'd gotten drunk. Obviously weighing not much more than a promise it didn't take much. Everything was a blur.

How did I get home?

The buzzing grew louder. It was my cell.

I rolled over the edge of the bed, grabbed it and rolled back to horizontal and level before my vestibular system was able to react. "Yes?"

"Takes you long enough to answer the phone, Loquess."

"What the hell do you want, Dooley?" I closed my eyes and leaned my head back on the pillow. Slowly.

"You're on shift in an hour."

"Right. It's Monday. I'm not on shift until Tuesday. I worked Saturday, remember?"

"You're half right. It is Monday. Gifford quit over the weekend."

Which meant Boston Police Department only had two flyers instead of three. Which meant only solo work, since Sneizek wouldn't fly with me. No loss there. The feeling was mutual.

Which meant I was on shift come Monday.

I felt queasy again for an entirely new reason. Sean Gifford might have quit because of me.

Welcome to Witchlandia.

I sat up and pulled on my robe.

"Loquess?" came Dooley's voice, tinny and faint.

"Yeah."

"When are you going to get in here? Horn wants to know."

The apartment had a porch that faced down over the Corridor Park and the Orange Line. I could have walked outside, wrapped myself in a flight bubble and taken off, just me and my stick. It was only a short flight. Even in bad conditions, all I had to do was descend down the hill and follow Columbus Avenue towards the city. That was the main reason David and I had found this apartment. Hell, Parker Hill was close enough to the BPD headquarters I could have *walked* it. I was safe enough; Parker Hill wasn't that rough. I was a cop and I carried a weapon. A small gun, to be sure. I'd managed to sweet-talk that out of Horn—mass counts. The smallest gun practical. Technically, as a police officer in flight I didn't even have to request clearance with either BPD or Logan, but it was important to announce the first flight of the day. That way traffic controllers knew who you were when the transponder popped up on the radar.

I looked around the room. Two years and I could still pick out a dozen items David had left when he moved out. A coffee cup emblazoned with shrimps and dragonflies we'd found in a pottery store. A pot showing a Van Gogh sun on the side and containing the dead stick of some long withered and unidentifiable plant. I'm not good with plants.

I'd replaced most of these relics while I'd been with Sean: a picture of Sean and me picking apples in Ipswich took the place of the picture of David and me in front of the Paquin Street Café in Columbia. In the east window a rose made of stained glass had replaced David's collection of lead crystal pendants. I considered Davidian artifacts as the remains of a dead civilization. They had no meaning and I refused to think about them.

I could see downtown Boston, gray and miserable, a cityscape of tall buildings, top half obliterated by clouds, base corrugated by three-story brownstones and houses. Last night the weather had been pleasant but overnight a front had rolled in. I opened the window: salt air mixed with something unnamed and unpleasant. The harbor at low tide with the wind coming from the sea. And misty. And wet. And cold.

"I could come get you?" Dooley offered.

"Okay. Downstairs in ten."

I hung up before he could take the offer back. *So I'm avoiding flying through a miserable Boston soup. Sam would be so proud. Sue me.*

In the shower and out again, dressed up in the oil slick uniform, cover that with the insulating coverall and a rain jacket over that.

It was October: leaves turned but still stuck to the trees. *Halloween coming*, I told myself. *Always a lot of parties at Conclave.* Be nice if I got it off. It made me think of something. I checked my calendar. Sure enough, this was the week Oscar Plante came to town. I made a mental note to drop by Faneuil Hall and catch his act. It's not common that one of the world's most famous jugglers would return to his roots as a street performer, but Plante did it every year. Turned on the weather radio and got the gist: miserable now but severe clear later in the morning. Never a dull moment with the Boston weather.

On with the official black sneakers. I grabbed my solo BPD stick out of the closet. Not as bulky, or as functional, as the team stick Gifford and I flew—*used to fly*—but still with the standard fittings for baton, radio and paperwork. Always the paperwork.

What did Gifford mean to me, anyway?

Ten minutes start to finish and down the stairs.

Dooley was standing, leaning against his car.

Dooley's name suggested some pale Irishman fresh off the boat. In fact, Dooley was half Samoan, half African. He towered over the world from six foot five and outweighed some small automobiles. He stared down at me from a great height wearing his perpetual expression of offense against the disorder in the world.

I stared back. "You made good time."

"I was here already. I had ample opportunity to view the vacant lot across from Heath Square. I thought if I were lucky, I could watch the junkies or observe a new body being taken away. There's always an opportunity for good police work."

Right. "Let's go," I said.

Dooley nodded and opened the door. "All right, then."

Dooley had been the handler for all the fliers for a year and a half. But Sniezek worked out of the North End and avoided any handler. With Gifford out of the picture, I was effectively getting in the car with my new partner.

Boston Police Department followed the partner system. It is my private belief that they would have partnered a flyer anyway. Normal people liked to humanize freaks. Sort of like partnering black cops with white cops a couple of generations back—not that Boston had ever been so proactive and forward-thinking.

I sat down in the passenger seat of Dooley's issue, leaned back and closed my eyes. Swaying gently in the early morning traffic. I knew the route so well I could see it, eyes closed or not. Around the square, vacant trees hanging over us. Parker Street to the Heath rotary. Down Heath Street towards Columbus Avenue, low bomb shelter apartment buildings opposite the vacant lot. Things looked different from the ground. Grittier. Nastier. I regretted my decision not to fly in to work.

Dooley glanced at me. "Aren't you going to ask me about Gifford?"

"No."

"He was your partner. Don't you want to know why he left?"

"No."

"Ah. I didn't realize he had left because of a cold lover's bed. Now it makes sense."

I opened my eyes and looked at him. "Excuse me?" I wondered if everyone in the department knew Gifford and I had been sleeping together or if it was just Dooley.

Dooley gave no clues. "Gifford took a job in Seattle."

"He'll hate it."

"That would be because?"

"He operates under visual flight rules just like me. He won't be able to fly half as much as he did here." I looked out the window. "Besides, Sean hates the rain."

Dooley didn't speak for a moment. "It is said that he announced he was giving up flying when he transferred."

"That's a lie."

"I saw the letter myself. Horn showed it to me. He'd apparently made his decision some time back and the two of them were waiting for the right moment to act on it."

Left onto Columbus Avenue, alongside the Orange Line and the Southwest Corridor Park. Opposite the park were first houses, then the open campus of Roxbury Community College. Everything looked open. A few people were moving quickly between shelters: coffee shop to classroom, classroom to ripoff grocerette. They watched us as we drove past, black faces turned out of the rain. Slab-sided brick buildings sprouting out of concrete, punctuated by thin trees.

When I came out to Boston it struck me as such an exciting place to live. I heard a new language being spoken at every street corner: French, English, German, Swahili, French again, Spanish. Everybody was so different from one another and I wanted to embrace it all, to bury my face in it. It made everything back home seem narrower. Back there we had blacks and whites, Catholics and Protestants, city and country. But the divisions I'd grown up with seemed so small compared with what I saw out here.

David had grown up in Gloucester, miles and miles from here. He seemed as far away from it as I was. We picked the Parker Street apartment and buried ourselves in the city. For a year it had been so exciting—a real Small Town girl comes to the Big City sort of story.

Now it just seemed like a place to me.

"And what a dismal place it is," I muttered.

"Yes," agreed Dooley.

"Sorry."

"Don't be. This isn't an easy place to live. You know about the pilgrims, don't you?"

"Mayflower Compact. 1627. Funny hats and shoes."

Dooley chuckled. "The hats were a later invention by those who didn't think the Puritans should be considered progressive. Only half of them made it through the first winter."

"You said this place wasn't easy."

"True enough, but that's not my point. Boston was built by those who lived. It took rough, dour, nasty, unsympathetic, intelligent, practical people to survive here." He waved out the window. "That's the way it's always been. Those that can't hack it leave. They go to easier places: Ohio. Kentucky. Missouri, New York City. Places where winter doesn't start in September. Places where the summers are always warm. Places where the day doesn't start out balmy and by midnight it's ten below. Those who stayed here were tough."

"There's got to be more to life than just surviving."

"A distinction meaningful only to those who have survived." He looked west. "And it's not always dismal." He pointed at the lightening sky. "Might see some sunshine today."

Both Sean and David had grown up here. Maybe I liked survivors.

Gifford and I: two years, off and on. First person I'd slept with since me and David split up. A big man—I like big men. He'd had that much in common with David. Big, that is, in a long wiry sort of way since, like me, he had to keep his weight down and muscle mass up for flying. But dark and quiet and as tone deaf as a man could be and still speak—a personal requirement of mine after living with a professional musician.

Tremont Street sideswiped Columbus Avenue and all of a sudden the avenue was no more and only Tremont Street remained. Names change all the time in Boston whether or not the thing itself changes. It was still early enough the rush hour hadn't really started.

Me and Gifford had been a flyer pair since I had moved out here. That is, the last two years minus three months. I stared out the window.

It should mean something when your lover moves three thousand miles away to get away from you. It should at least make you sad.

oOo

Geography is important to a flyer.

Boston was a small town. Route 128 bordered the city itself and the immediate surrounding suburbs. From top to bottom, the entire area was no more than twenty miles, and from left to right no more than ten. Boston proper was smaller than that. From the river and trees of the Esplanade down to Roxbury was no more than eight miles. Beacon Hill wealth, North End mafia and MIT intelligentsia—all within easy reach. Distance has no meaning in Boston. Things can change crossing over a foot of pavement or don't change for generations.

A witchflyer could be in the air from the BPD headquarters and reach the farthest point in no more than eight minutes without breathing hard. Faster if she (meaning me) used a JATO. And that meant point to point. From the roof of the Boston office to on the ground, gun drawn, in ten minutes, no siren necessary. Two minutes, if the flyers were paired.

That was the sales pitch for the Commissioner when they created the position. BPD headquarters wasn't the most convenient point of departure in the city—that would probably have been the Hancock or one of the other tall buildings. A flyer could start at altitude and ride gravity to the target.

But the Commissioner liked his luxury items where he could see them so flyers were stationed at BPD headquarters at Schroeder Plaza in Roxbury. We even had our own FAA-approved heliport: a six-foot circle next to the HVAC units on the roof. A single blue runway light mounted next to it. One time Sniezek had posted a silhouette of a witch with a red circle/slash through it on the HVAC next to the circle. We didn't get along.

Every time I left from Schroeder I had to fight planet earth for every vertical foot. Maybe it consoled the Commissioner since he really couldn't talk about us. Like deep cover officers, everyone knew we were there but no one identified us. A sort of paranormal don't ask, don't tell. I swore at him every time I took off from the low roof. I hoped he heard me.

The sales pitch was partially true. BPD headquarters or not, Gifford and I could take off and be ready on the ground crucial minutes before other officers could make it to the scene—even if those other officers were nearby. But there were only the two of us and Sniezek. That meant we had to be on watch most of the time, in headquarters, ready to run at a moment's notice. Such speed was rarely *that* useful. More often we were on standby, parked on top of a building during a special celebration—a visit by the president or some similarly high-profile individual. Somebody important enough that seconds actually did count. Most of the time we spent together was uneventful. So we talked. And did other things.

This meant we had a lot of time for solo work. Most of mine was intelligence and surveillance. I loaded myself with snoopers, and dressed in sheerest black or overcast camo and followed a Person of Interest through the city, noting their movements, listening to outdoor conversations with a parabolic microphone. It was exacting, precision flying— hours of high-tension boredom that at any moment could turn into seconds of sheer terror as the POI twigged to what was going on. Every time I hovered at altitude, not moving a foot in any direction while I took pictures, I thought of Sam. It was Sam that always insisted I never settle for just what would be necessary.

I wondered what Sam would think of me now.

I had no idea what I would be doing now that Gifford was gone and paired flying was out of the picture.

Once we reached the bullpen, Dooley wandered off to see what sort of assignments they would give us now that Gifford was gone. After being our handler, becoming my partner was a step up; one small incremental advance towards the rank of detective.

I pulled out my cell and called Gifford.

"Yes," he answered, his voice cold as stone.

For a moment, I thought I was talking to David. Two years ago. In the last days before I left. Tolstoy was wrong. Happy couples are different from each other. They become identical in misery. "Dooley said you quit."

"That's right."

"He said you're going to Seattle."

"There's an opening there."

"There's no flying in Seattle."

Gifford sighed. "That's not true. City flying is still permitted—the ceiling is rarely lower than six hundred feet. Higher flying is problematic."

"You hate the rain."

"I'll learn to live with it."

"Dooley said you were giving up flying."

The silence across the phone was deafening. "I didn't think Horn would make that public knowledge."

"Are you?"

Again, a long pause. "The opening in Seattle is for a detective. It's not a flight position. I've been told it's up to me. I'll think it over on the way out there and see if I change my mind."

I wasn't sure how I felt. Gifford had been nice. Pleasant. Loving. And comfortable—what was it I had against comfortable? David had been cozy but never comfortable. Exciting, maybe.

"When are you leaving?"

"I left yesterday. I'm flying over the Berkshires right now. All the rain is east of me. With any luck, I'll camp in Herkimer diamond country tonight. Tomorrow's a rest day. Think I might do some prospecting."

"You're taking the Long Walk."

"We always talked about it. Now I'm doing it."

93

Silence came between us. At that moment I truly realized Gifford was gone. "I still have some of your stuff."

"Yeah," Gifford said reluctantly. "The closing date on my condo is the twenty-fifth. I have to come back for that. I'll be in town for Conclave. I'll pick up everything then."

"I'll take you out to dinner," I said woodenly. "It'll be like old times."

"No. But maybe we'll get a little closure. Bye."

The connection went dead.

Closure.

Was that what I had with David? Did we have *closure?*

"Hey, Loquess." Dooley was standing right in front of me. "Life is better with a cup of coffee." And handed it to me.

I took it with a nod. "What's happening? Are we still on the D'Macy investigation?"

"Maybe," Dooley said softly.

"What?"

"Do you want to be a flyer all your life?"

I shrugged. "I suppose."

"I can't fly. But I *can* make detective. Hoffman and Rush are willing to throw us a bone."

"Go on."

"They have a homicide to cover. An old homeless guy they found over on Centre Street early this morning—only a few blocks from your building. Hoffman's been designated as investigator-in-charge. They're willing to let us do some of the leg work."

"Horn okay on this?"

"As long as A, it doesn't interfere with you doing any needed surveillance work, and B, Hoffman and Rush get all the official credit. Unofficially, if we do a good job we might be looked upon favorably when (and in your case if) we take the exam." He looked at me sternly. "I have ascertained that no immediate surveillance requires your expert hand."

I sipped my coffee thoughtfully. I looked up at Dooley. "You really want to be detective that bad?"

"Some of us are not gifted with the diabolical power of flight. We do what we must with our feet on the ground."

"Why don't you just follow up this homeless thing on your own? I'll be fine."

Dooley looked pained. "The captain feels that partners should work together. I must say I agree. Two sets of eyes are better than one."

I realized that in his own oblique way, Dooley was worried about me.

"Okay," I said. "Let's go check out a corpse."

oOo

The weather had cleared during the hour or so we'd been inside—I could see the cloudy remnants east of us still hanging over the taller buildings. The sky was clear blue and warm in the sun. The damp and misty smell of the early morning lurked in the shadows.

I drove while Dooley worked through the medical examiner's report. I hate driving. I can barely see over the steering wheel. It makes me drive like an old lady. I *hate* driving like an old lady.

As we crossed Berkeley, Dooley looked up from the file. "William Wallace."

"Governor of Alabama back in the sixties."

"That was *George* Wallace. This is *William* Wallace. Wasn't he famous or something?"

"Scottish revolutionary, seven hundred years ago," I said.

Dooley nodded and returned to the file. "This is pretty nasty. This guy was found by the super in the utility room of an apartment building. Hickey puts the time of death between ten and midnight last night." He gazed out the windshield thoughtfully. "He was tortured."

"Tortured how?"

"Whipped, it looks like. But it happened a while back. The marks have healed."

"Maybe he was abused as a child."

Dooley read further. "Hickey says no. They're adult injuries. There are pictures if you want to see them."

"I don't want to see them."

"Suit yourself." Dooley examined the examiner's pictures closely. "Didn't have anything to do with cause of death. Quick knife wound to the heart. Slashed the ventricle and aorta both." Dooley whistled. "Murderer was an accurate so and so."

"Sounds nasty."

"Oh, it's nasty all right." Dooley read carefully. "Last known address Kennedy Inn. We'll ask around the apartment building first, then the shelter."

The super was named Antonio Estevez. We found him in the furnace room cleaning the filters. "Going to be cold, soon." He put down the frame he was working on and wiped his hands. He was dressed in overalls and spoke perfect English with only the faintest of shifted vowels.

Dooley introduced us. "We're here about the homeless guy you found."

"Two detectives already talked to me last night. I was in the apartment all night with my wife and son."

Dooley nodded. "They're the front runners. We bat cleanup. We're here to collect statements from other people in

96

the building. But out of politeness, I thought we'd talk to you, first."

Estevez nodded. "Thanks."

"And we need a list of people in the building."

"I figured."

Armed with the list, we started at the top floor and worked down. Nobody had heard anything. Not the fat and pregnant single mom on the top floor or the gay couple in first floor west. The retired National Guardsman and model train hobbyist thought he'd heard something but under questioning he just wanted to show us his trains. His neighbor across the hall hadn't heard the murder but she *had* heard the model trains and complained about them bitterly. Nobody had heard William Wallace. Nobody knew William Wallace. Nobody had any interest in William Wallace. He died unloved and alone in the basement. After he had survived torture.

I had a sour taste in my mouth when we reached the lobby.

"Nothing," I said, disgusted.

"Yeah." The lobby had two benches. Dooley selected one and sat down. "It's strange."

I sat across the small lobby from him. "Strange?"

"Surprised he didn't make any noise."

"Maybe he was gagged."

Dooley examined the examiner's report again. "Doesn't say anything like that in the report. You should look at this. At least make an *effort*."

"I'm not the one trying for detective. It could be hard to hear anything from the basement."

"Yeah. Nobody recognized Wallace, either."

"Nobody we talked to, anyway. Some apartments didn't answer." I shrugged. "Maybe the basement was just a convenient spot to drag somebody."

Dooley didn't say anything for a moment. "Let's go look in the basement again."

Downstairs, we stepped past the yellow tape into the alcove where Wallace had been killed. "There's no outside door."

I walked to the other side of the basement and peered into the corners. "Nothing here."

"So the only entrance and exit is the basement stairs."

I pursed my lips. "So someone would have to drag Wallace down here without being seen, do the deed, and then leave him." I looked at Dooley. "The super?"

Dooley shook his head. "Why report it? Why kill somebody in your own backyard? Hauling somebody down those stairs would be a chore." Dooley tapped the file. He looked around the alcove. "No. Wallace was already *here*."

"What did the super say last night? Is it in the report?"

Dooley paged through the report. "You really should read this. It's more professional. The super said he didn't know Wallace. Didn't know who could have gotten down here."

I shrugged. "Let's talk to him again."

oOo

"All right. I did know someone had been coming in since the hard freeze the end of September." Estevez spread his hands. "Come fall sometimes, when it gets cold, I see signs of somebody sleeping down here. Nothing obvious—I'd have to do something about it if I saw a bed or a blanket or anything like that. But every now and then I'd notice the dust disturbed or water in the sink. What can you do? There are homeless people out there. It gets cold at night."

Dooley gave him a picture of Wallace. "You said before you didn't recognize him. Do you know him now?"

Estevez looked at the picture, then handed it back. "I never saw anybody down there. I certainly never saw this guy. Maybe he was the guy who slept down here sometimes. Maybe not."

Outside in the clear autumn air, Dooley shook his head. "Well, we learned he was in there when he was killed. We knew he was a homeless guy from Kennedy. So he hangs around in the area."

I had a sudden cold thought. "Let me see his picture."

"Which one?"

"His face. Let me see his face."

Dooley selected a photograph. I took it as if it burned. I stared at it a long time. Then gave it back.

"I've seen him before."

oOo

"This is why policemen should actually examine case folders *before* we question subjects." Dooley shook his head bitterly. "Who is he?"

"I don't know. William Wallace, I suppose."

"You're not helping."

"I didn't say I could help. I just said I've seen him before." I stared at my hands. "Around my apartment. He hangs out at the edge of Heath Square. I'm surprised no one recognized him."

"Heath Square is five blocks from here. That could be light years away from these people. If he wasn't begging them in front of the door every day they wouldn't recognize him. Maybe not even then. What did he do in the square?"

"He sang."

"He sang."

"Hymns, mostly. He has—*had*—a beautiful singing voice. Blues rough but right on key." I smiled at Dooley. "Something you learn to be sensitive to when you're living with a musician."

"Gifford was a musician?"

"I never lived with Sean and Sean is not a musician. This was a while ago. David Sabado."

"Sabado? The pianist?"

I nodded.

Dooley whistled. "You do hang out with the upper class."

"You know who he is?"

"Katelin, he sold out the Wilbur last fall. There were posters on every plywood construction front in town. They even put his face on the little Fourth of July flags on Longfellow Bridge. The only way I'd never heard of David Sabado is if I were *dead*." He tapped himself a couple of times. "No. Not yet. Therefore, I've heard of David Sabado."

I scowled at him. "Well, *I'd* never heard of him before I met him."

Dooley checked the case folder again. "We Boston sophisticates will just have to forgive you, being from Missouri and all. Kennedy Inn, next, Miss Katelin. You drive."

"Fuck you."

"My, how they talk down where you come from. Do you kiss your momma with that mouth?"

oOo

The Kennedy Inn was one of the better homeless shelters in Boston. Individual beds. Lockers. If someone managed to get a bed, they stayed on their best behavior to keep it.

Dan MacIlvey, in charge of the men's unit, checked his files for us. "William Wallace. I thought I remembered the name. He doesn't have a bed here."

"Really? We have an address for him here."

MacIlvey nodded. "We keep mail for him but he isn't allowed to stay."

"Does he have any mail?"

MacIlvey shook his head. "I already checked."

"Why isn't he allowed to stay here?"

"Looks like there'd been some trouble."

"What sort of trouble?"

"Religious. Turns out Wallace was some kind of Pentecostal. He had made it his mission to convert some of the men here—especially some of the Catholics. We have a lot of Catholics here. They didn't appreciate it."

Dooley chuckled. "I expect not. There must have been a final incident that got Wallace kicked out."

MacIlvey nodded. He lifted up the file. "Yeah. He had a fight with a Frenchman from Quebec named Dulac. François Dulac. I found the incident report after I heard about Wallace. Made a copy for you." He handed the file folder to Dooley.

"Any idea where I can find Dulac?"

"Yeah. Third floor. Bed six. He checked in twenty minutes ago."

Dooley wrote that down. "Anybody else know William Wallace? The staff, perhaps? Or some of the residents?"

MacIlvey shrugged. "I don't know. I'll have to ask around."

"You do that." Dooley fished out his card and gave it to him. "Call me later and tell me what you find. We'll go up and talk to Dulac."

Outside, I asked: "So why are there so many Catholics in Boston? From the Italians in the North End?"

Dooley chucked. "That happened much later. This was a strong Protestant town until the eighteen hundreds and the Irish immigration. The Irish ran this town until the eighties. Some of the gangs ran arms for the IRA."

"Ah," I said.

"Ireland is Catholic, you know."

"No! Really?"

Dooley chuckled again. "Is Loquess French?"

"Yes."

"Are you Catholic?"

"No. Methodist."

"Aren't most French Catholic?"

"Things change. Where did the name 'Dooley' come from? Are you Irish?"

"The name of the family that adopted me when my parents died," he said matter-of-factly.

I felt immediately miserable. "I'm sorry."

"No need," Dooley said.

Dulac was sitting on his bed, sorting through his things.

"François Dulac?" Dooley asked.

"Call me Frankie," Dulac said without looking up. "'François is too much of a strain for you."

Dooley sat on the adjacent bed.

Dulac glanced up at him quickly. "That's Tom Kelley's bed. Things might get sticky. Best not sit on it."

"Is there somewhere we can talk?"

Dulac led us to a common room. "You want coffee?"

"Sure," Dooley said for both of us.

Dulac brought us both what must have been coffee since it was black and at the bottom of a Styrofoam cup. There was little other indication.

"You knew William Wallace?"

"Fundamentalist prick ass. Yeah, I knew him."

Dooley looked up at him. "You didn't get on?"

"Fuck no." Dulac laughed. "Asshole kept trying to get me into his little fuckbag church. Like I wouldn't be caught fucking a nun first."

"Did it make you mad?"

"That he wanted me to go to his puswad church? Fuck no. It pissed me off that he wouldn't *shut up* about it. You make your bed and it'd be come to Jesus. You look at the moon and it'd be come to Jesus. You'd take a fucking *shit* and it would be come to fucking *Jesus*."

"What did you do about it?"

"Bust his fucking teeth in." Dulac held up his hand in a fist. "That scar there. Nine stitches. Worth every fucking one."

"Did you see him after that?"

"No. They fucking kicked him out. Would have fucking kicked me out, too, but MacIlvey put in a good word for me. Not a bad sort, MacIlvey. For a Protestant." Dulac admired his hand. "Nine fucking stitches. It was a fucking good hit."

Dooley sat back. "You never saw him afterwards?"

"Not a bit of it."

"Where were you Sunday night? After midnight."

"Fucking here." Dulac pointed back through the door towards his bed. "Back there. Checked in about eight. Wallace dead?"

Dooley didn't answer immediately. "Why do you ask?"

"Two fucking cops come in talking about fucking Wallace. Not like he's worth a bucket of piss. So he either killed someone or he got killed. If he killed someone you wouldn't be asking *me* where I was the other night so the fuck must be dead. Am I right?"

Dooley nodded. "You know you're a suspect."

Dulac waved it away. "Of course. I wouldn't piss on the fucker if he was on fire. You find out who killed him and let me know. I'll send him fucking flowers."

Dulac rose and went back to his bed.

"Okay," said Dooley, putting his notebook in his pocket.

We didn't talk until we were outside again.

"Did Wallace sing at the same spot every day?"

"Every weekday I was there. But I fly in to the station a lot."

"Did he ever preach to you?"

"Never."

"Interesting." Dooley thought for a moment. "This case is far more interesting than either Hoffman or Rush could have determined. I believe we might make it back to the station quite late."

oOo

Like gazelles around a watering hole, Boston's collection of street musicians collected around Boston's public transit system. There are three descending tiers: the subway, the trolley and the bus lines. For the subway, think a scaled-down New York system without New York's efficiency or pride of service. For trolleys, think buses on tracks. Boston has buses, workhorse trolley lines and subway trains.

I lived on Parker Street, at the edge of Heath Square, near New England Baptist Hospital. There was a T stop on

Huntington and down at Jackson Square, a fair distance. The neighborhood had been inconveniently left off the best Boston transit grid. There were no trains and the closest trolley was the bumbling and unreliable line several blocks away connecting the medical area, the museums and Mission Hill. Parker Street was served only by a decrepit and complex bus system—not a pleasant venue for the society of folk musicians, jazz guitarists and other street virtuosos that prowled the city competing for the generosity of transit patrons. If the subway was the moral equivalent of a great and beautiful lake to the performance crowd, I lived on the edge of a bug-infested swamp.

Wallace frequented Heath Square near the bus stop.

"There's nobody here," said Dooley looking around.

"The resident musician is dead, remember? He sang here. On this corner. Next to that park. Across from yonder church." I pointed across the street.

"'Yonder'?"

"That's just the way we talk out in the sticks."

Dooley didn't respond. "He sang hymns?"

"That's all I ever heard. Maybe that's the church Dulac was talking about."

"Let's check it out."

The door of *The Church of the Living Christ* was wide open. It was a broad space, filled with folding chairs and tables instead of pews, a door open to a back hallway where I could see the doors of other rooms. There was a plain wooden altar and cross opposite the main entrance, but other than that the space was devoid of ornamentation: plain white walls, linoleum floor, hanging electric lights. Two racks of lurid evangelist pamphlets braced the door. It reminded me of churches I'd been in back home.

A man was sweeping around the altar.

"Excuse me?" Dooley called to him as we passed the pamphlets.

The man stopped and straightened. He smiled at us. "I'm Tim Rabbitt. Can I help you?"

Dooley introduced the two of us. "William Wallace used to sing across the street. We're looking for people who knew him."

"You said 'used to'."

"William Wallace is dead. We're investigating his murder."

"Oh." The man sat heavily in one of the folding chairs. "Bill sang here last night."

Dooley pulled over a chair and sat across from him and pulled out his notebook. "I'm sorry for your loss. When was he here? When did he leave?"

"He sings—*sang*—every Sunday and Wednesday night at evening services. That went until seven o'clock. Then he left."

"Where did he go?"

Rabbitt shrugged. "As far as I know he has no fixed address. A lot of my congregation is homeless. I give out free meals when I can."

"You're in charge here?"

"As far as it goes. I'm the minister, groundskeeper, janitor and accountant. I live in the back." Rabbitt waved around the space.

"Where were you last night?"

"Right here. Evening services until ten. Bible study class until midnight."

"That's late for a bible class."

"It's a pretty dedicated class. We're studying Second Corinthians."

"Was Wallace in the class?"

"No. He was here for evening services and then left."

"At seven?"

"That's right. The bible class started at eight."

"So you were at loose ends between seven and eight?"

Rabbitt laughed. "A minister is never at loose ends. I grabbed a bite and read up for the bible class."

"You knew Mr. Wallace well?"

"Sure. He was here two, maybe three times a week. Since he moved into town a couple of years ago." Rabbitt watched me for a moment. "What did you say your name was?"

"Katelin Loquess."

"I've heard of you." Rabbitt smiled. "We have a friend in common. Sean Gifford."

"You know Sean?" I felt queasy with the sudden change in roles. Rabbitt was no longer a faceless source; he was somebody connected to me.

"Yes." Rabbitt gestured for us to sit. "Sean and I grew up together in Rozzy. For a while I thought he was going into the priesthood—both of us were devout in our own ways. But then he took the aptitude tests and discovered he had different gifts."

"I've never heard of you," I said flatly.

"I'm not surprised." Rabbitt gave me a slight smile. "Sean said there were… issues of connection between you. He probably never took you to the old neighborhood, either."

"No," I said.

"Let's get back to the subject at hand," Dooley interrupted. "You said Wallace came to town a couple of years ago."

"Yes."

"Where did he live before?"

"Columbia, Missouri."

I stood up and stepped back from them. I turned and went outside. I sat on the bench and watched the pigeons. Christ. I wondered if I had ever seen Wallace. Or if he'd ever seen me.

A few minutes later, Dooley came outside.

"What else did Rabbitt say?"

"Not much. He promised to ask his parishioners about Wallace. Hickey said Wallace was killed after midnight so he's a suspect with regard to opportunity. No motive I can see. We can leave it up to Hoffman and Rush to see if it's worth a warrant." He paused. "You're from Missouri, right?"

"Born and raised."

"Columbia?"

"That's where I went to school. I grew up south of there, down in Jefferson City."

Dooley looked across the street, digesting this. "You don't know him from Columbia?"

I shook my head. "I've been trying to remember. As far as I know, I never saw him before I moved here. Columbia's not a small town. It's the size of Framingham or Worcester. I could have spent my life there and never seen him."

"Yeah." Dooley bit his lip. "Guy moves out here and settles down not three blocks from your house, then joins a church where the minister grew up with your boyfriend."

"*Ex*-boyfriend."

"Yeah."

"It's an unpleasant coincidence."

"Yeah." He made a note in the notebook. "We can call Columbia and the state police. Maybe Wallace was followed to Boston by somebody that didn't like him."

I looked up. The church was a flat-roofed building. I unfolded my stick, wrapped myself in my own personal flight bubble and rode my stick up to the roof. I stood there looking around.

"Loquess?" Dooley called. "What the hell are you doing up there?"

"Trying to figure out where we are."

"Come back down here!"

I mounted the stick, stepped off and came down gently.

Dooley stared at me. "That is so unnatural."

"You've seen me fly before."

"You think I don't have the same reaction every time I see it?" Dooley waved it away. "Explain yourself."

"Checking distances. The Kennedy Inn is close to here. He goes to church here. He picks up his mail at Kennedy. He sleeps over at the apartment building."

"So?"

"Wallace stayed in the same area. I bet he didn't go far."

"So?"

"Nobody heard anything, right? Wallace was taking care of that sleeping space—he was careful not to leave traces. That means he understood the situation. Maybe he had some understanding with Estevez or somebody that knew Estevez turned him on to the situation. The point is he was protecting his space by taking care of it. Do you think he'd jeopardize it by letting in a stranger?"

Dooley thought about it. "Maybe he was asleep."

"Was there any sign of a struggle?"

Dooley consulted the file. "No. Cause of death was a quick knife to the heart—ventricle and aorta were slashed open. He wouldn't have had a chance to struggle. No skin under the fingernails. No abrasions on the knuckles. No marks of strangulation. Maybe he was asleep."

"Was he drunk?"

"No."

I thought for a moment. "Maybe he could have been asleep. Or, he could have known his attacker."

"It's an idea," Dooley said speculatively. "Not conclusive by any means. But worthwhile." He wrote it down.

"Okay, then." I smiled. "That was fun. Now, we write it up and give it to Hoffman and Rush, right? We're done."

"Not so fast. We can hold onto this for a bit. If we stay out of the office, we don't have to submit a report until tomorrow. We can find out lots more."

"What did you have in mind?"

"We can go back to the minister and grill him for more of Wallace's friends. Maybe we can even take him back to the station and talk to him there. If you're right about Wallace staying in one area, we can canvas the apartments here. That little store on the corner. The packie across the square. See if anybody's seen Wallace. Anybody who knows him. We could give Hoffman and Rush some real leads instead of all these notes and speculation."

I watched Dooley's earnest face. "You know, as interesting as that sounds, I've had a rough day. It's late and we've been doing this since early this morning. Our shift is over. What I'd like to do is give Hoffman and Rush the notes, clock out and go have a burger and a beer. Come on, Dooley. I'll front you the first beer."

"Some of us have to work for a living," Dooley said in a tight voice.

"Some of us want to make detective." I spiraled a finger into the air. "And some of us don't. Well, if you're not coming with me, I'm going down to Faneuil Hall for some crab bisque and a tall drink of something cold. There's a juggler there tonight. Oscar Plante. He only comes into town in October and plays in front of the hall because Boston is where he got started. I see him every year." I smiled at Dooley. "We all have our traditions, witches included." I pulled my stick out of the back of Dooley's car.

"You aren't going to amount to crap, Loquess." Dooley shook his head. "Come on. I could use your help."

"No. I've had enough for today. You go and get your man, Dooley. You'll make detective yet."

"I understand why Gifford left you." Dooley snapped out the words like breaking sticks.

"Then, you understand how it feels." I settled down in the saddle and started my ascent. "For the moment, I am leaving you. Welcome to Witchlandia."

"What the hell does that mean?"

oOo

I came into town over Exchange Place, my favorite place to perch in Boston. From the top of the Exchange you can see the city, a bit of the river, most of the harbor. You can see the bones beneath Boston, watch the buildings shrink as they approach the water and melt into the dumpy warehouses next to the harbor. Some of the hotels and apartments were designed to look like these old buildings—as if, somehow, the temporary storage of rum and bales of hay was the epitome of architectural grace. Others tried to outshine the adjacent granite or brick with soaring heights of glass and stainless steel. Didn't work. Somehow the old columns and severe angles seemed to glow while the newer buildings just looked like dressed up transients.

The best part of Exchange Place was to look down first over 75 State, an ornate gilded thing, and then down on the Customs Tower, a narrow, proud spire that came to a pyramidal point barely to the Exchange's shins. It didn't care. It always seemed to say *Screw you, Jack!* to the newer buildings. *I've been around nearly a hundred and fifty years.* Of course, compared to some of the other buildings in Boston, the tower itself was young. But it didn't care. It was an upraised finger to the rest of architectural Boston. I respected that.

Down and around the Customs House Tower, just over the rooftops and down in a narrow alley next to Butler Row. This close to Conclave, Bostonians were used to the occasional, if illegal, flyer. Even so, and legal as I was, I didn't need to advertise my presence. I still needed some degree of anonymity to do my work.

Bernoulli's had occupied the intown corner of Faneuil Hall since before I had moved here. Crab bisque had always been on the menu. David had introduced it to me when we first came to Boston. I had loved it. When David moved out, Bernoulli's had been the first restaurant I'd visited; eating the bisque with tears rolling down my face in some obscure act of defiance. Now it was mere habit.

Even so, Bernoulli's had a marvelous chef and for half an hour, I was able to lose myself to culinary excellence.

I paid my check, warm from both the bisque and half a bottle of wine, and strolled outside. The strings of Christmas lights decorating the brick avenue had seemed a wasteful extravagance when I came to Boston. That was before my first long Boston winter. Now, I viewed them as illuminated rage against the encroaching dark.

Plante always performed on Merchant's Row at the western end of the hall. I sauntered in that direction, enjoying the crisp autumn air, the electric blue of the early evening sky, the easy comfort of the crowds. I like crowds as long as I don't know anybody in them.

The crowd began at the edge of the hall. I walked up the stairs and looked down, expecting to see Plante's signature opening: Plante in a mask, sitting still next to a clock. He would look at the clock every few seconds and hold up his hands in a great exaggerated gesture: *five more minutes*. Or four. Or three. After a while, the crowd would be laughing, wondering what the next gesture would be and by the time he started his act, they would be ready.

Instead, I saw Hoffman and Rush, notebooks in hand, questioning a young boy. Someone from forensics I didn't know was examining Oscar's equipment.

Oscar Plante was nowhere to be seen.

"Loquess!" Dooley vaulted up the steps. "Where have you been?"

"Here. Eating dinner."

"Why didn't you answer your phone?"

I pulled it out. Sure enough, there was a *missed call* note on the face. "I didn't hear it."

"Come on. You can help take statements or something."

"Why?"

"Your friend, Oscar Plante, was found an hour ago not far from here. Killed just like William Wallace."

Chapter 2.2: Tuesday, October 19

The following morning, me, Hoffman, Rush and Dooley sat around a standard gray table going over each other's notes.

Hoffman was a big man, an athlete gone to fat. His big shoulders seemed to be the only thing keeping his enormous belly from falling down and striking the floor. Rush was tiny by comparison, only millimeters above the minimum allowed by regulations. The contrast always reminded me of one famous couple or another: Abbot and Costello, Laurel and Hardy, the Walrus and the Carpenter.

Today, I couldn't help thinking of Bugs Bunny and Elmer Fudd. If they had worked together. If they were deadly serious and devoid of humor. If they had been human—at least as human as the Walrus and the Carpenter.

"Okay," Hoffman said at last. "You did good getting Wallace's information. Horn wants to keep this case intimate. That way if anything new shows up in the press we'll know where it came from." He gave me and Dooley a pointed look.

Rush was silent as a rat, watching Hoffman.

"Thanks," Dooley said at last. "Let's get started."

"Plante was killed in a loft over on Melcher Street last night about eleven o'clock," Rush said softly. "The equipment was set up by an assistant, named Roche, before Plante was due to get there. Roche was hired locally by Plante's agent, a Frieda Wilcox. Roche was at a party last night and there are witnesses. He has an alibi."

"Wilcox?" I asked.

"In New York. That's where Plante is based these days," Hoffman continued. "Cause of death was a quick and *very* accurate wound to the heart. Hickey's initial opinion is the wound was produced by a similar weapon as killed Wallace. Unofficially, he says he thinks it was committed by the same person."

Hoffman nodded. "Did we get anything from the Missouri records?"

"Yes," said Dooley. "But it took a little wrangling. Fortunately, Katelin has family there and they were able to help."

"What did that cost us?" Hoffman watched Katelin.

"It didn't cost *you* anything." I tapped my fingers on the table in agitation. "I had to promise my family a week's visit." Deep breath. "Mr. Wallace owned a plastics factory. Devout. Went to church twice on Sunday and a couple of times a week. But that wasn't enough for him. He went in for scourging."

"Meaning?" Hoffman raised his eyebrows.

"Meaning the torture in the examiner's report was self-inflicted before he came to Boston. Apparently, it started about six years ago. His wife persuaded him into voluntary commitment. He spent some time in Mid-Missouri Mental Health Center convinced the treating doctors were demons. They treated him anyway. He got better just in time for his wife to have him declared incompetent and take the business.

Wallace didn't fight it. He just left the hospital and disappeared." I wound down.

Dooley chimed in. "Reappearing at *The Church of the Living Christ* a year later. He's been in Boston ever since."

Hoffman thought for a moment. "Did you check with the wife?"

I nodded. "She hadn't spoken with him since 1998. Just before he disappeared. Apparently, this makes her life difficult, but I wasn't clear on the legal issues."

"There's not much a homeless evangelist and wealthy juggler have in common. Likely, the killer knew both of them." Hoffman leaned back in his chair. The chair protested. He nodded across the table. "You looked into Wallace. Did you find any friends? Any connections?"

Dooley pulled out his notes. "MacIlvey didn't find anyone that knew him in Kennedy. The only real friends Wallace had were in the church. The pastor, Tim Rabbitt, knew him. Other members of the congregation might as well, but we haven't had a chance to interview anybody."

Hoffman nodded again. "Plante had a girlfriend and a business as well as an agent. We'll check into that."

"Loquess and I would like to continue checking the church angle." Dooley smiled.

Hoffman stared back without a shred of human feeling in those unblinking black eyes.

"Okay," he said at last. "Like I said, you two did a good job on follow-up. I'll send a couple of uniforms over to run down Plante's building." Hoffman glanced down at the pictures. His voice changed. "It's a damned shame, really. I saw Plante last year at the Colonial. He was amazing. It was like he was defying gravity."

"He was," I said quietly.

"Excuse me?" Hoffman turned his flat eyes on me.

"Plante was a telekinetic. He used it in his act. It's part of why he was so good."

"He *cheated?*" Rush sounded infinitely disappointed.

"Of course not," I said in a sudden fury. "You wouldn't expect a pitcher to use only one leg, would you? A catcher to use one eye? He used his gifts—*all* of them."

Hoffman ignored us both. "Crap. This means the federal regulations apply. We have to rule out the crime was related to Plante's paranormal standing or it could be a fucking civil rights violation." He rubbed his face. "Okay, Dooley. That part of it's going to be your job."

Dooley nodded.

Hoffman watched him for a moment. "I'm not doing you any favors. Ruling out paranormal connections is just a bump and grind: a lot of wasted time."

"I understand."

"Good." Hoffman shrugged. "It was a hell of a show, any way he did it. Hell of a shame. Let's go."

Hoffman rose and Rush followed. As he left, Rush shot me a sad glance.

Watching him, Dooley said with a soft chuckle, "Damn, Loquess. You should never tell someone there's no Santa Claus."

oOo

Once Hoffman and Rush left, Dooley said, "Plante was a paranormal. Think Wallace knew it?"

I stared at him. "What if he did?"

"Plante was using his gifts in his act. It's clear from Rush's reaction it was not common knowledge. Do you think it was something Plante was keeping secret?"

I thought about it for a long moment. "You mean you think Plante was *passing* for normal?"

"Wouldn't you?"

"I can't. Anybody looking up can figure out what I can do."

"True enough." Dooley leaned back in his chair. "But you chose to work in the police department, a profession well known to protect its own. Your work gives you a certain kind of anonymity. As you say, your… *ability* can't be masked. But you've chosen a profession that both defends and hides you."

"You're saying I'*m* passing?"

"I'm asking for your insight. If you *could* do what you love without revealing your gifts, would you be tempted to? By extension, would Plante?"

I tamped my temper down. Dooley had a point. Boston was easier than Missouri by a long shot, but it was never easy. "Maybe." I ticked objections off on my fingers. "For the idea to hold water Wallace would have to find out. He would have to want to try to hold it over Plante. And Plante would have to be threatened enough to kill over it. Not to mention we don't know if there is a connection between them. That's four points you have to make."

"Hickey thinks they were killed by the same weapon in the same manner." Dooley tapped the examiner's report. "He's pretty certain."

"It still seems pretty thin. Even if there is a connection, there are three points left."

"Just clutching at straws." He thought for a moment. "Which brings us back to the only obvious connection: the murder method." Dooley looked in the folder. "Wallace's test scores aren't here."

"We can look on line."

"Could there be more of a long shot?"

"You're the one trying to make detective. I'm just trying to help."

Dooley sighed. "Go on. I'll drink my coffee and watch."

The paranormal registry was voluntary—as much an article of pride as anything else. Nobody *had* to be on it. You could always request not to be placed there, and as long as you weren't in a sensitive position the federal government obliged. There were probably some conspiracy nuts that thought being on it was tantamount to registering guns, but it was unlikely they had the aptitude anyway.

Most paranormals, in point of fact, had a fondness for the U.S. government. After all, it was government-sponsored research of the forties and fifties that discovered how to refine our abilities out of raw aptitude. Rather than thinking of the feds as Big Brother, most of us thought of them as Big Coach.

The feds, for their part, considered the paranormals in the same ambivalent light they would consider any other public asset, like an educated electorate or a raft of draftable young men.

That said, the registry was, like many government lists, not easily open to public scrutiny. Looking up somebody else was intentionally gated the same as birth records, arrest warrants and school grades. But law enforcement, intelligence and Homeland Security agencies had unfettered access.

All I needed was Wallace's social security number, supplied by the Missouri records. Bring up the website, enter it in and wait for his scores to appear.

Dooley drummed his fingers on the table. "It *looks* like magic."

"What does?"

"What you all do. Your flying. His juggling. Making fire come out of a rock."

"But it's not."

"What does that matter? Why wouldn't someone think that it all comes from the devil or something?"

"You make me tired." I leaned back in the chair. "Sure, people think that. There are church sermons against abortion, evolution and paranormals."

"Evolution doesn't look like magic."

"Check out some of those weird insects in the Amazon and tell me that."

Dooley leaned forward. "But do you ever think there might be something to them?"

I stared straight at him. "You're on to me. I have to sacrifice a Christian baby every full moon to keep flying. FAA regulations. Section twelve."

"Come on!"

"People still plant corn by the moon and let astrology rule their lives. *It's not magic*, Dooley. Any more than Usain Bolt or Michael Phelps or Albert Einstein."

"Anybody can run. Or swim."

"Not everybody can even *think* like Einstein."

Dooley looked away. "You got me on Einstein."

I leaned towards him. "Look, every one of us has spent their entire lives fighting, denying or *ignoring* people who think we're magic. Or witches. Or possessed by demons. It's not magic. It's just a skill."

Dooley nodded. "Okay. But people act on what they fear. Maybe whoever killed Wallace thought he was paranormal. They *knew* Plante was paranormal."

Wallace's scores appeared and I turned back to the screen, grateful for an excuse to drop the conversation. I ran my finger down the column. They were all depressingly normal. "Normal."

"It was a long shot, anyway."

"Maybe." I drummed my fingers on the table. Damn it. He got me thinking. "It's not the real score, anyway."

"What do you mean?"

I stretched my back against the chair and sighed. "Did you ever take the initial aptitude tests?"

"Of course." Dooley shrugged. "It's just a word association test. I took it in school like everybody else."

I looked at him. "In school? In Missouri it's voluntary and online."

"It's voluntary and online here, too. Now. But when *I* was a child, back in the Cretaceous, there wasn't much of an internet. If you wanted to take the test, you waited until after school and sat in a classroom with a number two pencil. Voluntary or not, everybody took it. Who wants to give up the chance you might be Superman?"

I laughed shortly. "Hardly."

Dooley nodded. "I know that now. But that's not something you can tell a ten-year-old."

"You got a score back?"

"In the mail. Along with the analysis—it looked something like the SAT scores. This much is your score. This is your percentile. This is the bottom score for possible paranormal aptitude. Mine was not above that bottom score."

"Yeah." I picked up a pencil from the desk and twiddled it between my fingers. "My initial test was online—a word association test just like yours. It might even be the same test Bosch himself invented back in the thirties for all I know. My scores warranted a secondary test held up at the University in Columbia. I had to get my older brother to drive me. After that there are some further tests. If you pass those, you get skill training if you want it."

"So?"

"The initial test determines *possible* aptitude. The secondary tests show *applicable* aptitude. Here. Let me show you." I pointed at Wallace's scores. "See? Only one set. Big blank section over here. Now, I'll bring up my scores." I did and the blank section filled in. "Here are the kinetic scores. Thermal scores. Field scores."

"What's the difference?"

"Kinetic scores are those that involve direct manipulation of kinetic energy. Speeding things up. Slowing things down. Levitation. That sort of thing. Thermal is heat—fire creation, fire suppression. Field scores are direct manipulations of things like electricity. Magnetism. There aren't many of those." I pointed at my scores. "That's what they test for and so that's all they find. It's because of the horizontal whisky problem."

"Beg pardon?"

"Something Sam called it." I didn't say anything for a moment, remembering him. "He said if someone only had a talent for teleporting whisky from someone else's glass to our own, we'd never see it on any tests. Without knowing a talent for whisky teleportation exists, it's impossible to find."

"Telepathy?"

"There's never *ever* been any proof of telepathy. Or evil spirits. Or demonic possession. Dooley, we *had* this conversation."

"Just asking." Dooley looked cross. "What's that have to do with Wallace?"

I leaned over the keyboard and brought up my scores. I pointed at the screen. "Look. It says 'raw' on my initial scores." I brought up Plante's scores. "Here it is again. 'Raw.'"

I brought up Wallace's single page and pointed. "See? It says 'adjusted'."

"What does that mean?"

"It means that the aptitude showed something but not anything they understood. So they adjusted the scores to show normalcy."

Dooley thought for a moment. "Bring up my scores."

He gave me his SSN. Normal scores with the word "adjusted" next to them.

"Son-of-a-bitch. Why the *hell* would they do that?"

"Look. There could be some freak circumstance where you might do something out of the ordinary but they don't know what it is. And without training, it's highly unlikely you'd know what to do even if it happened. And if you did it by accident, in all likelihood you'd never know what it was you did. Hell, Dooley, for all intents and purposes you and Wallace *are* normal."

"I sure as hell would have liked to know about this when I was ten." Dooley finished his coffee, crumpled the cup and dropped it in the trash. "Wallace was homeless. Plante was wealthy. Wallace had been tortured. Plante is in perfect shape. Wallace's only friends were in a little church on the bad side of Boston. Plante was the toast of New York. Both were killed in the same way as to suggest the same person." Dooley fell silent for a moment, considering.

I looked at him. "Wallace is normal. Plante is paranormal. When we know method, motive and opportunity, we'll see that paranormality has nothing to do with it. This—" I pointed at the screen "—is just a mark on the checklist so we can say we conformed to the regs."

"Any common ground is better than no ground. Maybe we should talk to Rabbitt again just to see if we missed a possible connection there between Wallace and Plante. Who would we talk to about paranormal aptitude tests?"

I sighed. "Somebody down at the federal building? FBI? Don't we have a federal liaison or something?"

"Come on, Loquess. Let's try to make *something* interesting out of this. You must know somebody."

I smiled at him sourly. "You mean because *I'm* paranormal I must know about this sort of thing."

He looked uncomfortable. "With your vast experience—"

"Can it." I laughed. "Matter of fact, I *do* know somebody and this is as good an excuse as any to see him. His name is Eli Boor. The Bosch Institute has an office in McLean. That's where he works. He lives up in Salem. I can give him a call."

"You do that."

"You can't think we have a paranormal killer."

"Of course not. Are you stupid? We can go see Boor after we see Rabbitt."

I looked at him. "You do know we can just talk to him on the phone."

"I like to look them straight in the eye." He pointed two fingers first at my eyes, then at his own. "It's more detective-ish."

oOo

I called from the car. Tim Rabbitt didn't answer his phone. Nor was he at the church. But Boor answered his phone by the second ring.

"Katelin!" he boomed over the phone. "It's been months. How are you?"

"Not so bad, Dr. Boor," I said, a sudden smile on my lips. I always liked Eli.

"I'm hurt. You *used* to call me Eli."

"This is official business. I'm investigating the murder of Oscar Plante."

"Ah. I heard. Poor Oscar. How can I help you?"

I looked over at Dooley, driving. "I think it's better we speak in person."

"Hm. Let me check my schedule." A long pause. "I'm back to back here at McLean. But I have a private up in Salem at three. I can meet you up there by four thirty. Will that do?"

"Perfect."

I closed my cell phone.

We drove over to the church. Rabbitt was nowhere to be found, and the church was locked tight.

I stood outside. "It's an hour to Salem if we left right now."

Dooley shook his head. "I want to drop back by the office and see if Hoffman and Rush have anything. Maybe go over the case file again to see if I missed anything. Then, I planned to drive up there."

"Tell you what. I'll meet you."

Dooley glanced up from the file folder. "What? You're going to see some other juggler? We don't have enough murders?"

I tapped my fingers on my knee in agitation. Shook my head. "I haven't really flown in nearly two days. Like any muscle, it's use it or lose it."

"You have a flying muscle?"

I punched him gently on the arm. "You're an asshole. I've got to work out. A couple of hours might even make me human again."

"I live in hope."

I reached in the back seat and got my stick. As I unfolded it I said, "I'll see you in Salem at four."

"Where?"

I gave him the address. "Town center. You can't miss it." I adjusted my helmet, settled my ass on the stick and hovered for a moment, getting my balance right.

"You are a spawn of Satan," Dooley said quietly. "You do know that, don't you?"

"You say the nicest things to a girl."

I rose vertically and pitched east as soon as I was above the low buildings, keeping my climb until I was skirting the tops of the hotels. I hovered over Exchange Place in a cloudless blue sky. I could see the mouth of the Mystic River and a good portion of the Charles River pouring its heart into Boston Harbor. The water was rippling with sailboats even this late in the season. So clear that I could see the ring of hills around Boston and beyond them the horizon tints of taller hills beyond. Another thousand or two feet in altitude and I would have been able to see the mountains of New Hampshire, fifty miles away. The air was fall brisk and the light October golden.

oOo

I was on the radio to Boston Traffic before I landed on the State Street roof. Usually, I just worked through the BPD dispatcher. But this was October and Conclave was in two weeks. BPD would never get a word in edgewise.

In all the world there might be two hundred witches that are capable of true flight as opposed to many more that can lift a couple of inches or float in the air. Every year, most of those witches came to Conclave for the Salem Olympics along with anybody else that has the ability to levitate, move objects, light fires or magnetize iron, whether or not that ability was useful. Here flyers competed for little more than bragging rights in acrobatics, speed and endurance. Flying was not the only recognized sport, but it was the only one that required the use of most of the Salem Sound and Nahant Bay as a staging area. It was also the only one regulated by the FAA.

In July of every year the Air Venture air show makes Oshkosh, Wisconsin, the busiest airport in the world. Traffic controllers work their fingers to the bone and their voices to a scratch managing all of the takeoffs, landings and acrobatic stunts. It's a plum assignment. Participating controllers have a justifiable pride in what they've done. But the aircraft are still aircraft, not ninety-pound pilots flying literally cheek to cheek jamming a space smaller than one runway of the Boston airfield.

By tradition and inclination, Boston traffic controllers enforced scheduling and separation in both the practice and performance areas. It was hard, exacting work that had to be done visually—radar didn't have sufficient acuity. Most of it was done from the rehabilitated Marblehead Light with spotters at Winter Island, Forest River, Lynch Park and Salem Willows Park, along with a few boats. While they respected their brother controllers in Wisconsin, they considered the Conclave problems far more difficult and unique.

The night after Halloween was by tradition the Controller's Dinner, where the flyers hosted exhausted traffic controllers to an evening of seafood and beer. To me, this was one of the best parts of Conclave.

But now the controllers were just getting into the groove. The flyers were still disorganized and EMTs were moored out in Beverly Harbor trying to figure out if they could fish out an unconscious flyer from the cold water before he drowned.

"N75638. Boston Traffic request." All flyers had their own N-number since *they* were the aircraft and not their stick. The

'N' part signifies United States. For reasons that must lie in the fallows of bureaucratic minds—*I* sure don't know why— flyers always state the preceding N, though other pilots within the country of origin drop it. Go figure. I checked the ATIS: approach to the active runway was over the harbor. I'd be risking wake turbulence if I went up the coast that way.

"Boston Traffic, N75638."

"N75638: request terminal transit to Broad Sound and the Conclave practice area."

"N75638. Terminal transit denied. Too much traffic."

Aircraft were taking off over a corner of East Boston so they had to observe noise reduction rules. Maybe I could slip underneath. "N75638. What's my maximum altitude for an East Boston transit?"

"N75638. Eight hundred feet."

That was a bare minimum. I didn't like transits at low altitude. It was hard enough to remain the least bit incognito around Boston. Still, with Conclave so close, a flyer wouldn't be completely unexpected. "N75638. Request East Boston transit at altitude eight hundred feet."

" N75638. Transit approved. Set your transponder to 4338. I'll call your hand-off to Conclave Traffic."

"N75638. Roger."

I descended to the Westin on the water, sighted on the entrance to the Callahan tunnel and crossed the bay, turned and flew north following the Chelsea River until it dried up near the Revere Beach Parkway, then over to the beach and north east.

I didn't dawdle. I'd never been witness to the result of an encounter between a witch and the wake turbulence of a Boeing 747, but I'd seen pictures.

As soon as I came over Revere Beach, Boston Traffic came back on the line: "N75638: frequency change to 129.75 and hand off to Conclave Control."

"N75638 roger."

I changed the frequency and instantly there came the chatter: "N87JWH requesting acrobatic clearance."

"N87JWH: Proceed to Misery Island and hold. N88TH8: Finish your current sequence and vacate the Northeast Practice Area."

"N88TH8. I'll need another run on the routine."

"N88TH8: Hold in the staging area. There are four teams ahead of you. N87JWH: advance to the Endicott College practice area. You have forty-five minutes."

There was a pause. I took advantage of it. "N75638, request."

"N75638 proceed."

"N75638: request a solo practice area for tight sprinting."

"N75638: proceed to the Ocean Avenue entry by way of Swampscott and Atlantic Ave and hold."

The practice area must have been even more crowded than I expected. I had to skirt Nahant Bay by flying over Swampscott. Then I cut off the very lower tip off of Marblehead and landed in the parking area of the bird sanctuary. Conclave didn't expect me to hover while I waited for a spot.

Someone called: "Loquess."

I turned and smiled sourly. "Sniezek."

Bertrand Sniezek, the remaining BPD flyer, walked over to me, his black stick over his shoulder. He was bald, short and broad, heavier than a flying witch had any right to be. But every muscle was clearly defined—and on parade. He was wearing a skin-tight leotard to good advantage. There was no wind resistance against the body during flight; the bubble took care of that. It was pure affectation—and, of course, utterly different from when I did exactly the same thing in college.

When I had first joined BPD, it had been with the understanding I'd be a team flyer with Sniezek. But Sniezek had pulled me aside and made it clear in no uncertain tones that he was only interested in solo pursuit. Team flying was not one of his interests. Not to mention, he would never fly with such an underpowered partner.

"Heard you talking to Conclave Control. Are you entering this year?"

"No. But I wanted to get a good workout."

Sniezek nodded. "Good. I'm going for the zig-zag. It's going to be hard enough without competing against a waif like you."

I could feel myself bristle. He always found some way to get at me. "I've been thinking about changing my mind."

He held up his hands in conciliation. "I meant no offense. I was referring to the mass difference. I have a lot of power but a lot of mass, too. It's tough on the turns."

I nodded, suppressing my irritation. Sniezek was mean-spirited and selfish but mass was mass. Flying still had to allow for Newtonian mechanics.

"I have a proposition," he said calmly.

"Yeah?"

"How would you like to run some z-sprints with me?"

"I thought I was underpowered."

"And a woman," Sniezek said comfortably. "In the straights I'd blow you away."

"Don't be so sure," I said, irritation returning instantly.

He waved that away. "We can do a straight race some other time. The z-sprint is something you're good at. Better than me."

"Really?" I lifted an eyebrow.

He shrugged. "Of course. No mass. You way more maneuverable than I am. If I can work against you, I'll do better. Besides, it's more fun to compete against somebody than work out on your own."

"Generally, I like to work out with someone I like."

He grinned. "Life is full of disappointments."

In spite of myself, I grinned back. It would be nice to hand Sniezek his head. "Make the call," I said.

A moment later he turned to me. "The z-sprint area is going to clear in fifteen minutes. Ready?"

I nodded. The starting area for the z-sprint was just over the water in Lady's Cove so we didn't have to transit. Sniezek took the chance to stretch out but I felt pretty limber. Pretty soon, they called our numbers and we glided over to the starting point at the Marblehead Yacht Club.

Unlike the rest of the flying events, the z-sprint is specifically over a combination of water and land. It's a sprint over uneven terrain—think of it as a slalom course for skiers, if they were skiing in the air and could go up as well as down. It was always a hit with the crowds—a collection of ten or twenty high-speed witches shooting forty miles an hour a hundred feet over their heads.

This course was about five miles long. There were six colored pylons starting at the yacht club. The course proceeded straight from the club to Dolliber Cove and a near 180-degree turn—almost a reverse. Then down to Fort Sewall and a merely difficult 90-degree turn to the west. Past the beach at the foot of the Waterside Cemetery and another mild turn, this time to the south. A fairly long leg to the Marblehead High School but a screaming reverse turn back towards the center of Marblehead and the Village School. Then, another screaming 180 and the flyers ran the same course in reverse. A ten-mile course in total.

Like in slalom skiing, you had to pass the pylon on the outside of the turn—cutting inside lost you points. The reverse was tricky since the leader then had to thread back through the pack without a collision. The z-sprint had the most injuries of all of the events, but no witch had ever suggested the reverse be eliminated.

We hovered over the start of the z-sprint.

"I have a countdown timer." Sneizek set it. "Ten seconds?"

I nodded.

I leaned down against the stirrups, holding myself loosely against the handlebars. *Relax,* I told myself. Never lose energy from mere tension.

The timer rang and we were off. I ticked off the markers in my head. Crocker Park, John Glover House, Alpha Whisky.

As I expected, Sneizek pulled ahead quickly. This was a part of the course that favored raw strength—something I couldn't match.

But the pylon on the island in Dolliber Cove was marked green, meaning a minimum turning altitude of two hundred feet. Sniezek had to start his ascent early to account for the extra mass he carried.

I didn't bother but kept accelerating, barely over the water when we passed the Hood Yard. By the time I had to start trying for altitude, I had passed under him.

Then I pulled up and quit trying to keep up speed—I just added a strong vertical vector. This had the effect of lifting me like a bullet and sacrificing horizontal speed I needed to dump for the turn anyway.

I peaked just over the required height a scant second behind Sniezek—better than I had feared but not as well as I had hoped. Sniezek turned out, but I had the vertical momentum. I looped back upside down and flew directly toward Fort Sewall. We were neck and neck.

With the advantage of a straight descent, Sniezek began to pull away. I didn't try to catch up, just kept the gap as small as possible. This leg was short. He didn't have time to muscle ahead.

As we approached Fort Sewall, Sniezek again had to step outside to make the turn. I had no ascending advantage at this point.

Still, I didn't slow down. I blew past him. This pylon required a quarter turn west. I counted down the distance and started a hard snap roll to the outside. I timed it perfectly: my head spun past the midpoint and was coming back around towards the pylon as I turned, killing side momentum when I started the turn. I pushed high off the stick to get the most benefit of the roll and felt the g-force pulling at me, slowing down the roll but keeping me in the turn. I came out of the turn rolling upright, dizzy but unbowed, lined up for the next pylon across the town.

I glanced back. Sniezek had not only had to go wide to preserve his speed. But without the momentum transfer of the roll, he was forced to slow down and then re-accelerate.

I gained ground until he came back around from the turn, but this was a medium leg followed by the long leg of the course. I lost ground on the straight but regained some on the turns. Now, we were on the home stretch of the first round, getting ready for the reverse. I had another trick up my sleeve.

I shot towards the last pylon, glanced back. Sniezek wasn't far behind. I jogged to the inside and low to the ground of where I had to run to make the turn. Then, I abruptly goosed the stick into a quick ascent. A vertical 180 twist and now I was flying *backwards*. I held on to the stick with my legs, spread my arms wide, and stopped flying.

The wind, held back by the bubble, suddenly roared against my back. I held my arms wide as long as I could, feeling the wind slow me down, then grabbed the stick and wrapped the bubble around me. I killed the remaining momentum and accelerated back up to speed going south on the reverse.

Sniezek shot past me, his mouth wide open.

I had a good lead now but I needed to conserve my energy. I was breathing hard and sweating like a pig. *Like a sparrow flies*, I thought. Pushing for speed and then release, just holding the bubble to cut wind resistance. Just enough to let me catch my breath.

Sniezek caught up with me as we reached Fort Sewall. But I got my lead back on the next two turns.

Now it was straight along the edge of the water, speed against speed. But I'd been resting as much as I could since the reverse and Sniezek had been forced to use up his wind closing on my lead.

I leaned on the stick and *pushed*.

I was able to hold six feet of lead, but Sniezek was creeping up. Four feet. Three feet.

It wasn't enough.

I passed the Marblehead Yacht Club pylon with a foot to spare.

Sobbing with breath, I didn't even try to use anything to slow down. It was all I could do to keep myself above the water as I shot over the Lady's Cove and curved slowly back to Ocean Ave.

As soon as I was back over land, I eased the bubble. The wind slowed me down and I settled onto the crusty beach, dropped the stick and stood, hands on my knees, barely able to breathe and trying like hell not to throw up.

Sniezek walked up a few seconds later. He waved to me and collapsed on the sand, unable to speak.

Finally, he grabbed a bottle of water from the storage compartment of his stick and weakly tossed it to me. I weakly caught it. He pulled out one for himself.

"That," he said between deep breaths, "was a damned fine run."

I nodded, still catching my breath.

"That roll into the turn looked dangerous as hell. But the wind stop—is that even *legal?*"

I grinned at him and shrugged, speaking between gasps. "I don't think it's ever been tried." I looked around. There were a few people watching from up on the hill but most were down on the piers following the acrobatics. "You be the first. Maybe you'll get some points."

"Where did you learn it?"

"Sam Kozak taught me the snap turn when I was sixteen. But I can't say I learned it then. I spent a week running snap turns over the Missouri River and I fell in more than once. It takes a lot of practice to keep from getting disoriented in the turn. I discovered the wind stop by accident when I lost the bubble and went sailing about forty feet."

Sniezek watched me for a minute, sipping his water. "Sam was my teacher, too."

"Until the day he died, I think Sam had a hand in the training of every cop flyer still flying."

"He must have thought a lot of you, teaching you at sixteen."

"Yeah," I said. Maybe he did; maybe he didn't. He probably wouldn't now. Had it been seven years? No, eight. I met David in 1994. I met Sam in 1991. Sam died in 1993 .

I stood up and shivered. I hadn't thought to bring a towel with me and I was dripping with sweat.

"I have a towel you can use. If you want." He gestured towards his stick but wrinkled his nose.

I laughed. "Thanks but no thanks."

"Don't forget I offered."

I regarded him with something approaching friendliness for the first time. "How come you're always such a bastard to me? And why not now?"

Sniezek sipped his water and capped the bottle before answering. "There's a story, eh? You're a good flyer, Loquess. Very good. But I never thought you were serious about anything. Even with Sean—*especially* with Sean. First you were with Sabado. Then, when that went south, you started playing around with Sean." He put the bottle back in his stick. "I'm a flyer and I'm a good one. More importantly, I'm a cop. My daddy is a cop in Framingham. My granddaddy was a cop over in Poland before he came over here. I'm a cop first and a flyer second. You were always hung up on your men first, then your life, then your flying, and somewhere at the tail end of things came BPD. I can't trust someone like that. Dooley was *your* handler, not Sean's or mine. Because you needed one."

I was stung. I picked up my stick. "Then, why be nice today?"

Sniezek stretched. Looked around. "I don't know. Maybe because it's a beautiful day. Maybe because you are such a damned fine flyer. Maybe I'm getting old. Or maybe it's because you're really working a case with Dooley and acting like a real cop. For once."

"Thanks," I said shortly and mounted my stick.

Sniezek waved at me languidly. "Have fun."

oOo

I cancelled myself out of the practice area and requested a transit across town. After I was cleared, I heard Sniezek request more time.

Eli's house was on Essex Street in Salem. The minimum altitude for the non-practice area was six hundred feet from ground or forty feet from the tops of buildings. I followed the waterfront, just off of the water and above the boats. Salem and Gloucester were two places in the world where I didn't care about being seen. Every witch in the world was on parade this week. I was a needle among needles.

I was tired, aching in every bone. It had been weeks since I'd had a workout like that. I was out of shape.

I had won the z-sprint by luck and deceit rather than by skill. If the course had been forty feet longer Sniezek would have pulled enough ahead to beat me.

Okay, I told myself. *No more drinking. Back to the gym and the high-protein shakes. Wouldn't hurt to increase my run a mile or so. Yeah. The way I've been acting for the last couple of months? Time to start running again.*

Eli's place was an old captain's house. I came across the ferry terminals and over the Peabody-Essex Museum, up Essex Street, landed gently on the widow's walk and collapsed on the bench, breathing heavily.

Eli had built a trellis around the widow's walk for privacy—Eli was no stranger to flyers. Or to me.

Of course, the fact that Eli had been David's therapist from the time he was six until he was discharged at twelve gave him a certain familiarity.

How long had it been since I'd been here? Since David had left? Had it been *that* long? Surely I had come up here to visit at least once since then. I couldn't remember. The wind and the sweat made me shiver. I remembered meeting David up here one night when we first moved to Boston. The trellis had given us some privacy. We took advantage of it. I wondered if Eli knew how we'd abused his hospitality.

I stood up and found the key hidden in the planter, opened the door and took my stick inside.

Once out of the wind I quit shivering. I checked my watch. Dooley wouldn't be here for at least an hour. If Eli was here, he'd be in his office with a patient. That room was so soundproofed Armageddon could happen outside and they'd only find out when they finished. I had a brief image: "I think we've made great progress but it's time we wound down. Why don't we pick up next—*oh my God!*" I found myself grinning.

I went down to the basement and undressed, threw my clothes into the dryer so they'd at least be comfortable to wear even if they smelled. Then, into the shower and blessed hot water.

Half an hour later I was in the kitchen wearing clothes only slightly damp and somewhat salt-encrusted and eating a slice of homemade bread.

"Here I was worried you wouldn't make yourself at home."

I looked up and Eli was watching me. Without thinking, I stood up and hugged him—or as much as I could, given that he was round as a basketball.

Eli hugged me back and kissed me on the cheek. Then, he held me at arm's length and considered me critically.

"Not sleeping well enough. Nor have you been eating well. Or exercising." He cocked his head. "And drinking too much." He sighed. "Well, at least I can feed you."

Eli pushed me towards the table and sliced some more bread and put it in the toaster. Then, he pulled out mozzarella cheese, some tomatoes, a bit of basil and garlic and some olive oil. Ten minutes later, he had a bowl of bruschetta. He handed it to me.

"Eat. I'll make espresso."

For a moment it was as if every cell in my body had been waiting its entire microscopic life for that bruschetta. I licked the spoon, scraped the bowl with the bread.

Eli had sat down across the table and watched me. He gave me the tiny espresso cup. "How have you been?"

I shrugged. "So-so. Working on a case that might involve paranormals. That's why Dooley is coming over."

Eli checked his watch. "We have half an hour. You are unhappy. Why?"

"Sean and I broke up. He left."

"Did he leave? Or did you push him away like you did David?"

"That's not fair!"

Eli shrugged and didn't say anything, waiting for me to answer.

I composed myself, sipped my espresso. "I suppose I pushed him away. That's what he thinks, anyway."

"Did you?"

"Yes." I leaned back in the chair. "It's been two years since David and I broke up. For *whatever* reason. That's over. Sean was different. But I still couldn't make it work. I can't make anything work out here. Things have been crappy since I moved out here. I've been here three years. Three years of crap."

"Boston is a hard place to live."

"I don't have any friends. Back in Columbia, I had Arnold, Anita, Mattie, Carl. Sandy never let me have a boyfriend she liked, but she was pleasant enough. Out here..." I raised my hand and let it fall.

"Do you have police friends?"

I shook my head. "Sean was a friend until we started sleeping together. Now that's over. Dooley is a colleague. The other cops don't want to have much to do with me."

"Why?"

I shrugged. "I had a workout with Sniezek this afternoon. He said I didn't take the job seriously enough."

"Do you?"

I shrugged again. "Not really. I mean, it's a good flying opportunity. I've learned more about flying since I came here than I ever thought about before. But the cop stuff?" I thought for a minute. "If I could keep the flying but do something different, I'd do it."

"The thrill of the job is gone."

"Pretty much."

Eli studded the wall behind me for a moment. I knew what he was going to say before he said it. After all, he'd said it before.

"I could get you a job over at the Natick research labs, you know. Or even at MIT."

"As a lab rat."

He nodded. "Can't argue with that. Or the need for human experimentation. But though most of the flyers have donated time at one point or another—you included—we're coming to a point where we need someone permanent on staff. You could be that person."

I thought about it. This wasn't the first time Eli had hinted at something like this, but it was the first time he'd made such a bald offer. I had to take it seriously, even though it deeply disturbed me.

"No. Not yet, at least." I shivered.

Eli caught it and smiled wanly. "You think about it." He rubbed his hands together. "Back to the subject at hand. You know this whole thing is familiar, don't you?"

I grinned at him sheepishly. "You mean like David was with the piano when I met him?"

"Exactly."

I shook my head. "I don't think they're the same thing. David had lost his belief in his talent. That it was something more than just hammering keys. All he had to do was realize he *reached* people. Even I could see that. Me: I'm a good flyer. But it's not art or anything." I looked over at him. "What do you think?"

Eli stood up and stretched. "I think you and your insurance card should come over to the hospital and see me a couple of times a week."

"Can I afford you?"

"We have a sliding scale for civil servants." He stroked his beard for a moment. "Seriously, though. You sound very unhappy. There's no reason for someone as bright, young and talented as yourself to be that unhappy. I think I could help. It doesn't have to be official therapy. Just come on by and spend some time with an old friend." He smiled craftily. "Did I mention I put a pool table in the basement?"

"No!"

"I did! Blond wood with a charcoal gray felt. Flat as a promise. Come on over. Drink my beer. Play pool with me. We'll talk about things."

"You're a wicked man, Eli."

"I admit it." Then, his expression suddenly turned professional. "And Officer Dooley has just arrived."

oOo

Eli took us into his office. He gestured towards two chairs facing his desk and sat across the desk from us.

It was a large desk, glass-smooth and made of a deeply grained wood so dark it looked almost purple, empty but for a tasteful black monitor to Eli's left. The desk put a distance between us that forced formality. Dooley and I on one side; Eli on the other. We were police officers. Eli was a material source of information.

It made me uncomfortable. I'd always been welcome in this house. So welcome, I'd come in today unannounced and, without a second thought, taken a shower and eaten a meal knowing Eli was enthusiastic about me being there.

I suddenly realized Eli had brought us into his office on purpose. The enforced formality was intentional.

I looked around the room. Eli had furnished it sparsely. Two chairs. A sofa on one side. Some framed diplomas on the wall and a pair of ancient Japanese prints. I knew without investigation they were original and expensive—Eli would have nothing less. Cabinets of the same elegant wood as the desk lined one wall, a similarly made bookshelf lined the other. Two tall and narrow windows on opposite walls and a great bay window behind Eli's desk, framing him as he looked at us. The office was on the top floor and the house was on a slight rise. Through the window, if I looked past Eli and over the neighboring houses, I could see the bay.

"What can I do for you, Officers?"

Dooley spoke up. "We've been checking into two murders that seem to be related." He pulled out his notebook. "One of the victims was a paranormal—"

"Oscar Plante."

Dooley sighed. "There's a natural give and take to these things, Dr. Boor. If you wait and let me ask the questions at my own pace, it will go faster."

"Sorry."

"Since one of the victims was a paranormal, we are obligated by federal regulation to make sure the crime wasn't paranormal-related. We had some questions about the paranormal testing process."

Eli looked surprised. "Really? Katelin's been through it. There's not much more to know."

I spoke up. "I can get the scores of the secondary test and the final training exams. We're interested in the primary screening."

Eli looked at us blankly. "Whatever for?"

Dooley consulted his notes. "We're interested in high-scoring people who had no predisposition for selection."

Eli leaned forward. "Why?"

Dooley watched Eli without moving for an uncomfortably long time. Then, he shrugged. "It's likely a lead that will go nowhere. Federal regulation indicates we have to look at all possibilities."

Eli nodded. "All right."

"Do you have access to the pre-test scores?"

Eli nodded again. "Of course. Part of McLean's contract is to update the primary test regularly to prevent gaming."

I was surprised. "People try to game the test? Why?"

Eli smiled at me. "Spoken like someone who truly has been through the whole selection process successfully. There are lots of reasons to game the test: status, prestige, money—"

"Money?" asked Dooley, suddenly interested.

"Sure." Eli chuckled. "There are only a few thousand able paranormals on the planet. If someone can get to second-level screening, there are those who would believe that's enough evidence of *some* ability even if it's not enough to be selected. Gaming the system lets the unscrupulous take advantage of the gullible." Eli shook his head. "It's not even true. Second-level screening is intended to weed out those who got through first-level screening. We only do full testing on those who pass through both levels."

"These are false credentials, then."

"You could call them that." Eli looked out the window for a moment. "At least, they are false in that the first-level screening didn't weed them out. We're fairly certain candidates who have managed to pass through two levels of screening have something we want to examine."

I leaned forward. "I was told during testing that first-level screening only winnows out people who have abilities that can be tested for."

Eli stared at me. "There are those who believe that," he said reluctantly.

"So people with new abilities—abilities for which there are no tests—might show up in the primary test."

Eli cocked his head at me. "What do you mean?"

"If someone had an ability but it didn't fit any of the normal applicable abilities, would it show up on the primary test?"

Eli sighed. "It's not that simple. Do you know how the testing works?"

I sat back. "Of course. I took the tests—"

"No. I don't mean how the test is administered or the nature of the test. Do you know how the test actually *works?*"

Dooley interrupted. "Even if she does, I don't. Explain it to me, Doctor."

Eli fiddled with a pencil on his desk. "Bohr and Heisenberg first legitimized witchery. Bohr's mother was a demonstrable paranormal. The two of them presented a paper in 1937 showing that witchery was a physically reproducible phenomenon but had no more in common with relativity than it did with quantum physics. Physics has been in a strained state ever since. We have three competing models of how the universe operates: the Standard Model, Einstein's Relativity and whatever dismal mathematics passes for a model of how the paranormal works. The rest of the physics community has managed to muddle on quite nicely by ignoring us." Eli chuckled. "Oppenheimer said, 'God may or may not play dice but he's not above fixing the game.'"

Eli continued. "But to investigate the phenomenon, you needed to actually find experimental partners. For whatever reason, we have been unable to reproduce paranormal effects in a laboratory or a particle accelerator. They can only be examined in the messy and unscientific human brain. How do you find such people? How do you train them? Herbert Bosch was a young physics *and* medical student in Copenhagen. He sought Bohr out and they both worked with Ellen Adler until she died in 1930. Bosch finished his degrees and moved to England. Bosch thought he could find behavioral markers that would show people of talent. Later, Bohr came to England as well to avoid the Nazis. He refused to work with Bosch and the paranormal. Instead, he worked on the bomb project. He preferred the simplicity of particle physics."

Eli leaned forward against the desk. "The brain is a single organ that does many things. They all affect one another. If you're excited in one part of the brain, another part of the brain raises your heartbeat. If you're upset about your wife, deep down in the amygdala, it affects your tennis game. Bosch was a physicist and physiologist. One area of his research was studying electrical behavior of language in the brain. He thought word associations would show a statistical pattern in talents that would be absent or different in the untalented. He developed the first pre-test—of course, at that point, it was the only test that seemed to work the least little bit. What it does is measure a pre-disposition towards the paranormal. No more than that."

He leaned back in his chair. "Initially, the test was only marginally successful. But it did winnow out a population that could be examined. That led to refinement of the test. Barry Stevens developed some training for the abilities we were discovering—telekinesis, pyrokinesis, such as that. It was Stevens who first articulated the horizontal whisky problem."

Dooley glanced up. "I've heard of that."

"It was a big debate in the sixties between Stevens and Skinner. It's largely been resolved."

"There's no horizontal whisky problem?"

"No new abilities have been discovered in twenty years. Just further refinements of what we already know. Regardless, Bosch refined the test against the results. By the middle fifties, it was administered right alongside achievement tests. Now, it's all over the world."

Dooley wrote something down in his notebook. I tried to read it but couldn't see the page.

Dooley finished and looked up. "So the primary test can reveal ability even if you don't know what ability that is."

"It can show *pre-disposition*. Not ability."

"If they show *pre-disposition*, the candidates are brought in for secondary testing?"

"Usually."

"Usually?"

Eli crossed his legs. "Look, the scoring of the test is a work in progress. A result that might be considered meaningful in 1961 could be determined to be insignificant in 1972. Or a result might be intriguing but useless in 1979 and could be shown to be important in 1982. The test itself changes. How do you reinterpret past results when the tool that created those results has itself changed? It's hard work."

"So you don't bring in everyone."

Eli nodded. "Through experience, we've learned that some result patterns show a pre-disposition that doesn't manifest in secondary screening. Maybe it's an ability—the 'horizontal whisky' problem. Likely not. Since we can't do anything with it, it's meaningless."

"They don't pan out."

"Right."

"So nowadays, you don't even bring them in."

"Exactly."

"But their scores are high."

"The scores are reported as numbers similar to the SATs: six hundred, seven hundred, eight hundred. If someone scores a seven hundred on a pattern we know to be intransigent, we reduce it with a handicap."

Dooley watched Eli for a moment. "My score was five-fifty-six. You're telling me I could really have a score of seven or eight hundred?"

"It's not a meaningful pattern. We downgrade the score to correct it."

"What's the top score?"

"The test is designed to the concept of a perfect score of a thousand."

I interrupted. "How do we get the raw pre-test scores? Before you downgrade them."

Eli gestured to the monitor. "They're all on line."

"All of them? All the way back to the sixties?"

"Yes."

"Good. I'll need access."

"Okay." Eli looked at us both. "This sounds like it goes beyond federal mandate."

"It's just due diligence," said Dooley, putting his notebook back in his pocket.

oOo

Dooley stood outside, disk in hand. He tapped his notebook against his other palm, watching me. "Are you flying back or coming with me?"

"I'm beat. I'll come with you." I looked at him when I got in the car. "Due diligence my ass."

"Yeah." Dooley took a deep breath and let it out. "I was just pissed off my scores were downgraded. I wanted to make him pay a little bit. Petty of me."

"You don't know they were downgraded. It just says 'adjusted.'"

"You'll tell me later." Dooley pulled out his keys and put them in the ignition. He didn't start the engine. "What is your relationship with Dr. Boor?"

"Every paranormal knows Eli Boor and Martin Miegle. They're the two leading researchers into paranormal physics. Eli's the psychologist and neuroscientist. Martin's the quantum physicist. I bet most of the Boston witches have met Eli personally."

Dooley looked exasperated. "That much you told me. But now I am asking you something different. What is your *personal* relationship with Dr. Boor?"

"He's a friend."

"You can give me a little more."

"What? You think I'm *sleeping* with him?" I was nearly shouting.

Dooley was unperturbed. "Or maybe you slept with him in the past. It's obvious you have some kind of prior relationship."

I looked out the window for a moment. "David suffered from multiple personality disorder when he was a kid."

"Really? I didn't read that in the liner notes."

I nodded. "It's not publicized. It's bad enough he was in a mental institution when he was growing up. But MPD has significant media presence. David never wanted anybody to know about it."

"And Dr. Boor?"

"David was at McLean. Eli was David's therapist. When David got better and was released, he and Eli stayed friends. More than friends. David's father was absent a lot—he was a fisherman out of Gloucester. Between being in McLean and his dad being out at sea, David didn't have much in the way of a father. So he latched onto Eli. Eli latched back. They've been close ever since."

"Why was David committed?"

"David set fires in old houses. Almost killed a retired couple. He was caught, declared mentally incompetent and sent to McLean."

"Interesting." Dooley fell silent.

"Why?"

"McLean doesn't do criminal cases. They handle research into paranormals and boutique mental patients. Criminal cases are sent to Bridgewater."

"David was a kid."

"Criminal juvie mental cases go to Roslindale. Usually they get farmed out—and not to McLean."

"Maybe Eli liked him. He might have known the family. I don't know all the particulars."

Dooley shook his head. "It doesn't matter. It has nothing to do with this case."

"Neither does any 'relationship' I have with Eli."

"Which I notice you never clarified." Dooley grinned at me.

"I told you about David!"

"I didn't ask about David, did I?" Dooley laughed. "But, as you say, at this point it has nothing to do with the case."

oOo

Rabbitt was still not in the church. Reluctantly, we returned to the office.

Bored, I booted up Dooley's laptop and brought up the site Eli gave us. I checked my own scores, of course. Preliminary test gave me a seven-fifty. Plante was a full eight-sixty-five. Dooley was a seven-seventy, which surprised me.

Wallace and Rabbitt were both in the middle eight hundreds. On impulse, I put in David. His score was eight-ninety-five.

"They all showed promising results on the pre-test before the test scores were corrected."

Dooley thought for a moment. "What does that mean?"

"Not a thing."

"Let's throw it in the pot and let it stew. We don't have enough to hang anything together."

Hoffman and Rush were working at the table, going over something on a laptop.

"Did you talk to the preacher?" Hoffman said without looking at us.

Dooley didn't speak up so I answered. "He wasn't there."

"Not surprised." Hoffman planted one fat finger on the laptop and looked at them. "We talked to Plante's sister."

"Yeah?"

"Plante's been going to church here in Boston. Devout, even. Tried to convert her. Guess whose church?"

Dooley answered right up. "Tim Rabbitt's."

Hoffman made a gun from his finger and pulled the trigger. "Bang on. We have a connection between the two murders. The DA's getting us a warrant. Soon as we have it, we're going to go bust down a door or two. Want to come along?"

Dooley nodded. "Hell yes."

"Me, too," I said, surprising myself.

"No doors for you."

"Why the hell not?"

"You're going to watch from the air." Hoffman turned back to the laptop. "If he's the killer, I want every advantage I can get. Things might get nasty."

From the outside of the building there was no evidence that Rabbitt was in the meeting area or the tiny living quarters in the back. But Hoffman took no chances. He stationed uniforms near the windows and in the back alley. He looked up at me and gave a signal.

"On it," I whispered over the radio. I was high, in the dark and covered in night camo. Rabbitt couldn't have seen me with night goggles.

I know my abilities. I'm quick and acrobatic. I really am a very good flyer. But one skill I prize above the others: stealth flying.

Witchflying in and of itself is quiet—the bubble dampens most of the turbulence. We have no engines. No propellers.

But we can be seen.

Clouds had rolled in covering what was left of the moon, but the city lights lightened the color of the sky to a light gray. I came in over the church and did a three-sixty wearing infra-reds: two-story, flat-roofed warehouse. One roof door next to the HVAC cooling stack. Various pipes. Narrow, human-sized alley on one side. Loading dock on the side. Open space and fence in the back.

No body signatures on the roof or in the surrounding alleys. I flipped up the infra-reds so I didn't get disoriented. I eased down along the roof line and circled again so I could see a little into the windows. Nothing obvious. The inside was dark.

I came up to the first window and flipped upside down so I could see inside the corner of the window from the top—people look down out a window more than they look up. Flipped down the infra-reds. Nothing.

Next window. Same result.

I eased around the top floor and didn't find anything. Bottom floor: same result.

I took my station, high enough to see most of the back but low enough to see clearly. I keyed my microphone. "I'm in position."

"Okay, then," said Hoffman. "Still no movement or light?"

"No movement whatsoever. No infra-red. Unless he's in an inner room, this is an empty building."

"I hope not."

Two uniforms stood on either side of the door, one holding the battering ram. Hoffman pounded on the door and stepped to one side. "Open up!" he cried. "Boston Police Department. We have a warrant to search these premises."

No answer.

Hoffman nodded to the policemen. They picked up the ram and stood on either side, getting a good swing going. Then, they slammed it into the door. With a shriek and a splintering crash, the door burst inward. Hoffman and Rush entered first, guns drawn, followed by the uniforms.

I drifted in a slow circle so I could watch the three sides of the building other than the front. Lights flashed out the windows as police spread through the church.

Twenty minutes of slow hover strongly resembled twenty minutes of isometrics. I was covered with a light sweat when Hoffman's voice came over the radio.

"No one here, Loquess. Anything to report?"

"Not a thing."

"Okay. Come on down."

I dropped in a low glide, feeling relief at the sudden movement. I collapsed the stick and slung it over my shoulder.

Inside the meeting room, Hoffman was talking to Dooley. Rush was nowhere to be seen.

Dooley waved me over. Hoffman was writing in his notebook. He glanced up as I joined them.

"You spoke with Rabbitt day before yesterday, right?" Hoffman closed his notebook and put it in his coat pocket.

I glanced at Dooley and nodded. "Yes."

"He didn't seem agitated or upset?"

"Some. He was unhappy about Wallace."

"Right. The homeless guy."

I looked from one of them to the other: one white, one black, both hugely towered over me. "What did you find?"

"Not much," said Hoffman. "A computer. Some sermon notes. No evidence of violence. No weapons. You saw Rabbitt about four in the afternoon?"

"Right."

"Dooley says you went to dinner."

"Yes. By myself."

Hoffman nodded. "Plante was killed not long after that."

"You have an idea?"

Hoffman shook his head. "No. I'm thinking that Rabbitt must have left from here to kill Plante right after you two talked to him. We can account for all calls on both of their phones and they didn't talk. Which means Rabbitt must have known where Plante was staying and known when Plante was going to be there. You don't need to ask questions you already know the answer to." Hoffman grinned at me. "You didn't know where he was staying, did you, Loquess?"

"No, Detective."

"Good." Hoffman rubbed his cheek, thinking for a moment. "So by the time you and Dooley were talking with him he'd already made his plans. Did he talk about anything *other* than Wallace?"

Dooley spoke up. "He mentioned a longstanding friendship with Sean Gifford."

"Really?" Hoffman was surprised.

Dooley nodded. "He said Sean had talked about Loquess a great deal with him. Rabbitt and Sean had known each other when they were kids."

"Isn't that interesting?" Hoffman pulled his notebook back out and wrote that down. "One victim from your home town and the other a paranormal. Our best suspect was a childhood friend of your ex-lover. What do you know, Loquess? The world really does revolve around you."

"Columbia isn't exactly my home town."

"Mere details."

oOo

Two network vans arrived and had set up by the time Hoffman and Rush were done and forensics started taking apart the scene. Cameras and lights were focused on the entrance to the church.

Dooley and I watched from the window. Dooley eyed the crowd sourly. "My car is over there so I *have* to go through them." He looked at me. "You, however, have other options. I can meet you back at the office."

"Okay." This was no time for bravery. I worked my way to the back of the church, carefully stepping around forensics, and slipped out the back door. The alleyway was dark. I pulled out and extended the stick, settled onto the saddle and ascended quietly into the night sky.

I gained a few hundred feet of altitude before I banked towards Schroeder Plaza. I kept to a leisurely pace—not much more than a light run.

Hoffman wasn't far wrong.

The sheer *connectedness* of the case unnerved me. Wallace from my college town. Living (and dying) down the street from me. Wallace and Plante both attending Rabbitt's church. Rabbitt old friends with Sean.

I switched the radio over to cell and was about to call Sean but stopped. What was I going to say? *Oh, by the way Sean, your old friend Tim Rabbitt is wanted for murder.*

Sniezek's face swam up in my mind. *Are you a cop or aren't you?*

I dialed the number. It rang several times before Sean answered.

"What do you want?"

"I need your help."

Pause. "Okay. What for?"

I thought for a moment, trying to think of some easy way to lead in. Fuck it. "We need to find Tim Rabbitt. He's wanted as part of an investigation. I understand you're friends so any help would be appreciated."

Sean spoke slowly. "Tim's in trouble?"

"You could say that."

"What's going on?"

"Come on, Sean. You know I can't—"

"We used to be partners," he said, doggedly. "We used to be... whatever it was we were. I worked for BPD, too. What the hell is going on with my friend?"

I sighed. "He's a person of interest in the Plante murder."

"Plante murder?"

"Listen to the news. Oscar Plante was murdered. Rabbitt's been implicated."

"You think Tim *killed* him? Tim's a minister, for God's sake."

"I know. We need to find him."

Sean didn't say anything for a long time. I watched the houses I drifted over. It was dark. Lights shone through the windows. In an apartment, I saw a man and woman setting the table. In another, a man was reading a book, sipping a glass of wine. Several windows had the definitive blue glow of televisions. No one looked up. No one saw me. People went about their business with no idea I was watching them.

"I don't know where he is," Sean said at last. "The last time I talked to him was a week before I left. And then it was *me* talking to *him*. About leaving."

"Where are you?"

"I'm coming up on Black Bear Pass. I don't know why they call it a pass; it's over twelve thousand feet. I'm camping at Ouray tonight. I plan on an ascent tomorrow."

I nodded, even though he couldn't see me. "Hoffman will want to talk to you."

"He's the detective in charge?"

"Yeah."

"Okay. I'll lie over in Telluride. He can call me in the morning. I don't want to do a full interview in flight."

"Okay. I'll tell him."

"All right, then."

"Sean?" I stopped for a moment. "Are you coming back for Conclave?"

"I said I would. I have to close on the condo."

"I'm looking forward to seeing you."

Sean didn't say anything for a moment. "Good," he said, and hung up.

I had no idea how to interpret that. Regret? Revenge? Sentimentality?

Even so, the conversation had been mostly cordial. Impersonal. And completely full of crap.

The clouds parted and the cold and flaccid moon shone on us all.

Chapter 2.3: Thursday, October 21

"Witch murder" fit the *Herald* like a glove—after all, it just wouldn't do to be too much like the *Boston Globe*. Better to trumpet unsolved murder cases and take an opportunity to dump on city government. The *Herald* headlines screamed, "Witch Murderer Still Uncaught!" The *Globe* said sagely, "No Leads in Plante Murder." The Metro had a Plante obituary in time for the Wednesday commuters. Nobody was interested in Wallace's murder; he wasn't important enough. So far we'd kept that connection secret—both papers would have loved to report *that*.

Then, by Thursday, Conclave pushed it all onto page three.

Boston has three major holidays. First, there's Christmas. Everybody celebrates Christmas, of course. There's nothing particularly Bostonian about it. Doesn't bring in the tourists from out of state. If you want a big Christmas celebration, you go to New York.

At either pole of the year are First Night—New Year's Eve—and the Fourth of July. *Come celebrate Independence Day in the cradle of America's independence.* I suppose Philadelphia is the same. Christmas, First Night and the Fourth are the big three.

But fall is also big in New England. Every year the peak foliage report describes the rolling maple flames as they start up in Canada, burn over north New Hampshire and Vermont, then pop and curl down towards Massachusetts. Foliage train and bus tours are available starting in early September up through Columbus Day, by which time it's pretty much in Boston's back yard if it hasn't burnt out already. The news stations broadcast predictions comparing this year to previous years, weather watching and recommended weekends—if the media ever figures out a play by play, they'll put it on the sports news at six p.m. every night.

Conclave, happening around Halloween, puts a period at the end of that sentence.

When they founded Conclave, back in the seventies, it was a little thing with maybe three or four events and a dozen participants—barely worth a note in the "What to Do Around Town" column in the *Globe* and no mention at all in the tourist books.

That was then. This was now.

Over its seven days, Conclave attracts perhaps as many as a hundred thousand visitors into Salem with a bleed-off into Boston. It's not as big as the Big Three but it's the largest thing Salem and Gloucester have to offer. No merchant in New England turns up his nose at a week-long celebration a month before Thanksgiving.

It starts the week before Halloween and ends on Halloween night. The contests are heavily weighted towards telekinetic events: lithe flyers in z-sprints, relays and endurance runs, hulking foreign women in the heavy lifting competitions, curiously tall men in the no-motion skating courses, the fling, the toss and the hover.

The most televised events are, of course, the pyrogens. Everybody likes a fire.

To us, Conclave is seven days where any witch capable of lifting, igniting or suppressing a burning toothpick while drunk could show up, qualify, and take home a medal and a moment of glorious television.

While I would be working in Boston.

Was I bitter? Of *course* not. It was even raining, which made the day complete.

Horn broke the news to the assembled detectives in the conference room: leaves were canceled. Holidays rescinded. We were going to continue working until Plante's murderer was caught. Conclave started on the twenty-fifth and this was the twenty-first. If I wanted to go to Conclave, we needed to find Rabbitt in four days.

Dooley and I dutifully hunkered down and tried to cover ground. We had the names and addresses of everybody who lived in or worked in the building where Plante's loft was located. We had the landlord who rented the loft to Plante. We had Roche, Plante's assistant. We asked (ever so politely) that Wilcox, his agent, come up for an interview. We found nothing.

We did find Tim Rabbitt's only surviving relative, Bonnie Rabbitt.

Dooley said they should not have been so coy and just called her Bunny. I said they were cruel and unusual people.

But Bonnie was a dead end: she hadn't spoken to Tim for over a year. Phone records confirmed this. And she had been in Ontario for vacation while this was going on.

I complained to Dooley: what the hell kind of suspect has a sister that goes to godforsaken Ontario for a vacation in October? Even so, an alibi is an alibi.

It had been three days since Plante had been killed. Dooley was huddled over the computer trying to find somebody, anybody, connected with the case when Hoffman and Rush came in.

With a big grin, Hoffman planted his ass in a chair across from me. Rush sat behind him on the desk, looking somehow proper and embarrassed.

"I just visited with Ted down in computer forensics. On Rabbitt's computer."

Dooley pulled his chair from behind his desk and rolled it over. He sat down next to me. "Do tell."

"Yeah. Have you ever heard of *WheresKatelin.com?*"

I stared at him. "A website?"

"Yeah."

"About *me?*"

Hoffman laughed. "That's right. Rabbitt had cleaned out his computer pretty well but he'd left a few cookies in the trash bin. Turns out he was one of your fans."

"How many…" My voice faded out. I didn't know what to call them. Fans? Observers? Stalkers?

"The word is *subscribers,*" Hoffman said carefully. "It's a pay site. Expensive. And there aren't many clients. Only a few people even know about you or care."

"There are videos," said Rush, staring at the ceiling.

"What kind of videos?" I asked faintly.

"Tasteful. That's the right word, isn't it, Ron?" Hoffman looked at Rush. Rush nodded.

"Christ." I stared at my hands.

Hoffman's voice became suddenly crisp. "Okay. Enough fun. The site is managed by a Cybertech Investigations. A PI services firm over on Winter Street. Rush called them up. They're sending the site manager—who is also the associated PI—over to say hello. Some guy named Dobbs."

Dooley nodded. "That might be a real lead."

"Yeah. We found Rabbitt was a subscriber. Also Plante. Also Wallace."

Dooley spoke up. "Wallace was a subscriber? How did he pay?"

Hoffman chuckled. "I have no idea how a homeless man manages to subscribe to an expensive service. That's one of a whole string of questions I want to ask Dobbs. But Wallace was listed. Better yet, he was signed on the day after he was dead."

Dooley whistled. "Neat trick."

"Oh, it gets better." Hoffman turned his glance on me. "Another local subscriber is David Sabado."

Rush looked at me sympathetically. "You're very popular."

oOo

Dooley hustled me out of the office and down the street to the Dunkin' Donuts.

"What do you want?" I said in a tight whisper as we walked down the street.

"Just shut up for a minute."

We went inside. Dooley ordered me coffee and a doughnut I didn't want and coffee and a cruller for himself. Then, he led me into the corner and sat me down. He planted his monumental hulking body across from me.

"Loquess, you have to listen to me."

"I'm listening."

He sighed. "No, you're not. You're doing your Loquess thing where you say you're going to listen and then whatever you hear gets all twisted up in the spider's knot you call a mind. Instead, you hear echoes of something your father said or your brother or David, reflecting Sean reflecting your father or your mother, reflecting some flying teacher you knew. I need you to put all those people you like to have talking to you in another room. This needs to be just between you and me."

"Say what you want to say."

"Do I have your full and complete attention?"

I closed my eyes and breathed deeply. "You do."

"Something stinks."

"That's what you wanted to say to me?"

"Something stinks and it's *attached* to you. I can buy one old homeless guy that came from your home town. But that's about seven coincidences back. Katelin?" He looked at me hard.

He'd never called me by my first name before. I stared back at him. "Yes?"

"This has something to do with you."

"Can we move off of the obvious stuff now?"

"Did you *hear* me?"

I looked away and breathed for a minute. Then, I turned back. "Yes."

"Okay." He leaned back in his chair and took a bite out of the cruller.

"*This* is where we stop talking?"

He swallowed. "I'm pausing for effect. And I wanted some cruller."

"Consider me affected."

He nodded and wiped his lips. "Okay, then. What do we know?"

I ticked them off on my hands. "Wallace was from Columbia. Wallace, Rabbitt, Plante and Sean knew each other. Jesus." I shook my head. "Do you think *Sean* is mixed up in this?"

Dooley shook his head. "He's out in Colorado, isn't he? Could he be running from something?"

I pulled out my cell phone. If he was mixed up in this I'd have it out right now.

Dooley reached over and closed it before I could dial. "Let's just list things for now. Put Sean down in the 'may be involved' column. He's not the murderer. He's got too good an alibi. Besides, Hoffman had a phone interview with him this morning and decided he's in the clear."

I put my phone away. "Wallace, Plante and Rabbitt all had accounts at that website."

"Plus David Sabado."

"Yeah," I said sourly.

Dooley leaned forward. "Hoffman and Rush are going to grill you *before* they bring in Sabado."

"How come?"

"For fifty reasons. To get a handle on how to manage him. To make sure they have their ducks lined up in a row before they haul in a celebrity. To make sure there are no surprises."

"Ah. That's why you hustled me down here." Light dawns on Marble Head.

"What's interesting is Hoffman let me. That suggests you aren't a suspect."

I suddenly felt small. "Do you think I am?"

Dooley shook his head. "Motive would be too thin. Besides, Hoffman wouldn't be playing with you if you were.

He'd get all the evidence together while he was smiling and acting like he was a good old boy. Then, when he had enough, you'd find yourself in the little gray room facing the two of them across the table. But he let you come with me to let us know that *he* doesn't think so."

"Can't you guys just *say* things? Out loud? With your mouth?"

Dooley grinned. "Where's the fun in that? You need to use your mythical witch powers on us."

"I'm just a simple flyer."

"You're not trying hard enough." Dooley thought for a moment. "Did you check Sabado's pre-test results?"

My cheeks burned. "Yes."

"Don't blush. It interferes with good police procedure. What was it?"

"Eight-ninety-five."

Dooley whistled. "You'd think that was significant. What were the other scores?"

"Wallace, Plante and Rabbitt were all in the eight hundreds."

"But not as high as Sabado?"

"No."

"What were you?"

"Seven-eighty-two."

"How the mighty have fallen."

"Hey! You were a seven-sixty."

"Which shows you how reliable the pre-test is." Dooley swore under his breath. "I do not like to underestimate myself. I wish I had known the scores were manipulated."

I sipped my coffee. It had grown cold. "You got the score they needed to give you. Since they didn't know what you were good for." I grinned at him. "Jury's still out on that, too."

Dooley ignored me. "What were the corrected scores?"

"Plante stayed in the seven hundreds, of course. But Wallace and Rabbitt were downgraded to the five hundreds."

"Who would ever get much below that?"

I shook my head. "I think five hundred is a sort of zero. Below that you'd have some different kind of influence."

"What? Some kind of spawn of Satan?"

"Of course not. *I'm* spawn of Satan. Remember?"

"I stand corrected. How long were you and Sabado together?"

"Three years. Two years in Columbia while I finished my degree. Then, we moved out here. We were here a year and then broke up."

"You haven't been sleeping together since?"

"Dooley!"

"Hoffman's going to be worse."

"I haven't *seen* David Sabado in two years."

"No phone calls? Accidental meetings?"

"No."

"Common friends?"

"Eli Boor. Carl Spotts. Martin Miegle. David's family didn't like me and I didn't like them so we didn't maintain contact."

"I know Boor. Who's Spotts?"

"Carlton Spotts is music director at the University of Missouri. He's a friend of the family."

"Still there?"

"Unless he's moved in the last six months."

"Martin Miegle is Boor's physicist partner. Tell me about him."

"He lives out in Western Mass somewhere. I've never met him."

"You said he was a common friend."

"Well, I've talked to him on the phone a few times. He's a little creepy but not in a bad way."

"How can you be creepy in a not bad way?"

"You talk to him. You'll understand."

"Any friends you made out here?"

I shook my head. "Not other than Eli and Martin."

Dooley wrote that all down. "Why did you break up?"

"He was on tour a lot," I said shortly. "I was working a lot. After a while we didn't have anything to say to one another."

Dooley gave me a *look*. "There's more to it than that."

"Nothing that's relevant."

"Hoffman is going to drill right into that. He wants to know everything about you."

"I'll take that under advisement."

"Okay." He sighed and wrote that down. "Was it an amicable separation?"

I snorted. "I was so mad I took off for home to cool off. If you know *anything* about my family, you'd know that was an act of last resort."

Dooley tapped his pen on the book. "That was the leave of absence you took? I thought someone had died."

"Yeah."

"But you're still friends with Boor and Martin." He glanced at his notes. "And Spotts."

"Sure."

Dooley watched me for a moment. "You do realize how completely dysfunctional that sounds, don't you?"

I shook my head.

Dooley continued. "You spend three years with a man. You learn his life. He learns yours. The two of you get entangled. Normal separations are ugly. Ragged. Full of loose ends. But not you. You have a couple of friends in common. Everybody's cordial except for you and David. You just don't speak to each other. Very clean."

I looked at him for a long time. "Martin said something like that. He said David and I were 'entangled'. Now we're not."

"Any idea what he meant by that?"

"Something to do with physics. Everything Martin says has something to do with physics."

Dooley nodded and wrote more in his notebook.

I watched him for a few minutes. Then, I got fidgety. "So: how's the case, counselor?"

"Thin. All we have is a tangle of loose ends. Unless Hoffman and Rush come up with something pretty special, we got nothing."

"Until he kills again."

"Until he kills again." Dooley finished what he was writing. He closed the notebook and put it back in his pocket. He pointed at my doughnut. "Are you going to finish that?"

oOo

Hoffman was every bit as rough as Dooley had said: snide, insinuating, accusational. But the questions were the same. At least he didn't have Rush in with him—he gave me that much respect. The Hoffman/Rush Bad Cop/Good Cop routine was the stuff of legend around the office. By questioning me by himself he acknowledged that since I was a cop the routine wouldn't be effective. Oddly, it made me feel good.

Like Dooley predicted, he zeroed in on it.

"Why did you and Sabado break up?

I gave him a nasty smile. "You know how it is, Albert. You're at work all the time. Your spouse gets tired of it. You've been through that what? Twice now? Three times?"

Hoffman stared at me with disbelief for several seconds. Then, he burst out laughing. "Nice shooting, Loquess." He drummed his fingers on the table. Bad cop was gone. Now it was just Hoffman. "Both victims and the possible murderer are in this *'Where's Katelin'* ring. Along with your ex-boyfriend. Why the hell are they stalking you?"

I leaned back in the chair. "I don't know. Maybe it's just because I'm a flyer."

Hoffman shook his head. "It's more than that. There's no *'Where's Sniezek'* site. No *'Where's Gifford'* site. Just you."

"They don't look good in tights."

"Rush thought of that." Hoffman shook his head. "There's a mess of Conclave sites with profiles and pictures of all the athletes. Sniezek is there. Gifford has been blogging about his long walk. But they're public figures. And the hits are low and it's not private. Your stealth work kept a low profile so the public pictures are few, far between and unattributed. *Where's Katelin* is a private site run by a PI firm. That's different."

"When's Dobbs getting here?"

Hoffman checked his watch. "About twenty minutes ago. Rush is interviewing him now."

"You wanted to talk to me by yourself? I'm touched."

Hoffman chuckled. "Professional courtesy. Don't worry. It'll never happen again."

"Look," I said, seriously. "Can we get Cybertech on this? I mean, punish them for watching me?"

Hoffman smiled at me, suddenly feral. "Oh, don't worry about them. We don't like anybody stalking cops. Even a halfway cop like you. The mayor is already on the phone to the head of the company. This isn't going to stand. When Rush gets through with Dobbs there won't be enough left to pick your teeth with. I'm just a cop who likes his job. Rush is *mean*."

oOo

Dooley was sitting in my spare chair when I got back to my desk. He was leaning back in his chair looking satisfied and thoughtful.

I sat across from him. "How was it?"

"How was what?"

"Didn't you watch Rush grill Dobbs?"

"I did." He still looked thoughtful.

"How was it?"

"I'm still digesting it."

I sat down and waited.

He turned his chair to me slowly. "Have you ever seen a really good prosecutor in action?"

I shook my head. "I've seen prosecutors. But I can't say they were really good."

"Most of them aren't," Dooley said matter-of-factly. "Like lots of things, the profession doesn't pay well enough to really attract top talent. You get good idealists, if you're lucky. But you also get a lot of lawyers who aren't good enough or imaginative enough or brave enough to go out on their own. Or worse: you get lawyers who consider prosecutorial duties as a stepping stone into public office." He shuddered at the last.

"You've given this some thought."

"It was in the mix of considerations when I graduated law school."

I felt shocked to the core. "You went to law school?"

Dooley nodded. "You see? One learns something every day."

"What are you doing here?"

He stared at me levelly. "Are you saying this is not an honorable profession?"

"No."

"Then, are you saying this profession is beneath me?"

I shook my head.

"Good." He waved his hand at me airily. "My reasons for being here are not your concern, but I understand your curiosity. Law school taught me some things about myself. I would not be a good defense lawyer. I lack the character flaw that would enable me to defend someone I knew was guilty. Civil law is boring. Corporate law is Hell's seventh level of boring. But I do like the idea of justice—or what passes for it in our system. I thought about becoming a prosecutor. One gets some choice about cases—presumably one would not pursue a felon one did not consider guilty."

"What happened?"

"I wasn't hired. Apparently, I was too good, imaginative or brave."

"Ah," I said as if I understood.

"But you asked about Rush." He peaked his fingers together. "Rush has all the theatricality, drama and pointed intelligence of a good prosecutor. He led Dobbs by telling him what he already knew, managed to get a few self-incriminating tidbits under the guise of professional camaraderie." Dooley glanced up at me. "Did you know your apartment was bugged?"

"No," I squeaked.

"Apparently, it was. There are recordings. Rush ferreted out hints and then pointed out what Dobbs had revealed, neatly trapping him in a *federal* violation. Then, Rush reversed his hold and suggested that Dobbs go into full detail. Dobbs cracked open. I've never heard so much detail about something in which I was so little interested."

"Bugged for how long?"

"Dobbs wasn't sure. At least the last year."

"A year?"

"Perhaps longer. Available video didn't cover all that time, of course. Apparently, it was extensively edited."

"A year?"

"Enshrined in a DVD that Rush now has in his possession. According to Dobbs, the bugs should be gone within the hour."

Oh, god. Which was worse? The fact that the footage existed at all or the fact that Rush had it? "He didn't destroy it?"

"He will deliver it to you by close of business today. Intact. Without copy. Rush is an honorable man. But this is the age of the internet, dear. Nothing can be destroyed. Do we have the complete material?" Dooley shrugged. "We'll see." Dooley pressed his lips thin and stared out the window.

I wanted a drink so bad I could taste it. Were the fights I had with Sean on the disk? Sex scenes? Did it go back to when David and I were living together? Did it capture when he packed up and moved out? And all of those little things people do when they don't think they're being watched. I shuddered. What did they see? What did *David* see?

"I'm curious, though," said Dooley, oblivious to me at that moment. "It was such a wonderful performance I can't help but wonder what Hoffman contributes."

oOo

Dooley called David. I sat at my desk staring at my computer screen, every ear cell aquiver trying to listen to the conversation. I could not think of David without thinking over what we did together. I could not think over what we did together without framing it in a view of a webcam, transmitting it all back to a pay-per-view porn site.

Dooley had his back to me and spoke softly so I couldn't hear what he was saying.

He hung up and turned around, looking out the window thoughtfully.

"Well?" I asked.

"He's out west in California someplace. He's working his way back to Boston. Middle of next week he'll be in New York, performing. He'll be back before Halloween." He looked a question at me.

"He's always up here for Conclave."

Dooley lifted an eyebrow at me.

"At least, he was when we were together," I amended grudgingly.

"Are you following his concert schedule?"

"I'm on his mailing list. He's a fine pianist." It sounded false, even to me.

Dooley watched me for a moment, saying nothing.

I snarled at him. "Like you've never checked up on an old girlfriend or an ex-wife."

Dooley nodded. "Just keeping you honest, Loquess. Certainly, *he* checked up on *you*." He chuckled.

I felt wretched. "So, what did he say?"

"As soon as he gets in town, he'll come here." Dooley leaned forward. "I talked to him and checked his concert schedule, too. There's no alibi in it. He was here in Boston for both murders."

I didn't know whether to feel excited or sad. Then I remembered Dobbs and I just felt angry.

oOo

Dooley and Hoffman went home. Rush came by my desk on his way out.

"Here," he said and gave me the disk.

I took it and stared at it.

Rush had his coat on. He was going home. I could go home, too. To my bugged apartment.

I sure as hell wasn't going home. I wasn't sure I could ever set foot in that apartment ever again. It dawned on me I had no place to go.

"Albert thought you might want this," Rush said. He put a key on my desk.

"What's that?"

"It's the key to one of Albert's rental apartments. It's in Mission Hill—not too far from your place. Albert kept it after the divorce from his second wife. But he doesn't use it. He thought you might not want to go home." Rush grabbed a pen and wrote down the address. "Doesn't have a roof door, though."

"I don't need a roof door." I took the key. "Thanks."

Rush nodded, embarrassed again. He left.

I held the key up to the light. You just never know about people.

I put the disk in the office microwave and watched it crackle and burn. Then, I took my stick up to the roof and used my special key. I walked dutifully over to the circle lit in blue by the single runway lamp. Sniezek's drawing had long since blown away. The rain had cleared. I just stood there and looked around, trying desperately for perspective.

The facts of the matter were not in dispute. But I realized I had once thought so much better of David now that I realized I thought so much less of him.

oOo

David once told me that Boston had no skyline when he was a kid. On those rare treats when he was home from the hospital, his mother would sometimes bring him down to the city on the train for some special occasion—like the Saint Anthony's festival or First Night. Never Conclave, of course— to see those events, all David had to do was walk down to the park, tune his radio to WGBH and listen to the coverage.

The skyline seemed to just suddenly appear one night when he was in Paris or New York or Missouri. He returned and a dozen hotels, high-rise offices and bank buildings had emerged perfect and whole from some deep wound in the ground.

I had come out for Conclave when I was fourteen, relying on a vague invitation from Sam during a training clinic that summer. I showed up on his doorstep the week before he took three golds in a row: z-sprint, free ascent and marathon. Maybe I impressed him. Or maybe he just thought it was something I needed. Regardless, he invited me back every summer until he died.

When Sam finally persuaded me to fly into the city with him, I saw Boston as a huge collection of spires and columns towering over deep canyons of brick and marble. It sure was a skyline to a young Missouri girl like me.

Now, it was merely a collection of buildings.

I stood, watching the city at night.

As I looked towards the harbor I saw every now and then the firefly light of a witch flying here or there—illegally, of course. They could not have had clearance to fly in the city itself and certainly not at that altitude or at night. If they were caught, it could be a fine or grounding for the full length of the games.

But nobody had ever arrested a witch for an illegal flight during Conclave and I wasn't going to be the first. I remembered Sam and I discovering a furtive back alley a surprisingly short distance from Faneuil Hall, a quick dizzying full vertical ascent to a steady hover, looking down on people shopping, driving down the street, listening to the babble and mutter fade in and out like the sound of the ocean.

"It's a fine city," he had said, a faint Chicago twang still left in his voice.

And I remembered watching the city at the end of my first shift after David had moved out, standing in this very spot, about to hover over the earth, held up only by my will, wishing I could share that sensation with him. If I had been able to, would he have left? And now was I glad he did?

I unlatched my stick and pulled out the radio, got clearance for a patrol flight—which meant I could fly anywhere in the city I wanted. I toggled the roof lights and took off in a haze of blinking white and green.

But I didn't turn on my own running lights. My transponder was on and if there were other aircraft in the vicinity, Boston control would let me know. I flew over to where I had seen the fireflies.

Sure enough, two witches were sitting in the corner shadow of Exchange Place watching the lights on the Customs Tower. I came down behind them, tracing one corner in a vertical descent. I could watch them and it would be unlikely they could see me.

"It's not so big. Atlanta is much bigger," said one, a girl, in a sweet drawl.

"Really?" The other was a boy. "Bismarck is tiny."

"Well, it is way out there in Minnesota."

"North Dakota," said the boy in an easy voice suggesting he'd been making that correction all evening.

I guessed neither was more than fourteen—no older than I was coming up here with Sam. Fearless—or at least not admitting to fear—sitting with their legs dangling over a ten-story drop, holding their sticks lightly beside them as some sort of magic talisman.

And, should either fall, of no further use to them than that. I doubted they had the experience to remount in time on a free descent. They would hit the street just about the point they realized they weren't going to get airborne.

I thought about just leaving them there. But Sam had taken care of me—if I had fallen, Sam would have raced gravity down to save me and died before giving up. Who was going to look out for these two kids?

I descended in front of them—if they got scared and fell, they'd fall *backwards* onto the roof and not forwards to their inevitable death. They scrambled away from me.

"Hey," I said gently. "It's okay."

"Don't report us—" started the girl.

I waved her silent, came over the parapet and set down beside them. "Katelin Loquess, BPD."

"Crap," said the boy bitterly.

They proffered me their pilot's licenses without me asking for them. The boy's name was Sarjit and the girl's Naomi. "It's a long flight from Salem. Do you know how to get back?"

"Sure," said the girl confidently. "We came down here this afternoon."

"Give me your log books."

They did and I made a show of pulling out my flashlight and going over them.

"You're athletes?"

Both nodded.

"What events?"

Both in acrobatics—not surprising. Acrobatics favored young, light, lithe bodies: low mass.

"Staying in the athlete's village?"

Both nodded.

"Do you have regulation night lighting?"

They looked at one another. Naomi looked defensive. Sarjit shook his head.

"Radios?"

Again, the head shake.

I gave out a theatrical sigh. "So, you're flying in a municipal area and transiting a Class B airspace without notification or fulfilling a Minimum Equipment List."

Now, they looked miserable and scared—which is exactly how I wanted them to feel. When Sam and I had done the same thing, Sam had made sure we weren't in violation of anything except athlete's village curfew. These kids were joyriding—and I was going to let them get away with it, provided I put the fear of god in them first.

I pointed at Sarjit with his log book. "You don't have much experience in municipal flight. You could use inexperience as an excuse. But you—" I pointed at Naomi with hers. "You have a municipal endorsement. Forget all the FAA violations, uncleared flight in Boston is 'flying to endanger'. Hefty fine and possible jail time."

Naomi had been looking ready to argue with me but when I brought up FTE, she went pale. The FAA regulates witches just like it regulates any other aircraft, but within urban airspace, control is delegated to the states—which, in the case of Massachusetts, is further delegated to the cities. This meant I had real authority to enforce federal, state and city regulations on these two.

Which both of them knew in the abstract—being on the supplement to the FAA written exam—but Naomi had the municipal endorsement so it must have been drummed into her by her instructor.

I let them think about it for a moment while I finished looking over their logs to see if I'd missed anything.

"Follow me down to the pavement. If either of you exceed two hundred feet a minute—"

"We won't," Naomi said quickly.

We *walked* to South Station. I watched as they bought tickets on the Rockport line back up to Salem. "You take a cab back to the village. I don't want you a millimeter in the air before practice tomorrow." I gave them back their licenses and logs and left them there. From a narrow alley near the Garden, I took off and started flying over to Hoffman's apartment. Maybe tomorrow I'd go over to Parker Street and pack up a few things. I could look for a new place. There were no chains that tied me to Parker Street. Nothing tied me down but my own mind.

I thought of the kids, probably congratulating themselves on getting off scot free.

I smiled and thought of Sniezek: Was this what it felt like to act like a cop?

Chapter 2.4: Friday, October 22

In our investigations we had created a sketch of the lives of Wallace, Plante and Rabbitt. Now, Hoffman and Rush had us all work on a timeline of what the principals had been doing for the last two weeks and an understanding of what they had been doing for the last two years.

Hoffman and Rush took Plante, since it involved both a celebrity and a trip to New York.

The common thread between Wallace, Plante and Rabbitt was Rabbitt's church—the task given us by Hoffman and Rush. Computer forensics had found a set of spreadsheets listing donors but they were coded or numbered: one, red, blue, thirty-two. Forensics was unable to connect the dots and tell us who they were.

We obtained Rabbitt's bank records. Sure enough, there were deposits corresponding to the spreadsheet entries, but when we looked up the cancelled checks, they were all cashier's checks and money orders made out for Rabbitt himself. Small checks. A couple of thousand here and there. It didn't amount to much. There was a conspicuous withdrawal on the day of Plante's murder but it was only a couple of thousand dollars. A man couldn't go far on just that.

"Is Rabbitt rich?" I said. "Did he fund the church himself?" The screen was filled with different checks. "Maybe he has an account we don't know about."

Dooley shook his head. He pointed to numbers on the check images. "That's a bank routing number. Here's another one. They correspond to the issuing agency and they're all different." Dooley leaned back. "Looks like he cashed the checks into money orders and cashier's checks. Probably used one of those paycheck cashing places. We would have to find the issuing agency, find the deposit corresponding to this particular check and then find out whose check that was."

"Can we do that?"

Dooley shrugged. "I don't know. Maybe. The regulations aren't terribly well enforced on these places. They have to keep records but they're probably on paper. It'll take time. I expect he was trying to preserve his donors' anonymity." He thought for a second. "It's a good way to sock away money for yourself."

"What do you mean?"

"Say Matilda the Donor Lady gives you a check for five grand. You go down to one of these check cashing agencies and split the check into two checks. Each of them for twenty-five hundred dollars. Each of them to you. Then, you deposit one check into the church and the other one you send somewhere else."

"Wouldn't you have to show records? Tax purposes?"

Dooley shrugged. "Probably. But I bet Rabbitt's church doesn't get looked at all that closely. And if the mythical dummy organization isn't that big and doesn't get the attention of Homeland Security, it could hide for a long time. If there were a lot of small checks across several donors over time, you could collect a pretty sizeable nest egg without anybody noticing. It would require a lot of cross-checking by the IRS to make sure all of the tax-deductible contributions were accounted for."

I pointed at the computer. "If that's what he did, his take was a lot better than fifty-fifty."

"Or," said Dooley slowly, "he had all of the contributions made out to a different organization and had *that* organization donate. That keeps his church safe."

"And it means if we can trace back these checks to Rabbitt, they might point to where the real money is."

"If this isn't complete supposition, that is."

"Yeah." I rubbed my eyes. "Let's give it to the financial guys and let them figure it out. If it's there, they'll find it."

Dooley nodded. "Might take a while but it's worth doing." He made the call.

oOo

We started pulling facts together. We didn't know where Wallace was after church and before he was murdered that Sunday. But we were able to collect facts on Plante. He'd taken a cab to the church and returned. He'd had breakfast the next day in the hotel café and returned to his room—card use confirmed that. Then, he'd been discovered. There were no calls to or from the room that morning. He'd made two calls to his manager in New York and one to his helper, Roche. Then, nothing until he was discovered. There was nothing unusual in his bank records for the couple of weeks prior to his murder—or, at least, that was the story we were sticking to until the financial forensics guys got back to us.

"Maybe Plante saw something. Maybe he saw Rabbitt kill Wallace. Rabbitt figures it out—or maybe Plante contacts him."

Dooley looked over the table at me. "You think Plante was blackmailing Rabbitt? I think Rabbitt could have gotten all the money he wanted out of Plante without blackmail. Besides, there's nothing in the phone records."

I nodded. "Spiritual crisis. Plante comes over to see Wallace—"

"No record of the trip."

"No *cab* record. He walks this time."

"Why would he walk?"

"I don't know. Maybe Wallace told him something he needed to think about—he takes a walk to clear his head and ends up at the church. But Rabbitt isn't there. So he crosses the street to look up his friend Wallace."

"He knows Wallace is staying in the basement?"

I nodded. "Say he does. Plante comes over to see Wallace and catches Rabbitt in the act of murder. His religious leader has committed a horrible act. He flees. Rabbitt tries to contact him—"

"*Still* no record of contact on any cell phone we know of."

"Rabbitt *doesn't* try to phone him. He comes over—he knows Plante's habits. He knows Plante is going to be resting before the act."

"Does he?"

"I rest before a meet. I bet Plante rested before a show."

"After he's witnessed a murder?"

I shook my head. "Right. That wouldn't make sense."

Dooley waved me on. "I bet after witnessing a murder Plante would be doing anything *but* resting. Let's say he goes back to the hotel room to think."

I pointed at Dooley. "Rabbitt tries to persuade Plante it's all for the greater good. He fails. They join in prayer and when Plante is kneeling, Rabbitt slips him the knife."

Dooley pulled at his lower lip in thought. "Without a doubt the broadest and most speculative piece of detective work I've ever heard."

"It's not feasible?"

"I bet it's not even close. Let's get back to the church records."

I thought for a moment. "I've got an idea."

"Always a dangerous thing."

"We need a window into Rabbitt's church."

Dooley nodded. "Yes."

"There aren't that many checks. Probably only a few moneyed donors supporting a largely homeless congregation. It could be the donors didn't even attend the services. But Wallace did attend and he was homeless—"

"And still managed to pay for the *Where's Katelin* service."

"Maybe one of the donors paid for him. Or maybe Wallace never actually signed on at all—it was Rabbitt. That would explain how we saw a record of Wallace's sign-on the day after he was killed. But forget that for a moment. If we want to know Wallace's background, we need to be able to find the people who *came* to the church. We need a window into the church population."

Dooley slitted his eyes. "Okay. Go with that."

"Let's talk to Dulac."

"The Frenchman? He *hated* Wallace."

I nodded. "I know that. But he wasn't the only person at PSI Wallace tried to convert. I bet Dulac knew other people who were more receptive. Maybe even some who were going to Rabbitt's church."

Dooley shrugged. "We could open the church on Sunday and see who shows up."

"This is Friday. What do you want to do? Take the day off? How's *that* going to help you make detective?"

Dooley sighed. "There are some apartment buildings nearby. We could canvas them."

I just looked at him.

He stood up. "Right. Let's go find Dulac."

oOo

Dooley called MacIlvey from the car. Dulac had gotten a construction restoration job in Back Bay. He gave us an address we could check.

"How come MacIlvey would know the address where Dulac was working?"

Dooley eyed the street and pulled out into traffic. "I don't know. But it makes sense. If something happens to Dulac they need to have someone to call. Maybe Dulac has children somewhere that need to know where he is. Or maybe he has child support obligations and *has* to report where he's working. Could be any number of reasons."

The address was on Bay State Road in the bowels of Boston University. Dulac was part of a crew gutting one of the brownstones.

I was ready to go right inside but Dooley held me back. There was a bench next to the building. We sat and waited. After a minute, a man walked up with an extension cord slung over his arm.

"Excuse me," Dooley called out.

The man stopped. "Yeah?"

"Do you know Frankie Dulac?"

"Yeah."

"Can you tell him Abraham Dooley and Katelin Loquess are down here? We need to talk to him. No problems or anything. Just need a little bit of his time." Dooley smiled.

The man looked Dooley up and down, then nodded and went inside.

"What was that all about?" I asked.

Dooley watched the light falling through the trees. "Think about it. Dulac's from Quebec. Probably here illegally—I can't imagine he has a green card or work visa. He's getting catch as catch can work—which means he is likely getting paid under the table. If you're paying a guy like that, you don't want cops poking around. Any smell of trouble and the first thing you're going to do is fire the guy. But if we sit down here, we ask one of his co-workers—*not* the boss." He waved around. "Just enjoying the fall air. Not flashing any badges. We could be anybody. We could be social workers. We could be friends from the old country. We could be family. Not somebody the boss necessarily wants around but not a real threat either."

About ten minutes later, Dulac came down covered with plaster dust. He looked at us both for a minute. "I got to run a line in the basement. Come on down there if you want to talk."

We followed him inside and downstairs. He closed the door after us. "What the fuck do you want?"

"We need your help," I said. "Do you know anybody that Wallace won over when he was trying to convert people?"

"Fuck, no. Asswipe never got anybody to go to church with him. Nobody I knew, anyway."

Dooley leaned forward smoothly. "We're looking into the church carefully. There doesn't appear to be any sort of membership roll or mailing list."

Dulac snorted. "Fuck right, if they recruited shithounds like Wallace. What the fuck you gonna do? Call him for donations?"

"Exactly," I said. "If you knew anybody that was taken in by Wallace, we would like to know. We could talk to them and then, through them, find other people in the congregation. We might find Wallace's killer that way."

Dulac looked at me, then at Dooley. "Son of a whore called me a papist like it was something filthy. Fuck. I'm glad he's dead."

"I know." I tried to speak soothingly. "But someone who kills a homeless man like Wallace might kill someone else. This time it might be someone you like."

Dulac stared at me with tiny dark eyes. "Yeah. It's not like we get any fucking *police* protection." He pointed at Dooley. "Get your little fucking notebook out. I don't know where she lives but the little slut has an apartment or something near the church. Wallace talked about her once or twice. She was the church manager."

"Her name?" asked Dooley patiently.

"Sandra. Sandra fucking Kohl."

oOo

I managed to keep it together. I smiled at Dulac. I smiled at Dooley and said, "I'm going outside for a minute." I stood up. I went outside. I unstrapped my stick, sat on it and executed a perfect vertical rise to the top of the tallest building on the Boston University campus. There, standing in the shadow of some devious structure shaped like an immense golf ball, I landed.

Then the shakes began.

Was every fucking person I had ever known trying to make me lose my mind? Every element of this case, every thread, every clue led straight to me. Now, Sandy *Fucking* Kohl? My college roommate? The blue-eyed menace?

Who else was going to show up? My fucking brother? My fucking father? My deceased mother? Arnie? His wife Mattie? His daughter Anita?

I pulled out my cell. My shaking hands made it difficult to find Arnie's number—would he even be home now? Maybe not. No answer—just voice mail. I called my brother. No answer. Voice mail. Maybe they were all in Boston. I called Mattie.

"Hello?" came the warm voice over the phone.

"Mattie! You're there!"

"Katelin? Is that you?"

"Yes! Are you at home?"

"Of *course* I'm at home. You called here, didn't you? Radio phone doesn't even make it to the driveway."

I sat down on the gravel. I felt like weeping. "I'm glad you're there. Where's Arnie?"

"At work, of course. We aren't rich enough to retire yet."

"And Anita?"

"Katelin, is something wrong?"

"Where's Anita?"

Gently now. "She's at college—"

"Where?"

"Washington University. You know that."

"You know that for a fact?"

In an ominous voice like thunder. "She sure as hell better be with all the money we're paying. You're scaring me, Katelin. Tell me what's going on."

And I told her, everything, going back and forth, telling about this case, how I felt awful about Sean leaving. How terribly inevitable it finally became between me and David. How Dooley was shaping up to mean more to me than a partner but at the moment less than a friend, how I thought I wanted someone as a friend up here. Someone different from everybody else I knew. How I missed Missouri and that maybe coming up here was a mistake but now I didn't think I could ever go home.

All the while, Mattie soothed me, asked questions, laughed gently sometimes, sniffled others.

Finally, Mattie said, "Well, what are you going to do now?"

"Finish the case, I guess."

"Oh, I have no doubt you'll figure *that* out. You're a smart girl. But you've some bridge repair work due in your life. With that boy Sean. With David—though it may be too late for that and he'll need more than just a little talking to. Paying to bug your apartment indeed."

"I don't think that's what he intended."

"I said bridge repair work and there's some there with that boy. But there might be some *demolition* there, too, if you catch my meaning."

"I do, Mattie." I grinned into the phone. "I'll have to do something about both of them."

"And honey?" Mattie said softly. "You've been apart from your family way too long. There's some bridge building you need to do there, too."

I felt tears coming again. "I know."

"Are you listening to me now, honey? I'm serious. Family got to take you in when you have nowhere else to go. Rough as they are, they'd take you in a heartbeat. You know that. You owe them for that."

"I know, Mattie."

"Promise me."

"I promise."

We spoke a little more and then I hung up. I stared at the phone for a moment. I wasn't ready to call my father or brothers. Not yet. But there was someone I owed a call to that could not wait. I called Sean.

It went to voice mail of course, but I didn't think much of that. He should have finished the Long Walk by now. If he was flying he wouldn't be answering. But even so, he might not want to talk to me. I didn't know if I wanted to get back together or not. But I sure didn't want it to end like it did with discarded pieces all over the landscape. Like me and David.

I couldn't say any of that into a voice mail message.

"Hi," I said, feeling awkward. "It's me, Katelin. You said you were coming back to Boston to close on your condo. We said we'd get together and talk about things. We didn't set a time. Let me know. I'd still like to get together. "I couldn't think of anything else to say. Then, "I'm sorry I didn't treat you very well."

Which was the long and the short of it, really. I'd never treated Sean well. Never gave him a chance.

My phone beeped. Two text messages. One was from Dooley: *Where the hell are you?* The other was from Sean: *Got your message. Be in town Wednesday. Bernoulli's, 7pm.*

There it is, I thought. You can make up any story you want about something like that.

oOo

I called Dooley and told him I'd meet him back at the station. The air was crisp and I wasn't quite ready to be inside.

I stepped off the BU roof and dropped fifty feet to get up some momentum. Then, I pulled out and shot over the Pike, Brookline Ave and Fenway Park. I ripped through a dozen snap rolls until I was dizzy, then pulled up the nose and flew straight up into the sun.

Time to live a little.

Dooley was waiting for me at my desk when I came down the stairs. He watched as I sat down across from him.

"So, what's the plan?"

"Who's Sandra Kohl?"

"My roommate from college."

Dooley shook his head. "You should have told me—"

"I didn't know. Last I heard, she got her Ph.D. and moved out west. Something to do with electron microscopy."

"West where? Missouri?"

"Colorado, I think. Maybe California. I forget."

"You haven't—"

"*Seen* her. *Talked* to her. Or had any communications with her *whatsoever* in four years."

"Jesus. Who the hell *else* is coming out of the woodwork? Your father? Your mother?"

"My mother's dead."

"Do you think a little thing like that would *stop* her?"

I laughed. I couldn't help it. "You know? With my mom, maybe not."

Dooley called the station from his car and got Sandy's address. It wasn't far from Rabbitt's church—no surprise there. We drove over. It was a nice little brownstone with a roof garden. I stifled a sudden urge to fly up and look it over.

Dooley knocked on the door.

The zombie equivalent of my college roommate answered the door.

194

Sandy had been beautiful. A curvaceous, blue-eyed wonder whose very appearance had sheer physical impact on anyone that saw her. She had been tall and there wasn't a man alive with the willpower to keep his eyes above her neck for more than five minutes.

This woman was bulbous, round rolls of skin crowding her wrists and elbows. Her head seem to grow organically from a mushrooming pad of fat swelling between her shoulders. She smelled of sweet acetone and solvent, indicating some deep metabolic disorder I couldn't even begin to understand. But I could still see Sandy's eyes and cheekbones buried deeply in the buttery flesh.

She looked at us, one to the other, for several seconds, not immediately registering me or the badge in Dooley's hand.

"Detectives Dooley and Loquess. Are you Sandra Kohl?"

She nodded. "Loquess?" Then she saw me. "Katelin!" she squealed and enveloped me in a soft aldehyde embrace. "Is it really you?"

"Yes," I said, awkwardly patting her back.

"Come in! Please come in."

"Do werewolves kill you when they invite you into their house?" Dooley whispered to me as we walked inside.

"That's vampires and you invite them in. Not the other way around."

The room was dark and the air heavy with some deep and abiding stink, a mix of incense and decaying onions.

"I'd heard you lived here now." Sandy sat on an old threadbare sofa partially covered by an ancient cotton print. I could see half the face of Jesus peeking over the back. "Please. Sit down."

"Ms. Kohl—" Dooley began.

"Oh, call me Sandy. Are you with the police department, Katelin?"

"Yes." I found it hard to breathe.

"I'm not at all surprised." She set her hands on her knees. "You were always hanging out with that security guard. And working for the police department back in Columbia."

"Ms. Kohl—" Dooley began again.

"Sandy," she said shortly, sudden steel in her voice.

"We're looking for Pastor Rabbitt. We were told you might know something about his church." Dooley glanced over at me. *Jump in any time.*

She calmed down at once. "What do you mean?"

"We understand you take care of the books."

"No," Sandy said distinctly. "Only Pastor Rabbitt took care of the money."

"We're not interested in the money," I said hurriedly, trying to warn Dooley off with my eyes. "We need a list of the members of the congregation."

"Why?"

I glanced down, trying to look sad. "You remember William Wallace?"

She smiled. "Oh, yes. He had a beautiful singing voice."

"You know he was murdered?"

She looked down and pursed her lips. "Yes. I heard."

"We're looking for the murderer."

"No." Sandy shook her head defiantly. "No member of Pastor Rabbitt's congregation could ever do such a thing!"

"Of course not," I said soothingly. "But they might know something we can use. Something that can point us to the killer."

Sandy nodded doubtfully. "Pastor Rabbitt did say to help you any way I can."

Dooley sat up straight. "He said help the police—"

"Oh, no," Sandy said. "He said help *Katelin*."

"When did he tell you this?"

"Monday." Sandy thought for a moment. "Yes. It was Monday."

Dooley pounced. "That's the day Plante was killed. Did he say where he was? Can you reach him?"

Sandy's eyes narrowed. "I don't think he intended me to help *you*."

"Quiet, Dooley," I said. Back to Sandy. "It's important that we get in contact with him."

Sandy smiled. "You were always so serious, Katelin. You should lighten up."

"I know. Do you know how to put us in contact with him?"

"I can give him your number if he calls. But he said he might not be able to call again for some time." She laughed quietly. "You're both so serious."

Dooley started to interrupt but I glanced at him and he shut up.

"Okay," I said. "Let's get back to what we said before. Do you have an address list of the congregation? Something we can use?"

Sandy shook her head. "Nothing like that. After all, half the congregation doesn't have a fixed address. I have a list of names and some contact information. I don't know if it will be of much use—"

"Just let us have what you can."

She nodded and went to the back of the apartment. I could feel the floor give as she moved.

I followed her. I didn't think she was going to run or anything but I'd given up predicting *anything* about this case. "How are you feeling?"

Sandy was rummaging around in a box of papers. "Oh, fine. Now that Pastor Rabbitt cured me of cancer."

"You had cancer?"

She nodded. "Breast cancer. But he cured me. He laid his hands on me here and here." She pointed to her breasts. "Now I'm all better."

"You've put on a little weight."

"Oh, yes. From when I was sick, but I'll get over it." She pulled out a few pages. "Here's the contact information. The congregation wasn't very big—only fifty or so. But Pastor Rabbitt always said you had to start small." Sandy handed it to me.

I ran my eyes over it quickly. I saw Sean's name. And Sandy's. But no one else I knew. Thank heaven for small blessings.

Chapter 2.5: Monday, October 25

That was Friday.

We worked over the weekend—we even staked out the church. But somehow Rabbitt's flight had worked its magic on the congregation. Only a few showed up and they knew nothing.

We put a tap on Sandy's phone. Nothing. Rabbitt didn't call over the weekend, anyway. But we had hopes for the week. And we had hopes he was still in the area. All of the calls to Sandy last Monday were from pay phones local to the church: one at the Brigham, two at the VA Hospital. We didn't know where he was *now* but at least he was nearby *then*. We questioned businesses around each phone but no one remembered seeing Wallace, Rabbitt or Plante.

By Monday, though, Dooley and I had managed to trace down some of the congregation—harder work to do than talk about. Half the contacts were out of date. Those that were still valid—sisters, landladies, parents, shelters—often didn't know where the candidate was, didn't care or, in a couple of cases, didn't want to know. One woman was surprised that the candidate was alive, much less that he had listed her as a contact. A couple of people said they didn't know the candidate at all. We didn't believe them but at this point it didn't look worthwhile to trace them down.

From the contact list, we found half a dozen candidates for interviews. From *those* we gained a more thorough timeline.

Tim Rabbitt had started the *Church of the Living Christ* a decade before. Surprisingly, he'd attended Harvard Divinity School. He'd worked in social services for a few years, then started the church. We were able to find the two original donors—a couple of young Brahmins living up on Beacon Hill. But they had no new information for us. They hadn't been connected with the church for years.

Nothing interesting until William Wallace arrived in Boston from Missouri and joined the church. Wallace had brought in a Pentecostal flavor to the congregation. Some of the members liked it; some didn't. Rabbitt was an early convert. Subsequently, there had been a substantial shakeup in the membership. Those that remained either embraced the new dogma or at least didn't find it offensive. The others moved on.

Rabbitt became an enthusiastic Hell and Damnation preacher. From the interviews, he might have had some "undue influence" with some of the younger women in the congregation. Dooley smelled incipient cult and I agreed.

The congregation went through another winnowing at this point. Those who didn't accept Christ, and Rabbitt, as their personal savior left. Rabbitt was in charge and Wallace his right-hand man.

"Why did Wallace stay homeless?" I asked Dooley as we put this all together.

"I have no idea." He leaned back and looked over the whiteboard where we were listing all of these events. "It doesn't make much sense."

Tim Rabbitt was still connected to the homeless shelter network. He trolled funding parties for new and wealthy cult members. This is where he met Oscar Plante.

At this point, we went back to Sandy. Sandy had been finishing her dissertation when she was my roommate. She finished it shortly after I met David. She moved out west and joined up with a firm in Silicon Valley doing something with electron microscopy and chip inspection—I never got an answer out of her I understood. Apparently, there had been a messy divorce from someone named Robby, or Robo, or Roberto. Sandy used all three names as a synonym for "fucking asshole bastard." Most of the IPO money went to the divorce. She attended an industrial conference in San Jose to find comfort sex.

Plante performed at the same conference. He saw Sandy (who must have looked more like she had in college) and the rest, as they say, is history. Plante planted Sandy and persuaded her to come to Boston. Subsequently Sandy planted Rabbitt. Rabbitt persuaded her that his cause was just and good. Sandy invested what was left of her meager IPO winnings in the *Church of the Living Christ*. She may or may not have had breast cancer and Rabbitt may or may not have cured her. I did manage to get Sandy to tell me the name of the diagnosing physician who, upon subsequent investigation, proved not to exist. No one named "Emilio Gonzalez" practiced medicine in a rundown warehouse over in the waterfront district. I smelled fraud. If I ever found him he might just accidentally fall down a flight of stairs on his way to a hearing. Regardless, Sandy had been sent by Rabbitt to the Brigham to see if his "healing" had been successful. After Sandy allowed me to see the records, they showed what

I suspected. She had no diagnosable cancer—and had likely never had any such thing.

It's amazing how stupid people can be when they're in love.

At some point Sandy put on all the weight. Maybe the disorder was caused by what Rabbitt and Wallace had put her through (not to mention Plante) or maybe it was just another indication of poor Sandy's disintegration. But it was all in service to Rabbitt's plan: gather enough followers, enough money, and move south. Sandy thought she had persuaded Rabbitt that Missouri was a good place.

But Wallace didn't plan to leave.

Wallace began hanging around the Kennedy shelter. This was not in keeping with Rabbitt's plan. Wallace was converting people but, according to Rabbitt via Sandy, they were the wrong people. They were homeless people who couldn't pay for their own place to live, much less Rabbitt's. There were many arguments.

Then, last week Wallace was murdered. The day after that, Plante was murdered. Rabbitt told Sandy to help me (*ME?*) and then disappeared himself.

If you neglected my connection with everything, Rabbitt was looking more and more like the villain in this story. Even Dooley said so.

Chapter 2.6: Tuesday, October 26

The next day was overcast and rainy. Not a nice warm rain. This was October and the rain was a frigid foretaste of November. I could have flown in anyway—visibility was sufficient—but it would have been miserable flying. Even though the flight bubble kept out the rain, it didn't keep out the cold and the damp any more than it kept out oxygen. Not to mention the rain on the roof when you take off and the rain on the roof after you land.

I put on my rain coat, sweater and hat—I will *never* get used to Boston weather—and caught the Mission Hill bus. It made me think of the bus that went by Heath Square—right where Wallace used to sit and sing. The thought of Wallace's dead corpse brought the day low. Remembering that Wallace, Rabbitt and Plante had spent their spare time following my every move brought it lower. Recalling David's involvement burned the day into a deep red glare. Only the thought of Peet's warm coffee near the station drew me to work.

Fortified with powerful stimulants from a cup the size of my head, I entered the BPD headquarters and made my way to my desk. Dooley was already there, reading an examiner's report.

"A filthy habit," I said as I took off my coat. "Police porn."

"Don't you read NTSB reports?"

"That's completely different."

"So you say." He put the report down. "Hickey wants to talk to us. Something to do with this." He tapped the report. "I've been waiting for you."

"Why?"

"Because we're working together. Seeing the medical examiner without you would be rude."

"Yeah. I meant why does he want to see *us*? Why not Hoffman and Rush?"

"They're busy right now preparing for the Sabado interview Thursday."

I didn't say anything for a moment. I just looked at him.

He looked away. "Well, they told us they expect us to analyze any information and report to them. We're just holding onto it for a little while. To help. We're not keeping any secrets."

I didn't say anything.

"We're not keeping them for long, anyway," Dooley said defensively.

"What does Hickey want to tell us?"

"If I knew that why would we have to go down there?"

Hickey's office was on Albany Street near Boston City. I half expected we'd have to meet in the morgue and for him to haul out dead bodies in some nasty show and tell. But he was already over here and met us downstairs. He just had pictures.

"Remember I said the wounds on Plante and Wallace were identical?"

"Yes," said Dooley. I nodded.

"I was right. And I was wrong." Hickey held up two pictures showing the wounds. There was an angle of entry drawing printed over the picture. "The wound is identical: same instrument. Same accuracy. Same force applied. But the angle of entry is different. Here on Wallace's body—" Hickey pointed to one picture. "The angle is high. On Plante's body the angle is lower."

I looked at the pictures. "What does that mean?"

"It means the perpetrator was standing at different heights at the two murders." Dooley picked up both pictures.

"Wallace and Plante were both seated when they were killed," I said. "Could that make the difference?"

Hickey shook his head. "If anything, that would make *less* of a difference in angle. In men, most of the difference in height derives from the legs. Seated, the two men would be nearly the same height."

"Okay," said Dooley. "What's *your* opinion?"

"I haven't got one. If it weren't for the solid evidence of the wound itself, I'd say that we had two perpetrators: one taller than the other. But both the force applied to the wound and the location of the wound indicates just one."

"What if the murderer was stooped over? Or kneeling?"

Hickey shrugged. "Maybe. I wouldn't have thought so—stooping or kneeling would make a difference in the force applied in the strike and change the nature of the wound itself rather than just the angle. But who knows?"

We left Hickey and went back upstairs. We were alone on the elevator. "What does it mean?"

"Beats the hell out of me. Maybe Rabbitt has one leg shorter than the other and strikes differently depending on where he's standing."

"And you thought *my* ideas were far-fetched."

"Speculative, Loquess," Dooley said carefully. *"Speculative.* As in complete fiction. Far-fetched just means it's a complete wild-assed guess."

"Maybe Hoffman and Rush can figure it out. After all, *they're* detectives."

"You hurt me, Loquess. Hurt me deep."

oOo

"Your fingerprints are all over this case," said Hoffman in a low, ominous rumble. Rush sat next to him. Dooley had stepped outside to take a call.

It was bad news, bad news, good news. Bad news that Rush and Hoffman were acting like they might really think I was a suspect. Bad news that Dooley wasn't here to give me moral support. Good news that Hoffman hadn't said a word until now. It meant they didn't really know what to make of it.

"Yeah," I said.

"You've *got* to have an opinion on this?"

"I think God has a sick sense of humor."

Hoffman raised his eyebrows. "You think this is all coincidence?"

I shook my head. "No. But I don't know what's driving it. Maybe they all were part of the famous *Where's Katelin?* phenomenon."

Hoffman shook his head. "Kohl wasn't listed."

"She's the only one."

"Yeah." Hoffman stared at me for a long minute. "If I thought you were in this, I'd take you out back and beat you with a tire chain. But you *can't* be. Kohl was in California two years ago. Wallace was in Missouri. And there's no connection between you and Rabbitt *except* these people."

"There's Sabado," said Rush suddenly.

"He's got no connection to Rabbitt," Hoffman said sourly.

"He doesn't need one," Rush insisted. "He lived with Loquess. He slept with Kohl."

"I didn't say that," I said hotly.

"Oh, please," said Rush. "It's obvious you think so. Sabado has a connection to the two of them. They have a connection to everyone else."

Hoffman looked at Rush. "You think Sabado killed Wallace and Plante? For what?"

Rush smiled. "I didn't say he killed anybody. I'm saying he's at the center of this. Whatever *this* is."

"And what do you think *this* is?"

"I don't know." His smile turned cold and nasty as a barracuda. "But I can't *wait* to ask him."

Hoffman chuckled. "Yeah."

I left the conference room looking for Dooley. He was nowhere to be found. I found a note on my desk saying he was checking out a lead but nothing more than that.

At loose ends, I sat down and tried to think like Hoffman and Rush. Rush could be right. All of this could be centered on David. But Rush was biased. Being a cop, he didn't want to think about a fellow cop in trouble. At least, not in any legal trouble. I suspected that neither Hoffman nor Rush would ever lose sleep if I suddenly resigned from the department.

I remembered something Sandy had said about the night I met David. Okay, maybe they *had* slept together. Both had said it hadn't happened. But Sandy had pursued him and if he got away he'd be the first. Even if it hadn't happened that night, David and I had been apart for two years. Who knew what had happened between them since? I hadn't even known Sandy was in town.

Sandy had a carnivorous streak. She'd said back then she'd wanted to own a piece of him. Could someone have been thinking of using Sandy's impulse to get to David? Of course, once the weight had set in she wouldn't have been worth much as a *femme fatale*.

Or would she? I looked down at my own thin frame.

The spirochete wandering of my mind twisted further. To be completely honest, I stood as much chance of being at the center of this as David did. Sure, maybe David slept with Sandy back in college. I *certainly* slept with David. Sandy was my roommate for better than a year, and that was perhaps a stronger connection to me than an abortive one-night stand with David.

I shook my head. The problem was this case had no structure. You had to have a model of a case, a theory, something to hang the facts on, a solution. She killed her husband because he was sleeping around. He killed his brother over money. The shopkeeper died because it was a robbery gone wrong. Elementary stuff: method, motive and opportunity. Here: two murders by a cult leader who killed his right-hand man and one of his chief donors.

It didn't make sense.

The phone rang and I answered it. "Loquess."

"Find Dooley and meet us at Rabbitt's church." It was Rush.

"What did you find?"

Rush snarled over the phone. "Tim Rabbitt."

oOo

I called Dooley. No answer. I left a message to meet me at the church. Then, I ran up the stairs, checked in with dispatch and sailed off the roof at a dead run. It was a short flight at that speed. Fast as I was, I could see down on the street I was racing the WBZ and WFXT camera vans. I barely had enough time to check out with dispatch before I was in my descent and landing in the alley next to the church. I had time to tell the uniforms to set up a perimeter to keep the inevitable press out of the soup. Then, I went inside.

Rabbitt was lying backwards in a pool of blood. It looked as if he had been kneeling, was stabbed and fell backwards with his ankles beneath him. He looked uncomfortable, thin as a knife and worn out. Being on the run hadn't agreed with him.

Not that Hickey wasn't there crawling over the body. He beckoned me over.

"Yeah?" I said, squatting next to him.

He used a probe and gently pulled back the torn cloth over Rabbitt's heart. The wound was small but thick with blood.

"See? Same weapon. Same targeting. Different angle."

After three murders, I could see it even without Hickey's contributing expertise. "Rabbitt was kneeling. Could that make a difference?"

"Maybe that's it." He returned to his examination.

I walked through the main hall, in the back, through the living quarters. Nothing had been disturbed from the last time I'd been here.

Returning to the front hall, I saw Sandy coming in the door, a uniform on either side.

Hoffman and Rush didn't see her immediately. I walked quickly over to her.

"Thanks, Officers," I said. They nodded and went back outside.

"What are you doing here?" I hissed.

"I saw the camera lights," she said dully, staring at Rabbitt's body. "Is he dead?"

I glanced back at Rabbitt's body, twisted and bloody, motionless beyond any possibility of life. "Yes." Sandy looked stricken. I took her arm. "You had nothing to do with this."

She looked at me blankly. Smiled. "You were always looking out for me. Funny the way I turned out as soon as you went away."

I held her shoulders and gently shook her. "You got mixed up in something you didn't understand. When this is over, I'll take you home. All the way back to Columbia. It'll be all right. I promise."

She nodded.

Behind me, I could feel Hoffman's presence.

"Miss Kohl was here to see what all the commotion was about," I said to him.

"Was she now," Hoffman said.

I stood out of the way and he looked down on the both of us.

"How long have you been here, Miss Kohl?"

"She just got here," I interrupted. "I saw her enter."

Hoffman swung towards me. "That'll be all, Loquess. I'll get back to you if I need your help."

He turned back to Sandy and started to lead her away. I grabbed his arm.

"*Detective* Hoffman," I said in a low voice. "A word."

Surprised, he let me pull him away.

"What the hell—"

"Listen, Hoffman." I glanced back at Sandy. "Leave her alone."

"The day I let you—"

"She's the *only* person we have left that had any intimate connection to Rabbitt. Everybody else is either out of town or dead. She's really fragile. If you and Rush pound on her you're going to break her into little tiny pieces. From then on she's going to be useless. Leave her alone and we might get something from her. Use your usual ham-fisted approach and we'll get nothing."

Hoffman stared at me for a good half minute. "You know, Loquess," he said slowly. "If I didn't know better I'd say you were thinking like a cop."

He left me and motioned to one of the uniforms, then turned to Sandy. "I'm sorry you had to see your friend this way. You go home and take care of yourself. Officer," he paused, glanced at the name tag, "Schmidt here will stay with you and make sure everything is all right. Got that, Schmidt? You stay with her until tomorrow and make her feel safe. We'll talk then." Aside, he said to me, "You're not averse to making sure she stays around, are you?"

I shook my head. Knowing Sandy, I knew what would make her feel safe. I hoped Schmidt wasn't married.

oOo

Dooley didn't answer the phone all while I was walking up the street and looking for witnesses. I must have interviewed a dozen people on either side of the church. After three murders it was like we were all reading from the same hymnal: Did you hear anything? Nope. Didn't hear a thing.

That night I turned on the television in my room and flipped between the Boston stations like a football junky. They had lots of pictures of the church, milling crowds, milling policemen controlling said crowds and long shots of what little of the crime scene they could see through the door. No good pictures of me.

The *Herald* front page trumpeted the Conclave Ripper, forever tying the Conclave and murder together. The organizers protested. The *Herald*, as usual, ignored them. There were no good pictures of me. I looked through the *Globe* as well. I saw a few gray blobs in the background, any one of which, or none, could have been me. Still safely anonymous. So far.

Chapter 2.7: Wednesday, October 27

I brought breakfast to Sandy on Wednesday. A thick sausage in a biscuit: fat wrapped in butter wrapped in fat covered by a thin carbohydrate shell to keep in the fat. I figured if she held the thing in her hands for a minute she'd gain two pounds. I brought a milkshake to wash it down. We'd work on her weight later. Right now I wanted her to feel comfortable.

She was alone when she answered the door. I figured either Schmidt had managed to keep his professional integrity intact or, more likely, had run off at the crack of dawn. She had a little cat smile I remembered from college, so I crossed off choice number one.

She held the biscuit in one hand and broke off pieces to nibble with the other.

"Tell me what happened," I said.

"Tim called me Sunday night. He said he needed a ride to Framingham. I drove him to this self-storage place on Route 135. He waved goodbye and I didn't hear from him until he called the next day. He said to help you."

"Right. He never called again? You never saw him?"

Sandy shook her head and nibbled the biscuit. Then she sipped the milkshake. Looked at it and then had a long pull on the straw. "This is good."

"How did Rabbitt get back into town?"

"I don't know. I would have given him a ride."

I left her and flew out to the storage facility. I called Hoffman on the way and he agreed to send out the forensics people. I was just to give it a quick look and tape it shut.

"Where's Dooley?" he asked.

"Working on a lead," I said, lying through my teeth as far as I could tell.

Rabbitt had paid a month's rent on a little shed the size of a tiny garage. I flashed my badge and got it opened. Inside was a cot, a few bottles of water and some food and a smell that suggested Rabbitt hadn't stepped outside until he returned to Boston.

"Didn't you notice the smell?" I asked the attendant.

He gave me a dead-fish stare. "No, Officer. I did not."

Meaning: *they don't pay me enough to care.*

I went back to my desk, making calls to people Sandy had managed to locate, getting wrong numbers and disconnected phones. Occasionally, I got a hit. Sure, they knew William Wallace. He was Tim Rabbitt's right-hand man. Shame about him. You mean Pastor Rabbitt is dead, too? What's the world coming to?

In other words, nothing.

I got a quick update from forensics on Rabbitt's shed: more nothing. But the financial guys had finally traced the deposits to the checks. Two and a half million unaccounted for. Enough motive right there for murder.

Dooley made it in near noon.

"Where have you been?" I said in a low voice. "I don't think Horn noticed you were gone, but I bet Hoffman and Rush sure have."

Dooley sat down in a rush and shook his head. Then, he shook it again.

"You okay?"

He looked at me for a moment. "No," he said. "Up late last night."

I got him a cup of coffee and he held it in his hand and stared at it, then sipped it slowly while I filled him in about Sandy and Rabbitt's shed and the money.

"I figure Wallace wanted to use the money for church stuff but Rabbitt had other ideas," I said. "So Rabbitt killed Wallace. Plante was a witness so Rabbitt killed him."

"Then, who killed Rabbitt?"

"Unindicted co-conspirator."

"Sabado?"

I shrugged reluctantly. "It doesn't sound like him."

"Where's the money?"

"Financial guys haven't found it yet. But they have some ideas."

Dooley nodded without saying anything.

I stared at him for a moment. "You look like hell."

Dooley nodded. "Ever observant, Loquess."

"What was the lead?"

He waved me away. "I'm not ready to talk about it just yet."

I felt nettled. "Well, did it pan out?"

"I'm not sure."

"You be sure to tell me if it does," I said, irritated as hell.

He ignored me. "I'll do that."

oOo

I clocked out at five p.m. sharp and went home—I wanted plenty of time to get my mind together before I saw Sean. I took a nice shower, agonized over what to wear and settled on slacks—a dress was asking too much, jeans were asking too little. I didn't know what to say to Sean or where we were going but I wanted to keep my options open.

I showed up at Bernoulli's at a quarter of seven. I went to the bar, looking for Sean. At seven sharp, I went to the hostess and asked if there was a reservation, first in my name, then in Sean's. Nothing. I took a table and left Sean's name with the hostess.

At eight, I was two drinks drunk and decided to eat. Katelin Loquess waits food for no man. But by nine, he still hadn't shown. I called him—voice mail. I texted him. No answer.

At nine thirty I called it a night. I was too drunk to fly. I made a stop at the packie around the corner from the apartment for a small bottle of tequila. If you're going to drown your sorrows, why use a puddle when you can use a lake?

I turned out the lights and looked out the window of the blank little room. It was a clear October night. Not a leaf on the trees. Nothing to stop the glare of the street lights from drowning out the glitter of the stars.

Chapter 2.8: Thursday, October 28

Thursday morning came, lit up by hangover flashes from Dooley's pounding on my door.

"Open up, Loquess."

I grabbed a robe and let him in, pointed to the sofa and left him there while I took a shower and got ready to go.

As I was coming out of the bedroom, Dooley handed me some coffee.

"Thanks," I said, surprised. He'd never brought coffee to the apartment before.

"No problem. Sabado is coming in this morning."

"What time?"

"Ten."

"Let's get bagels. Plenty of time."

"I suppose." Dooley shrugged. He seemed a little agitated.

"There's the Dunkin' Donuts over by Ruggles Station. We can park at the station and walk there."

"Okay."

I stopped in the doorway. "You feeling all right?"

He gave me an irritated look. "Of course. Why do you ask?"

"The way you acted yesterday. They way you're acting today. The way you like to drive around but today you want to walk. Are you sure a walk won't kill you?"

"I think I'll live." Then, a dry chuckle. "This time."

Dooley just drank coffee. He looked at me from across the table for a long time. "Why did you and David break up? The truth this time."

I didn't say anything for a long time. "That first year was amazing." I looked out the window. The clouds had broken to the east. Under them shone the rising sun, horizontal over the earth, lighting up the undersides of the clouds into incandescent gold. "Everything we did together worked perfectly and we did everything together. Over the summer, we got this little apartment on the east side of town. Two bedrooms in a tiny building across a one-lane bridge over the creek. Nothing around but trees. All you could hear were the birds and the sound of water. That fall he gave concerts all over the Midwest. He'd drive into Saint Louis or Kansas City or, sometimes, up to Chicago or as far west as Denver. He was happy doing that. He practiced while I studied. I liked that. He'd work on a section of some piece—some Bach or somebody. It would sound perfect. But he wouldn't like it so he would slow it down or speed it up or play it soft or play it loud, bits of it, over and over. You'd think that would drive me nuts, wouldn't you? But I'd be studying forensics or pathology or criminal law, snuggled under a blanket in the bedroom, half listening to him. He was *there*. And if I got bored with forensics or pathology or criminal law, I'd drag him to bed for an hour. We spent a lot of time doing that."

"Did you love him?"

"What? Are you stupid? Of course I loved him. He was the big musical furry center to my life."

"What happened?"

I fiddled with my coffee. "I think it actually started when we were still in Columbia but I didn't notice. Not till we came up here." I looked out the window again. The clouds were still ruinously illuminated. "It didn't take long to figure out life at the BPD was far from perfect. Sniezek refused to fly with me—he would have been the perfect flying partner, too. He was quick, strong. His sheer power would have complimented my finesse. I know now why he refused but I didn't then and it hurt. Sean wasn't a good fit, being all gangly and loose ends. He'd have been better as a solo flyer." I was still fiddling with my coffee. I stopped, clasped my hands together. "And there was resentment in the department. Nobody liked me—hell, nobody would *speak* to me. I was miserable. I came home spitting tacks, but David would just be nice and loving. Very supportive."

"You broke up with him because he was supportive?"

"I broke up with him because he didn't know I was there."

"I don't understand."

I leaned forward, trying to make it clear. "I'd come home a bitch. He'd pour me a glass of wine. I'd pick a fight. He'd make a nice dinner."

"So?"

"I'd come home in a great mood. He'd pour me a glass of wine. I'd do something good for him. He'd make a nice dinner. It didn't matter. The sex was great. He'd get me going and I'd go nuts. I'd do something for him—he'd think it was great. I'd do something different. He'd think it was great. It got to the point I started doing things *worse*—clumsy sex. I'd bite when I shouldn't, if you know what I mean. You know? He *still* thought it was great. *I didn't matter!*"

Dooley watched me for a long minute. "You're really strange. Do you know that?"

I shook my head. "On this I am absolutely clear. I know who I am. I'm a bitch. I'm self-involved. I'm half pissed off most of the time. The rest of the time I'm thoroughly pissed off. I *know* who I *am*. Maybe he was responding to some idealized version he had of me. Maybe he was responding to his mother. Or his aunt. Or his father. I don't know who it was he was responding to, but it was not me. And I wanted him to respond to *me*." I sipped my coffee.

"Even if he left you?"

I leaned back. "Even if he left me. If he knew who I was and I knew who he was, we could figure things out. As long as he was reacting to *someone else*, we had nothing."

"Did you fight?"

"Not often. He didn't like to fight."

"Do you?"

"Sure. Get something out in the open. Move things around. I've been tightly wound up in myself all of my life. A fight is one place I can get completely unwrapped."

"So you came to this realization. What happened then?"

I held my hands up to Dooley. "Look at these. I can drive a nail. I can shoot a gun. I can fly a stick. You know what David can do with his hands? He can make magic. *Real* magic. Not the crap people think I can do. He can move minds, break hearts, with nothing but the sound of a piano. *That's* a gift. I didn't understand what it meant."

I stared at the Formica table. "He'd been taking it easy while we were in Missouri. Just a few concerts here and there. David played for me—it was the one thing he did where I was absolutely sure I was the only person in the room. He needed that and so did I. But he had a career, too. He's a celebrity. In

Missouri, he was a big fish in a tiny pond. Boston is good but it isn't all that much bigger. He needed to get out there. Play bigger venues. Play with orchestras other than the ones in Boston. Places like Los Angeles, Chicago, New York, Atlanta, San Francisco, Denver. He'd had access to Chicago and Saint Louis from Columbia, but now he needed to tour. And as we drew apart, he needed the concerts more and more—David *needs* an audience. If one special person isn't there, well, half a thousand not so special people will do. But he was gone a lot and my job sucked and both fed right into the problems *we* had. Finally, it came to a head. I went back to Jeff City and stayed with my family for a couple of weeks—you remember that, right?"

Dooley nodded. "That leave of absence."

I grinned—well, I bared my teeth, anyway. "I only half lied when I said that to Horn. *Something* sure died on that trip. He came out. I wouldn't see him. I wouldn't talk to him. I wouldn't answer his phone calls. When I came back to Boston, he'd moved out. I haven't talked to him since."

oOo

We got into the office by eight thirty. Hoffman was going over his notes.

"Where's Rush?" I asked as we passed him.

"Preparing." Hoffman shrugged. "Method actors. Prima donnas, all of them."

"Beg your pardon?"

Hoffman gave me a look, his eyes deep in his face. "Get a sense of humor, Loquess. It's Rush's turn to get coffee." He turned back to his notes. "Sabado's coming in at nine."

"Dooley said ten."

"*Ten* is when we're going to start with him. *Nine* is when he gets here."

"What are you going to do with him for an hour?"

Hoffman gave me another look. "Room seven. You and Dooley can watch. No noise."

"The place is weird this morning," I said to Dooley in a low voice.

"Just this morning?" Dooley sat across from my desk. "Maybe it's celebrity jitters."

"You think so?"

Dooley shrugged. "I guess. It's not like Sabado knows anything."

"You don't think he's involved?"

"Of course he's involved—like Rush said. He's at the center of things just like you are. But the best we can hope for is he can make some connections for us that will lead us to what is *really* going on."

I watched him a moment. "So what happened yesterday?"

"Excuse me?"

"What was the big lead you went to check out?"

Dooley finished swallowing some coffee. "Like I told you. I'm not ready to say. When I do, you'll be the first to know."

"That pisses me off."

"I always try to do my part."

oOo

David showed up at nine sharp. He towered over the rest of us. He'd lost some weight and the result somehow made him appear even bigger than he had looked before. Stronger, maybe. He looked good.

He was dressed in a long coat, expensive but understated, warm but still right for October. He wore it easily, used to good things. When we were living together, he took pains not to dress any better than I did—some guilt about my money versus his money. He must have gotten over that.

I was surprised I didn't feel anything. There might have been some sort of pang inside for a brief moment but then, with his older face and lean body, he looked like a stranger. Or maybe that's how I wanted to view him: just another witness, just another suspect.

Hoffman brought him in.

David came in the room, listening to Hoffman. He glanced up, saw me and froze for a few seconds.

I watched him—I was prepared to see him. Clearly, he was not prepared to see me.

Hoffman stopped for him, watching. I realized that Hoffman had brought him through this area intentionally to shake him up.

"Officer Dooley and Officer Loquess are also working this case," Hoffman said, easily.

He swallowed. "I see. Hello, Katelin. Officer Dooley."

"Right," said Hoffman. "You know each other. Maybe you'll want to talk with Loquess after we're done. Come along."

I swear, Hoffman sounded like my old grandfather.

I glanced over at Dooley. He was watching David closely, almost hungrily. David didn't notice.

"We should go to room seven," Dooley said after they left the room. "Watch Sabado squirm for a while."

"Careful, Dooley," I said. "You'll get personally involved. Pretty soon you'll be protecting him."

"Not going to be a problem."

oOo

223

We let ourselves into the observation room about ten minutes before Hoffman and Rush came in.

"What do you think he knows?" asked Dooley.

"What is he? Your man-crush?"

Dooley chuckled softly. "In your dreams. Still, I understand *your* attraction."

"Not for years."

Hoffman and Rush came in the room. Rush was looking over the contents of a file. Hoffman came in with his hands empty. He sat down to one side of the table and stared at David.

"Detective Hoffman," David said easily, then faltered when Hoffman didn't respond.

"I'm Detective John Rush," Rush said, not seeming to notice. "This is Detective Albert Hoffman."

"Detective Hoffman and I have met."

Dooley pulled out his cell phone and stared at the screen for a moment. "I've got to go."

"*What?*" I hissed. "Are you nuts?"

"That lead I went looking for," Dooley said just as quietly. "It's panned out. Are you coming?"

"What sort of lead is it?"

"The best kind. The one where you find out who the murderer is."

I was torn. Here I had a chance to watch David eviscerated by Hoffman and Rush. Two masters of the trade. But Dooley was holding out a chance to actually solve the case without them.

"Okay!" I said in a loud whisper. "You better make detective for this."

Outside and into his car.

oOo

Conclave was in full swing up in Salem. But sometime in the late seventies Salem threw Boston a bone. The athletes got a one-day break between the trials and the finals. Participants who had been winnowed out and any witch who could lift a paper clip came down to Boston for the Conclave Parade. The preparations for the Conclave Parade were in full swing. All year long, witches pulled together scraps of cloth, glitter, LEDs, electronics and papier-mâché into costumes. All powered by humans; no cars or motorcycles. If it wasn't drawn, carried, lifted or flown, it wasn't in the parade.

The parade began in Chinatown, followed the waterfront to Faneuil Hall and then came back up by Government Center to Cambridge Street to enter Boston Commons from the north. It made crossing Chinatown a nightmare.

Overhead, I saw three of Sam's former students shoot down Columbus Avenue as we drove into town. Once we got to Kneeland Street, we got stuck. I watched one gentleman dressed as a clown bouncing a great orange ball, just staring at it. Down the street, a woman was flying paper airplanes in complex circles eight feet overhead.

Every third person was a juggler.

Dooley leaned on the horn until I reached over and popped on the lights. After that, we crossed Kneeland without any trouble.

Dooley turned onto Essex for half a block, then into this narrow alleyway and parking lot filled with trucks. He stopped behind the trucks, got out of the car and went to the trunk.

I got out of the car and looked around. I didn't see anything interesting. I glanced towards the back of the car. I could hear him rummaging back there. "What's in the trunk?"

"Special equipment."

I looked back to the alley, wondering where we were going. A sweet solvent smell and then his hand clamped a cloth over my face. I inhaled and I was gone, nothing left of me but tatters and light.

oOo

I woke with a headache and a nearly overwhelming urge to vomit. After a few moments, my stomach settled and I opened my eyes. Dooley was sitting across from me, watching me intently. He was silent.

"What's the..." My voice trailed off. There was somebody sitting in another chair a few feet away, the three of us making a neat triangle. He was leaning forward, unconscious. I didn't need to see his face to know it was Sean.

"What is going on?" My mind cleared and I stared at Dooley in horror. "*You're* the killer?"

Dooley didn't say anything. He pulled out a knife and held it. Short. A little wide—a small skinning knife, perhaps. I remembered what Hickey had said about the murder weapon: short, narrow and sharp.

He stood up and came over, looking down at me.

Without looking at Sean, he said, "Sit up, Gifford. I know you're faking."

Sean lifted his head. He looked at me, then Dooley, then back at me.

Dooley shrugged. "You two can speak."

I tried to but coughed. Then, I managed to say: "How long have you been down here? Are you *okay?*"

"So far." He shook his head, still dazed. "What day is it?"

"Thursday." I looked up at Dooley.

"It's still Thursday." Dooley smiled at me and his face was someone I'd never seen before.

226

"I've been here two days." He shook his head again. "I'm okay. I think."

Dooley stared down at me. "Another lover. Someone else you abandoned."

"What the *fuck* are you talking about?"

Dooley slapped me as easily as he might have slapped a puppy. The explosion made my vision dim and my ears ring. I tasted blood.

"Leave her alone!"

"Shut up."

Dooley brought his face down to within a few inches of mine. He grabbed my jaw with his hand and turned my face towards Sean. "What do you feel towards him?" He released me.

I jerked back to stared at him. "I'll kill you if you hurt him."

Dooley laughed softly. "You will *try*."

Dooley stood up. Watching me closely, he swung his arm in a broad backhand and slashed Sean's throat.

Sean tried to scream but only bubbled. He shook, thrashed—blood spurted across his chest, across Dooley, across me. I felt it in my heart, a controlled, cold death-dealing thrust, leaving me bleeding and lifeless.

I cried out. I tried to reach him, to rip through the cord and hold him. Instead, he died in front of me, both of us helpless, an inconsolable distance between us.

His life drained away and I was weeping, crying like a child lost in the dark.

Dooley took my chin and turned me to face him. *Kill me. Kill me, too*, said every part of me.

His face was filled with light and blinded me, deafened me to anything but his voice.

"We've never met before, Katelin," he said in a sing-song voice. "My name is Misty."

Part 3: David, 1999

Chapter 3.1: Thursday, October 28

Obsessions accrete slowly, like bones or the shells of crabs.

First, there's the breakup. The five descending stages of grief: anger, recrimination, regret, loneliness, depression. Was it my fault? Was it hers?

Picking up an object, any object, forgetting what the object is and remembering only the object's heritage: where we bought it or found it. The complete string of memories it evokes. An ancient, cheap lobster fork we found in a shapeless pile of silverware at the bottom of a rotting cardboard box holding down the floor in a junk shop, when we visited Provincetown for the first time. She insisted we watch the sunrise from the east side of the spit and then be sure to watch the sunset on the west side of the same day so she could watch the sun appear from the ocean and disappear back into it. A thin book discussing bamboo, written completely in Japanese, discovered in a garage sale on a trip to northern Missouri when she showed me land so flat I was morally certain I could see China if I only found the right spot and stared hard enough, her laughing at me as I stared, then grabbing me and pressing her face against my chest and telling me how much she liked the way I smelled. How much she loved me.

That sort of thing fades into the occasional surprise late at night or during the morning before coffee.

But the interest remains—nothing to be concerned about. After all, there's any number of reasons for a normal, healthy interest. And if that interest continues after the memories begin to fade—well, that's normal, too. Isn't it?

Then, when the interest doesn't really abate. If, in fact, you find yourself searching the net, Googling traces of your... *interest*, then that's okay, too. After all, everybody looks up old teachers. Girlfriends. Ex-wives. If everybody does it, it's still *normal*.

At some point, you cross a line. Maybe it's the pay-per-search sites—The person you're looking for is in Boston, Massachusetts! $29 to find birth records, deeds, marriage records!

But it's still all right. Okay, it's gone past *normal*, of course. But it's not really pathologic, is it? After all, nobody knows what you're doing. It's all legal—if it wasn't, how could they advertise so openly on the net?

Even when it's not a single search or even a regular search but you've purchased a continuously updating feed. It's still private. It's still legal.

You know you're in stalker territory, though, when you're offered a private deal. For a modest fee, you can watch private videos of her. At this point, there's no going back. There's no hiding it from yourself. You *know* what you're doing is rotten. But, you console yourself: I can't help myself. I'm *obsessed*. As long as no one knows, that's consolation enough.

Then, you have a change in perspective. A new light shines on you and it's as if you see yourself for the first time.

I knew my life was shaky when I got the call from Dooley.

I was in Saint Louis. Frieda had set me up with a short tour that ended in New York just prior to Conclave back home. It was a nice set of gigs. The one in Saint Louis was a solo recital. I'd been working through the Liszt piano transcriptions of the Beethoven symphonies again—I was finding a wealth of possibilities I hadn't understood before. Tonight, I would finish the concert with the Seventh. The *Allegretto*, with its pendulous and fallen grandeur like an unstoppable river flowing to the sea, never failed to move the audience. Or me, for that matter.

I was eating dinner by myself in the hotel restaurant. After dinner I would go upstairs, dress for the concert and take a cab to the hall. Drink a cup of coffee. Use the bathroom. Practice my warm-up exercises. All of those little rituals I had grown into over the years.

My cell rang. I didn't recognize the number but I answered anyway. Officer Abraham Dooley.

I agreed to speak with the Boston Police Department when I returned to Boston. I hung up the phone and stared at my salad. My hands and face felt numb. Without thinking, I started some finger stretching exercises. Scales. Arpeggios. I was calm in a few moments.

It had to be about *Where's Katelin*.

Should I have a lawyer present? After all, Katelin was a Boston police officer. BPD was very protective of its own, even if it didn't like them. You didn't grow up around Boston · without realizing that at an early age. On the other hand, I thought, what did I do that was really wrong? I watched some illegal videos. I'd always felt too squeamish to watch any of the bedroom files. Any half decent record of the site would show that. So I watched some records of Katelin flying around. Talking to locals. Drinking coffee. Laughing.

I would manage.

That night it hit me right in the Seventh. Right in the *Allegretto*, in the *dolce expressivo*, second line, fourth measure. For a moment, I couldn't remember the music at all. Just remembering all of the records I had seen. It would all be exposed: all of the searches I had made, videos I had seen. There would be interviews with other members of the site— sure, we know DAVID902. He was always watching. You couldn't sign on without seeing him there. Oh! He was *that* David? Wasn't he in a mental hospital? Multiple Personality Disorder? All of my flaws, all of my past, every rumor of me, every opinion of me, all visible and broadcast across the world. I'd be lucky to ever play a concert again.

But my left hand remembered the *expressivo* on its own and after a brief moment, my right joined it. My mind might be gone but my hands remembered their job.

A lawyer didn't matter. What records I had or hadn't seen didn't matter. One drop of data in the sea of the internet and I would be swamped. I had managed to avoid being eaten by the celebrity machine until now. If the BPD willed it, I'd be swallowed up. I was at their mercy.

I had no idea I could feel so vile.

That was as far as my mind got until I entered the station and met Detective Hoffman. He brought me through a back room and I saw Katelin and all the light seemed to be drawn to her. She looked at me.

And I understood at that moment that Katelin knew. Knew it all. Knew what I had done. Knew what I had become. Knew how small and ugly I really was. If there had been anything between us, her cool gaze said to me, it was gone now. I was just a witness. A perp. An offender. A criminal.

I thought I had felt as low as I could possibly feel. I was wrong.

Hoffman led me to a small gray room and left me alone.

I stared at the wall for a long time in wonder. *Ah*, I thought. *So* this *is bottomless despair.*

oOo

I was in the room an hour before Detective Hoffman came in with another man.

"Detective Hoffman," I said. I looked at him for some cheer, maybe. He stared back at me, his tiny eyes black and empty.

The other man spoke up: "I'm Detective John Rush. This is Detective Albert Hoffman."

"Detective Hoffman and I have met," I said, nausea fermenting in my stomach. I should never have eaten. I had a sudden urge to bolt—I was here voluntarily. I could scream for my lawyer. The room felt close, anechoic. The only sounds were our voices, the hiss of our breath, the rasping of our clothes, the minute squeaks and groans of our bodies as we moved in our chairs.

I glanced at Hoffman again. His expression was implacable.

Intellectually, I knew that Rush was playing a *good cop* and Hoffman was playing a *bad cop*. But it didn't make any difference. I found myself wanting to cozy up to Rush and frightened of Hoffman.

Rush sat down across from me and pulled out a folder. He opened it on the table with a slap. "You're a paid subscriber to *WheresKatelin.com*, right?"

I felt defeated. Ashamed. I thought about trying to explain it but there was no point to any explanation. I didn't say anything for a moment. The air in the room felt stale and devoid of oxygen. The lights seemed brighter than they had when I had come in here. I smelled something meaty like stale blood. Hoffman? I glanced at him. He was still glaring at me. He didn't seem to be sweating, and Rush looked as cool as a bird.

Rush leaned back in his chair and watched me. He slid a paper silently over to me. "Is that a copy of your credit card records? With the regular charge over to Cybertech Investigations?"

I nodded.

Rush passed another sheet over to me. "This is a paid subscriber list for the *Where's Katelin* website. That's your name, isn't it?"

"Yes."

"So, Mr. Sabado. Let's try that question again: are you a paid subscriber to the *Where's Katelin* website?"

"Yes."

"For the last..." Rush consulted the contents of the folder again. "Year and a half. Correct?"

"Yes."

"You do know that Katelin Loquess is a police officer, don't you?"

I nodded.

Hoffman stood up. The scrape of his chair was loud in the room. He turned away.

I was startled by his sudden movement and slid my own chair back. He glanced back at me contemptuously. Then, he pulled off his jacket and hung it on the door. His forearms hung loosely out of his short-sleeved shirt.

"Mr. Sabado?" Rush said, his voice like oil. "Please pay attention. I'm asking the questions here. Not Detective Hoffman."

But I could no more take my eyes off Hoffman than a deer could avoid looking at headlights. Hoffman pulled a tennis ball out of his jacket pocket and came back to his chair. He sat down and resumed his staring at me.

I didn't realize I was practicing five-finger exercises until Rush stared at my hands. I clasped them together and held them in my lap.

"You watched illegal videos of Officer Loquess?"

"I watched videos of Officer Loquess. I don't know if they were illegal or not."

Hoffman snorted. He started squeezing the tennis ball. Every muscle and tendon in his forearm bunched up to twice their normal size. The tennis ball bulged as if it were going to explode. I had never seen such muscles in my entire life.

Rush smiled thinly at me. "Point taken. Did you watch *videos* of Officer Loquess?"

"Yes."

"Videos of her on the street? In the air?"

"Yes."

"Videos of her in her apartment?"

I nodded, miserable.

Rush leaned forward. "Videos of her in bed?"

"No!"

Rush leaned back affably. "All right. All right. Did you know there's a record of every video you've ever streamed or downloaded?"

"I figured there probably was."

"We have that record. So if you ever *did* download some nice bedroom footage of Loquess—and who could blame you—we'll find out." He chuckled dryly. "She's a very pretty girl, isn't she? And you were together for a long time. I bet things were pretty spicy. It's natural to want to relive some of the good parts."

I didn't say anything. I thought of Katelin's eyes. *She* didn't think it was natural.

Hoffman squeezed the ball again. The strength in those hands.

I dragged my attention back to Rush. "Beg pardon?"

Rush smiled. "You were about to tell me how you missed the good parts of the relationship." Rush didn't give me a chance to answer but turned back to the folder. "Did you know any of the other subscribers?"

"No." I couldn't breathe. I burped something noxious.

"You didn't participate in the chat rooms?"

"I didn't know there were any chat rooms. Just a list of members on line." I could *hear* that tennis ball, a faint groan from the pressure.

"When you were in Columbia, did you know a William Wallace?"

"The plastics factory guy?"

Rush glanced up from his file. "You did know him?"

I shook my head. "I never *met* him. I'd heard of him."

"How did you hear about Wallace?"

I shrugged, feeling slightly more comfortable and on familiar ground even if I was confused. "I did a lot of local concerts when I was living in Columbia. Parlor room sets. School gigs. Even a wedding or two—there are a lot of people there with too much money and not enough taste. They'd want to hear Beethoven's Ninth at their daughter's wedding just so I'd play there. People talked about things and I'd overhear."

"What's wrong with the Ninth for a wedding?"

I didn't answer immediately. "It's too big for the occasion," I said carefully, not wanting to give offense.

Rush nodded and consulted his file again. "Why would people talk about William Wallace?"

I spread my hands. "Cautionary tale, I suppose. Columbia was a college town until the early seventies and the university budget crunch. Then, the town decided to attract business. Several factories were built—a pipe factory, a factory that built valves for the automobile industry and Wallace's plastic factory. He did very well but fell off the deep end with religion and then got caught up in a nasty divorce. The cautionary part depended on who was telling the story. If it was the wives—say, at a wedding—it was when to start divorce proceedings against a crazy husband. If it was the husbands, it was how to protect the business from a voracious wife. Anyway, the end of the story was always the same: Wallace ended up in a mental hospital and the plastics company ended up in receivership. Both Wallace and his wife ended up with nothing."

"I see." Rush watched me. "So you wouldn't recognize him if you saw him?"

"No."

"Here's his picture. Take a good look." Rush slid over a picture of a dead body lying in a pool of blood.

"I don't understand." The room felt suddenly cold. I felt dizzy. Every sound in the room compressed. My breakfast chased my coffee all over my insides.

"Did you know Oscar Plante?"

I shook my head. "The juggler? I've never met—"

"Ah. Here's his picture, too." Rush slid over another picture of a dead body. More blood. "Vice gets all the pretty pictures. Homicide is never quite able to get the right pose."

I stared at the pictures silently.

"Or Tim Rabbitt?" Rush slid a third picture over to me. "Surely you remember him. After all, didn't you kill all three of them?"

I stared at Rush. I stared at Hoffman.

Hoffman held up the tennis ball. Without taking his eyes off me, he squeezed the ball until with a gasp it ripped apart.

I threw up.

oOo

Both Rush and Hoffman jumped up out of the way. The morning's coffee and croissant spilled over the table, photographs and folder.

"Shit," yelled Hoffman.

Rush carefully snagged the papers by clean corners and pulled them off the table gingerly. "Well, *that* was unexpected."

They gathered up the papers and photographs—carefully, of course—and took them out of the room. I was left, just me and the smell of my own vomit.

I groped in the pocket of my coat and pulled out a napkin. At some point in my life I had apparently eaten at the *Au Bon Pain*. This napkin was evidence. I wiped my lips and cheeks, blew my nose and stood up. I got up and walked around the room. Noon came and went.

The door was locked—unsurprising. Interrogation rooms would be locked. I wondered what the rules were in case of a fire.

The door opened suddenly and a huge black man entered. "I'm Abraham Dooley. We spoke on the phone."

"Right."

"Something's come up, Mr. Sabado," he said with a smile. "We'll have to reschedule. Please come with me."

"Sure," I said, uncertainly.

"Good." He opened the door and led me out.

Down a hall lined with doors that I presumed opened into other interrogation rooms, to a back stairway and down stairs.

Dooley followed me all the way down—initially, I didn't think anything of it. I would expect to get escorted out of the police department. But we went past the first floor and into a parking garage.

"My car's over there," he said.

"I can take the T."

He waved me away. "Don't mention it, Mr. Sabado. With all you've been through, giving you a ride home is the least we can do."

"Thanks."

He didn't say anything as we drove outside. It was bright out. Blue sky. Glare off the white of the police building. I didn't mind getting a ride home; I'd come in on the train and it was a pain to go home.

"Did you know I was partners with Officer Loquess?" he said suddenly.

"No."

"But you did see me in headquarters when you came in?"

"You're pretty unmistakable."

"Yeah. I get that a lot. Well, we'll get you home."

Home was up in Gloucester. I'd *hated* the Parker Street apartment. When I'd moved out it was back into my family's place. Somehow, the idea of being in Katelin's jurisdiction just made me angry. I kept thinking what it might be like if she caught me speeding or jaywalking—not that she ever would. Flyers didn't do traffic patrol, and the last jaywalking ticket in Boston must happened before Prohibition.

Then, Mom died suddenly. Stood up one morning, got ready to go to work down at Addison-Gilbert Hospital, collapsed into a coma. They took her there and she never woke up. Dad had to hear about it over the radio since he was fishing off the Banks. He made it home in a few days and together we buried her. Dad sold the boat and lay around the house for a couple of months and then I found him downstairs slumped over the table: heart attack. I'd heard about one spouse dying shortly after the other but now I saw it firsthand.

Years later, I'm still there.

Being a passenger makes me reflective, I suppose.

Then, we crossed over the Charles River and he signaled to get off in Somerville.

"The best way to Gloucester is up I-93 and 128." I felt ridiculous. He *must* know this.

"Ah," he said. He glanced at me then back to the road. "I have an errand to make."

"You can let me off at North Station, then. I can take the train."

"No. I don't think so." He glanced at me again then back to the road.

"I need to get home." I felt my voice get high. I looked around. We were still on the off ramp. Maybe I could jump out of the car when he had to stop. I looked at him and he was watching me.

"Just stay in the car and everything will be fine."

"This corner's good," I started to open the door as he stopped at a light.

"Sweet Jesus in cashmere," he said in a tired voice that said he knew exactly what I was thinking. Dooley pulled out his gun—not pointing it anywhere. Just holding it. I realized how huge he was. He was a little taller than I was but with big shoulders and chest that looked like he could toss me over the car, much less in it. Without thinking, I raised my hands.

He held his gun so he knew I was looking at it. "This is a Glock 9 millimeter. Do you know what it will do to a man?"

I shook my head.

"Good. It's better not to know. Now close the door. I am not going to hurt you. But I need to take you someplace where we can talk."

I nodded.

"You are an idiot," Dooley said as he holstered the pistol in his jacket. "When an officer of the law says stay in the fucking car you stay in the fucking car, do you not?" He turned and stared at me. "Am I making myself clear?"

"Yes."

"Good. Now put down your goddamned hands."

I held them in my lap. "Where are we going?"

"Someplace you can tell me everything you know about Misty."

I stared at him, stunned by a name I had not heard for years.

oOo

It came to me then. "You did something. What?"

He looked at me slowly and turned back to the road. "Something bad. Or Misty did. I don't know which."

"That's impossible." I shook my head. "Misty was a figment in my head. A personality disorder—"

"I don't know what she was when she was in your head. But when she was in *my* head, she was real enough." Dooley shook his head. "This is no good. They're going to be looking for both of us soon. Once they realize I'm gone, they're going to want to talk to you. We need to find a place to talk. Private. Cozy."

I stared at him. "Are you coming on to me?"

Dooley snorted. "You wish." He grinned at me. "But a little perfume or a nice sun dress can do wonders."

That kept me silent the rest of the way.

oOo

Dooley pulled into a vacant spot in front of a disreputable-looking bar-front on Broadway. The windows were boarded over with plywood and the edges were separating. The roof was low—some of the shingles had fallen off and more than a couple were lying on the sidewalk in front. The closest thing to a name was a broken collection of letters hanging in the front window like some disheveled game of Hangman: "G__y R__b_d." The place didn't look functional, much less open. I said so.

"It's always open," Dooley said shortly.

"What is this place?" I asked.

"The Gray Rosebud," he said, looking at the place with evident satisfaction. "Owned by one of the last surviving members of the old Killeen gang."

"Who were they?"

"One of the Irish gangs from long before Winter Hill took over the underworld. In the first gang war it was the Charlestown versus Winter Hill. TKO for Winter Hill by virtue of having some remaining survivors. The second gang war was the Killeens versus the Mullins, a decided knockout by the Mullins. The third was the Whitey Bulger Takeover when Howie Winter retired. That lasted until Bulger ran off. This gentleman," Dooley gestured at the storefront, "had the good sense to leave town when the Killeens and the Mullins were in the ninth round. Howie Winter's truce included him and he came home."

"When was that?"

"Back in the seventies."

I appraised Dooley. "You're a little young."

Dooley shrugged. "I am a student of Boston history. Besides, he's my father."

oOo

"Pop!" yelled Dooley when he came in.

An old white man came out from the back. His face crinkled into a grin when he saw Dooley. "Son!"

They hugged one another and I stood off to one side in the traditional third wheel stance.

"Pop," Dooley said when they released one another. "This is David Sabado."

"Pleased to meet you," said the old man as he offered his hand. "Tom Dooley, like the song." It was absolutely clear he had never heard of me.

"Same here." I left the cognitive dissonance from an aging white Irishman being Dooley's father for another time. I had enough to worry about.

Dooley leaned towards Tom. "We're going to talk privately for a bit."

"Okay."

Dooley led me to a booth in the back. "Couple of Harps, Pop?"

"Coming up."

"We won't be bothered for a while," Dooley said as he sat down. "Pop doesn't open until two."

"I thought you said this place was always open." I sat down at the booth.

"It's always open to *me*."

The two beers appeared a moment later. Dooley held his up. "It's always happy hour somewhere."

It had been a rough morning. I nodded and clinked his glass with mine and drank a third of it. I put down the beer. I felt it roll through my empty stomach and my head went light. "So, what happened?"

Dooley nodded and told me about the William Wallace and Oscar Plante murders, how connected Katelin seemed to be.

"So," he said. "We'd pretty much tied all of the murders to Tim Rabbitt. Loquess came up with a sweet theory: Wallace was messing with the church congregation so Rabbitt killed him. Plante saw something or figured something out so Rabbitt killed Plante and split. Then, last Tuesday I get a call from Sandra Kohl." He stared at me, levelly.

He'd already mentioned Sandy, so I was prepared. I stared back.

Dooley broke it off with a wave of his hand. "Kohl tells me she has information that she wants to pass on. Information about Tim Rabbitt. I agreed to be the conduit. But it's not enough to talk on the phone. She has to meet me *in person*. Okay. But that's not enough, either. It has to be without Loquess."

Dooley tipped his glass towards me. "This, I thought, was a little much. I ask why. She says seeing Loquess was *too embarrassing*. I'd already heard what happened to Schmidt—"

"Who's Schmidt?"

"Officer assigned to take care of Kohl the night that Rabbitt was murdered. Apparently, appearances are deceiving: she's really not as weak as two sticks tied together with butter. Schmidt came in the next day looking like he'd been through a garbage compactor, a big grin all over his face."

"Ah." Not for the first time I wondered what I'd missed out on that one night with Sandy.

Dooley grinned sourly. "So I figured that was one possibility. More likely, I thought she might be trying to set up a meeting. She tells me she'll see me at the church."

Dooley stopped for a minute and drank down the remainder of his beer. "Can I get another one, Pop?"

The old man appeared from the back as if by magic. "Here y'go." He put two Harps in front of us. Dutifully, I drank the rest of my first one so I could start the next.

"I get to the church, right? Sure enough, Rabbitt is waiting for me. He looks like hell—like he hasn't eaten or slept in a week. Even so, I have my weapon out and covering him. He pulls out a knife and I tell him to drop it or die. He puts it down on the ground and lays face down. I kick the knife away. I cuff him. That's when it got weird." Dooley rubbed his face for a moment. "The instant I touch him, I feel strange. A little disoriented. A little dizzy. Then, it's like some thin smoke starts to fill the room—strands of it. Different colors, too: purple, red, green. *Food poisoning*, I think. Something. Suddenly, I feel *squeezed* inside. Like I'm pushed into a little bubble. I uncuff Rabbitt and put my weapon away. This is odd, I think. He comes up and kneels, looking at me like he's never seen me before. I walk over and pick up the knife. It's a wicked little straight blade—a skinning knife. I come back to him, looking at him. I can't figure out what's going on. I'm doing things but I'm not *thinking* about things. You know what I mean?"

I nodded, not knowing at all but unwilling to stop the story.

Dooley nodded back and sipped his beer. "Then, I lean down and slip the knife right into his chest. Rabbitt gives me a surprised look and falls back."

"You killed Tim Rabbitt?"

"It would seem so."

I felt oddly calm—not like I was talking to a killer at all.

"Inside I'm yelling but nothing's getting out. The colored smoke is everywhere so I can barely see. It's like trying to make your way through a burning fireworks factory. And I'm clumsy. Barely able to walk. I manage to make it to the back of the church, to where Rabbitt lived, and lay down on the bed, and then the smoke overwhelms me completely. When it clears, I'm not there anymore."

"Excuse me?"

Dooley nodded again. "This is the weirdest thing of all. I saw. I acted. Occasionally, I thought things. But *I*—me, myself and I—wasn't there at all. I remember everything perfectly from then on. No smoke. No dizziness. No confusion. But *I'm* not there. Someone else is."

Insane, I thought. I looked over towards the door. Pop was sitting behind the bar, a racing form in front of him. He was watching us. His face was cold and I suddenly remembered that this man was one of the survivors of the Irish gang wars.

"Someone else," I said, trying to figure out what to do.

248

"Yeah. Sounds crazy, doesn't it?" He stared into the beer moodily. "I was there when I reached Rabbitt's bed but when I woke up I wasn't. I was this... Dooley-thing. Dooley undead or something. Maybe that's the way to think about it."

"Okay," I said slowly.

Dooley looked up. "The Dooley-thing left and went to my apartment over in Allston. Slept the night through and went in the next afternoon. He talked to Loquess and pulled out all that stuff—" Dooley gave me a long appraising glance. "There is some truly fucked-up shit between you and her. When this all settles out, you two have got to get some serious counseling. And I haven't even *heard* your side of it. I bet that's going to be fun." He wound down for a moment, thinking.

"You talked to Katelin about me?"

"Not now. I'm not drunk enough. Then, this morning, you come in. The Dooley-thing is all hot about *you*. All excited. You get in and Loquess and the Dooley-thing go into the observation room to watch. Then, the Dooley-thing fakes a phone call and gets Loquess to run out on your interrogation. Part of some big plan—which I'm not privy to since I'm not remembering any *thoughts*. The Dooley-thing clearly has access to every memory I ever had but I haven't got *dick* from it."

I leaned back in the booth. I watched Dooley. He sure didn't look like any sort of killer. Oh, he had the big dangerous man thing down. But I got no impression of immediate threat. "What happened next?"

"Then, the Dooley-thing chloroformed Loquess and carried her, unconscious, into this basement in a nearby building, which, apparently, it had prepared beforehand."

"Oh."

"I know how all this sounds. I'm *not* a psychopath. I have a bachelor's degree in math from Boston University and I graduated from Suffolk Law School. I'm *not* crazy." He snorted. "At least, not yet. But I feel like I'm going to be."

"You chloroformed her?"

"Yeah." He sipped his beer. "Sean Gifford was tied up in the basement. I—*the Dooley-thing*—slugged him around for a little bit while it waited for Loquess to wake up. Then, they all talked for a couple of minutes. Then, it reached around and sliced Gifford's throat. Gifford died. The Dooley-thing grabbed Loquess and that damned colored fog rolled in. When it cleared, Loquess was gone and Gifford was still dead but *I* was back. I went outside. My car was still there. I raced back to BPD. I was going to tell Hoffman and Rush about it but I got scared. You puked and the two of them came out. They decided to let you stew for a bit—but *I* knew you were what the Dooley-thing was hot about. So I took you out of there." He stopped and looked at me. "You hungry?"

"I suppose."

Dooley finished his beer and put it down on the table. "Pop?" he called out to Tom. "I'm going in the kitchen." He rose and led me through the double doors in the back of the bar.

Tom nodded as we passed and went back to his racing form.

Dooley pointed to one of the stools at a long table. "Sit there."

Dutifully, I sat. "Where did you hear the name Misty?"

Dooley rummaged around in the cabinets and brought out mayonnaise, a few spices and a monstrous can of tuna fish. He ripped it open on an industrial strength can opener. "That was the last thing the Dooley-thing said: Hello, Katelin. You don't know me. My name is Misty." Dooley looked at me, his eyes red. "Who the hell is Misty?"

"A figment of my imagination." So I told him my story, all of it: Gerald, Amanda, Donald, the time in McLean, and of course, Misty. "Misty was the personality that told me how to get rid of the others. I pulled them out with my bare hands— metaphorically speaking, of course. She stayed. She was helping me with the piano, helping a young boy navigate the currents of life." I shook my head. "They were all imaginary, Misty included. Finally, the night I met Katelin I cast her out as well. It's just been me in here ever since."

Dooley slid a plate over to me. On it was a beautifully made toasted tuna sandwich placed *just so* with a radish next to it carved into the shape of a rose.

"This is lovely," I said around a mouthful of spicy tuna. "But I've never had tuna like this."

"It's the curry powder. Nobody expects it. I used to cook for Tom when I was a kid."

I decided conversation could wait until I finished.

Afterwards, he delicately wiped his mouth with a napkin. "Whatever was in my head was no figment," Dooley said quietly. "Or you've invented some sort of contagious mental disease."

"Well, if she's real, *what* is she?"

"I don't know. But I bet I know somebody who does."

I knew exactly who he meant and voiced the name: "Eli Boor."

Dooley's cell went off as we got up. He pulled it out, glanced at it and put it back.

I stopped and looked at him.

He nodded. "Hoffman. Trying to find me. We don't have a lot of time before things hit the fan."

oOo

We stepped outside into the afternoon sun.

"Hey, *coppers!*" came from overhead.

I looked up and Katelin was hovering maybe fifty feet up.

Dooley pulled out his gun and aimed it.

Katelin laughed. "Are you going to *shoot* me now, Dooley? Shoot your old friend and *compadre?* This is how you treat your brother officer?"

"Just come on down, Loquess," Dooley called up to her.

I could tell it wasn't Katelin. It had been years since I'd heard Misty, and then it was always in my own mind. But now, even with Katelin's voice and in the broad outdoors, I could still tell it was Misty talking down to us.

"Fat chance," called Misty. "So long, fuckers!"

She spun a vertical one-eighty and tore off up Broadway faster than I'd ever seen Katelin go.

Dooley slowly lowered his gun. "She knew I wouldn't shoot."

"Yeah. Misty's a smart... something."

"Should we follow her?"

I watched as Katelin reached the McGrath highway and ripped out a right turn. She didn't ascend over the buildings. "I think that's what Misty wants us to do. It's probably a trap."

"Why would she trap us?"

"I'm still trying to figure out why she let you go. She killed everybody else."

Dooley got in the car. "I know the answer to that one," he said as we strapped in.

"What?"

"She wanted me to tell you what happened." We pulled out. Dooley put on the siren and we raced up Broadway after her. "Now, why would she want me to tell you?" He glanced at me. "What do you have that she wants?"

"Back in? Whatever that means."

"Maybe."

We turned right and went up the McGrath. Sure enough, Katelin was hovering over I-93, waiting for us. She streaked over the interstate and we followed underneath into Medford. Over the Mystic and then after her up Route 16.

"Then, why would she want us both?" Dooley asked.

I shook my head, not understanding. Suddenly, Katelin appeared in front, flying directly at us. She had something in her hands. She let it go and went vertical.

"*Shit!*" Dooley swerved and skidded. The cinder block caught the window post of the car, bent it and broke the windshield, then rolled off onto the road.

The car skidded back and forth. It spun and slammed into the bridge railing. Cars honked and barely missed us.

We stared out the broken windshield, then looked at each other.

An old man in an ancient Camaro crept past us. "Drunken assholes!" he cried and shook his fist at us. Then, he was gone.

"Okay," Dooley reasonably. "I think that answers my question. She doesn't want both of us. She only wants you."

"How do you figure?"

"That cinder block was aimed at me."

"Pretty damned close one to call."

Dooley shook his head. "Give the girl a break. She's new at this."

oOo

The car was totaled. The engine wouldn't turn over and even if it had the right front wheel was bent out at a right angle.

"We get taken in, we won't get out again in a hurry," Dooley said. He kicked the tire. He looked around. "I don't even know where we could go. I live up on Winter Hill, but Loquess knows that." He kicked the tire again, savagely. "Shit. I've got a sweet car at home I've been restoring—1978 Lotus Europa. But we can't use it: it stands out. Even if Loquess didn't know about it, the car is registered to me. Car like that would get pulled over in an hour."

I looked around and saw the Orange Line. I couldn't see a train coming but I could hear it.

"Come on," I said, and we ran down the highway and then up the parking ramp. I managed to get out my card but Dooley just jumped over the turnstile. In the distance we could hear approaching sirens.

The train pulled into the station—inbound, exactly what I'd hoped. A little luck was with us. The train pulled out and as it left the station I could see blue lights converge on the wreck. Then, it was gone as the train pulled into a tunnel. We sat down. This car was mostly empty.

"Think Katelin saw us board the train?" I asked.

"Maybe. But she took off without hanging around. She's got something else in mind."

"She found you at your father's bar."

Dooley nodded. "I'm unclear myself on that one."

"Maybe she followed you."

Dooley sighed. "She certainly could have. Loquess can do surveillance. I'll give her that."

I looked out the window. "Maybe she went to get something to eat."

"Beg pardon."

"Did you see how she flew? She was *fast*. Fast as I'd ever seen her. Fast as I've ever seen any flyer—maybe faster. That takes energy. You don't eat enough, you'll starve to death."

Dooley leaned back, thinking. "Tim Rabbitt looked like he hadn't eaten. Do you think Misty just didn't feed him?"

I shrugged. "Or maybe it takes a lot to support two people in one body."

"Or one Misty."

Dooley thought for a minute. "Let's say Misty moves from person to person. Like a spirit or something."

"Okay."

"So she leaves you and enters Wallace. Wallace goes nuts and enters a mental hospital. A couple of years later he ends up in Boston. *He* looks fine. Anyway. She jumps to Oscar Plante and kills Wallace. The next day she jumps to Tim Rabbitt and kills Oscar Plante. Plante looks pretty rough but not terrible, but she was only in him a day. Rabbitt hides out for a week. Why?"

I shrug. "I'm not the detective."

"Neither am I. Yet." He stopped dead for a moment. "Oh, hell. There's a money trail. Financial forensics traced out all the deposits we were looking at. Two and a half million dollars leads directly to Tim Rabbitt. We knew that, right?"

I nodded.

"So we know Rabbitt has money—that's what detectives always look for. Follow the money. So if Rabbitt gets killed, it's likely because of the money. Hoffman and Rush think *I* killed Gifford. Loquess got away."

"But it was Misty—"

"Hoffman and Rush don't know that! The only person who knows that for sure is Loquess and she's Misty now. Hell, *I* fooled Hoffman and Rush when she was in me. Certainly, Misty can fool them."

"But you can tell them—"

"It doesn't matter. There's objective evidence that *I* killed Gifford. I'll bet you money Misty made sure to leave a lot of evidence, too—certainly she was none too clean with Gifford. It's not such a stretch to think I killed Rabbitt, too, since I *did*. Then, she leads us on a chase and tries to stop me."

"Maybe they won't believe her. They might believe you."

"Is there proof that *she* did it? No. Is there proof that *I* did it? Abso-fucking-lutely." He rubbed the top of his head. "It's brilliant. *Diabolical*. But brilliant. Welcome to Fucking Witchlandia," he said bitterly. Dooley looked at me. "Hell, I bet you'll be turning me in now."

I shook my head. "I believe you."

"Why the hell would you do that?"

"I know what Misty sounds like. That might have looked like Katelin flying around, but it was Misty talking to us."

"That's small comfort." He looked around the car. "Christ. If she's following us, they'll come *here*—stop the train at the next stop and arrest us. Or they'll come after Pop." He stood up. "We have to leave *now*." He sat down again heavily. "Where?"

"How long do we have?"

Dooley shrugged. "I have no idea. Minutes after Loquess talks to them. Might get a little time to manage the jurisdictional boundaries between Somerville and Boston but no more than that—scratch that." He looked out the window. "We're in Boston now. No jurisdictional boundaries at all. As soon as she reaches them, they'll be after us."

"Maybe Eli can hide us."

"They'll be staking him out, *too*. Loquess and I talked to him. Hoffman and Rush *know* that and Loquess will be sure to remind them."

"North Station. There's a train north to Gloucester in twenty minutes. If we can be on it I think I know a place to hide."

"We'll never make it." Dooley looked gray.

"If they catch us before we can figure this all out, it's a different fight. Until then, let's play the cards we're dealt."

oOo

The rest of the time on the train was just strange. Sitting there, nervous as hell, wondering if every T-cop was looking for us—it's amazing how many T personnel you see when you don't want them and how few there are when you actually need them.

Boston has two actual train stations: North Station and South Station, and never the twain shall meet. The timing was fortuitous for us. The Boston rail schedule is only set up to service going in and leaving Boston at rush hour. If you want to use the rail system for any other infernal purpose, the MBTA is just not there to help. Inefficiency, thy name is Boston.

I had a pass but I bought a ticket for Dooley using cash. It had been about thirty minutes since Misty had tried to drop a brick on our heads. We kept glancing upwards—which, I'm sure, was suspicious of something when viewed by a policeman or on security footage. But apparently, it didn't rise to the level of questioning us. We were able to get on the train successfully.

"She must not have told them yet," Dooley whispered to me after the conductor had taken his ticket.

"Why would she wait?" I whispered back.

"I have no idea. I can't imagine Hoffman and Rush didn't broadcast me." He thought for a moment. "Or maybe Horn held them back. After all, the Plante murder was big news. I know Horn was trying to keep the connections out of the media. It'd be real bad publicity if the murderer turns out to be one of their own. They may want a chance to get to me before the news breaks."

Dooley slapped the seat in frustration. "This makes no *sense*."

"Do murders ever make sense?"

"Sure. Method, motive and opportunity. *Motive* has to make sense. That's what I can't figure out: what does Misty want? To get back together with you? Are the murders going to help that? They sure as hell don't make her more attractive. And if they make her stronger, why pick such *public* people? Why not just pick off homeless guys? I mean paranormals are somewhat rare but there are a few around—it's like these are murders of *opportunity*. And the money. Does she want to retire to the Caribbean? Then, what's she doing hanging around here?"

"Welcome to Witchlandia." I remembered Katelin saying it. A smile sometimes. A rueful grin. A bitter scowl.

Dooley stared at me then looked away. He looked outside. The impossible blue of Spot Pond was on one side of the train. We could see seagulls and geese on the water. A steady wind blew tiny whitecaps on the water. He shook himself. "Yeah. Welcome to Witchlandia. So we get a brief reprieve. We have to go to ground and figure this out." He turned to me. "Where are we going?"

"My father's old boat."

"You're kidding me."

I shook my head. "I know the owner."

I wondered if it would be like coming home.

Chapter 3.2: Thursday Evening, October 28

Katelin had never seen the *Nonantum*. Oh, she'd met Mom and Dad—not a very warm meeting but she'd been the dutiful girlfriend. But she'd only been to the house. The *Nonantum* was something different. It was like bringing someone home and entertaining downstairs but never bringing them upstairs to the bedrooms. Too intimate. Maybe if Katelin and I had stayed together, Dad might have shown her the boat. But Katelin wasn't going to ask and Dad didn't invite her and we broke up so there it was.

But she had liked Gloucester and the sea and my mother. She loved to go fishing off the beach. The summer we moved back to Boston we took the family surf casting kit and came up to Plum Island on weekends. On the beach at dawn watching the sun come up. Katelin flew over the water looking for fish and I'd cast towards them. Or we'd cast at random and drink coffee. As the weather grew cold we'd huddle under a blanket if the air was too cold. If we were alone on the beach we'd do more than huddle.

I broke off the memory. We were coming into Gloucester Station.

The *Nonantum* was no longer Dad's but it was in port—I was in the habit of checking these things. After all, it had been the center of my father's life since before I was born. It had taken something as final and powerful as my mother's death to pull him in from the sea. Without it he'd withered and died. Or, at least, that's what I told myself when I was feeling romantic.

We walked over the hill to the piers—this was a real danger, now. Gloucester was small and I was well known— local fisherman's boy makes good sort of thing. But it was still fall and the spillover from Conclave had stuffed the town to the gills with a great bolus of tourists. There were enough crowds milling about that we were able to make our way to the docks more or less unnoticed. We didn't *blend,* you understand. We were both too big, for one thing. But we didn't stand *out* so much, if you take my meaning.

Dad had rigged *Nonantum* as a long line boat. She wasn't that big—barely a hundred tons—but Dad was a good enough fisherman to make up for the lack. He'd left me the house bought and paid for and left this world debt-free.

The boat was shaped somewhat like a scaled up lobster boat: lifted cabin and bow with a dropped flat stern. The long line equipment had been mounted over the flat stern with both lower holds and additional lockers bolted to the deck.

Now, the *Nonantum* looked naked. All long line reels and additional cranes were gone. Even the lockers were missing though the deck was clearly marked where the equipment had been fastened down. And the boat had been scrubbed with strong soap—I could still smell it. I had never seen the

Nonantum so clean. I wondered what Joey was doing with my father's boat.

The cabin was locked but I had kept a copy of Dad's key and the locks hadn't been changed. We slipped aboard and made our way down to the galley.

Dooley followed me down the stairs and through the corridor, carefully keeping his head down. The *Nonantum* didn't have an abundance of head room. He sat at the galley table. "Who owns this boat now?"

"Joey Cabrelli," I said as I rummaged in the cabinets. "First mate for my father. Dad sold him the boat when he retired. 'Fisher', we called him."

"Because he was a fisherman?"

I laughed briefly. "Short for Fishercat. Joey is as thin and mean as a weasel. Damn fine fisherman, though. Dad thought the world of him. He took my place on the boat when it was clear I'd never make a living on the water." I found what I was looking for. "Coffee?" I asked. "We have instant."

Dooley shuddered. "No thanks. Soda?"

"Coffee doesn't have to taste good. It just has to work." I looked in the fridge and tossed him a diet Coke. Then, I put the tea kettle on the range. The gas wasn't turned off. That meant Joey was sleeping on the boat and would be back before long.

"Isn't Mr. Cabrelli going to be a wee bit bothered at two strangers on his boat?"

"I'm not a stranger," I said. The water was hot and I poured myself half a cup of unpalatable caffeine and leavened it with milk. "It'll be fine."

"What about Loquess? Didn't she know where your boat is?"

I shook my head and sat down. The resulting coffee was off-gray and bitter. "She never saw the boat to my knowledge. Katelin didn't get along with my Dad. He seemed to think me not being a fisherman was somehow her fault, though it happened long before we met."

"Not his most brilliant moment, I take it."

"People thinking with their emotions don't usually come off as geniuses. He was a pretty bright guy. Hell of a fisherman and that's not stupid. Anyway, when Katelin and I split up it was a great excuse for them to never see each other again."

"Don't underestimate her." Dooley tapped the table for emphasis. "I've never seen anybody execute stealth surveillance like Loquess. She loads up with fifty pounds of observation equipment and disappears into the sky. Two hours later she comes back with every minute of the subject's life down to how long he took to shake it in the john. She could be out there right now and we'd never know it until Hoffman and Rush came down the stairs."

"Then there's no point in me not drinking my coffee, is there?"

"I guess." He finished his Coke. "Do you have a plan?"

"Is hiding a plan?"

"No."

"Then I got nothing."

Dooley rolled the can with his fingers. "I'm beat. Apparently, being possessed by the devil takes it out of you. Nowhere to go and nothing to do. Can I take a nap?"

I nodded towards the bow. "Bunks up that way. Pick one that doesn't have anything on it. I don't know if the crew has signed on but I don't want to screw it up for Joey if I don't have to."

"Too late," came from the doorway. Joey was watching us.

oOo

Joey hadn't changed since I'd last seen him at Dad's funeral. He was still a small, rat-faced man with a continuous and unslaked hunger written on his face.

"Hey, Joey," I said mildly.

"What the hell are you doing on my boat?"

"Hiding," I said equably. "This is Abraham Dooley."

Dooley nodded.

Joey's gaze darted from one of us to the other. "Who are you hiding from?"

"That's not important," said Dooley. He pulled out his badge.

"You have a warrant?"

I interrupted. "I let him in."

"Isn't that criminal trespass?" Joey pursed his lips. "Get off my boat."

"Mr. Cabrelli—" started Dooley.

"I don't give a *fuck* who you're hiding from." Joey edged over towards one of the wall lockers where I knew the pistols were located.

I stepped over to him. "You owe me," I said in a low whisper.

"Fuck if I do. I own this boat."

"You and the bank. How much did this boat cost you?"

Joey stared at me.

I bent down. I didn't want to tower over him any more than I would want to corner a rat. "When Dad quit the business he was all torn up. He knew you couldn't afford the *Nonantum*—not with all the equipment that came with it. He wanted you to have it and was willing to cut you a break, but that was his inheritance to *me*. It was me that persuaded him that I didn't *need* that inheritance. That I would be okay without it. It was *me* that persuaded Jerry Collins down at Bank of America that you'd be good for the loan. You figured it was Dad. But it was *me*, Joey."

Joey stared at me, eyes wide. "Why would you do that? We never liked each other."

"I didn't do it for you," I said, trying to straighten up in the low galley. "I did it for Dad. Because he wanted to do right by you. Now, I need a favor from you. We need to hide here for a day or two until we figure something out."

Joey licked his lips. "I can't go against the cops. I'd lose the boat."

I shook my head. "If the cops ask you about us, tell them we're here. But if they don't, you don't need to advertise the fact. We just need a place to light."

Joey nodded. "You can sleep in the bunks in the bow. Like David said."

Dooley nodded and went forward and I sat back down. Joey sat across from me.

I watched him for a moment. I had never gone out on the sea with my father. I had never helped him pull in a catch. I had never sat with him in the galley in the morning drinking coffee after being up all night through a storm nor stood with him in the pilot house watching Gloucester rise reborn from the sea as they returned home, holds full.

Joey had done all these things.

"Tell me about fishing with my dad," I said.

Chapter 3.3: Friday, October 29

I woke up in the early morning, hours before dawn. After talking with Joey for a while, I found the adrenaline of chasing and being chased by Katelin had worn me out, too. I staggered forward, found a bunk and collapsed for a few hours.

Dooley was sitting on the bunk when I woke up.

"How long have you been up?" I sat up.

"A while," he said. "Sleeping on a boat is easier than I expected."

"Is that so?" I stood up. The bunks were just a little short so I had to stretch in a cramped space. "Maybe in a bigger boat."

Joey had made breakfast. Nothing fancy. Just fried eggs and ham with some home fries.

The three of us ate in relative silence, knowing we were going to have to talk about serious matters afterwards. At least, that's how I interpreted what was going on. Joey was a fisherman. Dooley was a cop. I was a pianist. Men's men, if you know what I mean.

Joey lit up a cigarette after he'd finished. I stared at him for a moment, then looked back to my food. It had been a long time since I was in a place where casual smoking was commonplace.

"Okay," Joey said slowly. "Here's the deal. Today is the last weekend of Conclave—the official placement for final heats happens at nine."

"Salem Common," I said, for Dooley.

"I know that," Dooley said in a disgusted voice. "I grew up in Somerville. Not Jersey City."

Joey chuckled. "I make a little money taking people out in the boat to watch the races today. Later it's the fireworks and the Night Watch."

Dooley looked up. "What's the Night Watch?"

I spoke around a mouthful of egg. "Any qualifying athletes rest or practice for the final heats tomorrow. The athletes that *don't* make the cut go out and party—for the flyers that's a lot of dangerous stunts at night when the FAA is looking the other way. The sound is supposed to be completely clear of traffic or—" I looked at Joey "—boats, so no one gets hurt."

"There are a few boats allowed on the water with minimal lighting," Joey said defensively. "I make a fair amount taking people out but a lot gets used up in fees."

"Fees?" asked Dooley, raising his eyebrows.

Joey stared at him. "*Fees.*"

"So you can't put us up on the boat after today." I drummed my fingers on the table. I looked at Dooley. "Do you think I could put you up at my house?"

Dooley shook his head. "*You* might be able to pull it off by yourself. They have a suspect—me—and you would be questioned to corroborate. They never really thought you had anything to do with the murders. The evidence was too tenuous. But now they have me."

Joey took a drag on his cigarette. "You're wanted for murder? Is there a reward?"

Dooley scowled at him. "You wish. I didn't do any murders. It's complicated."

Joey looked at the two of us, lingered on me. "I'm not surprised."

"I have a concert Sunday evening," I said. "Rehearsal is tomorrow."

"You'll have to miss it," Dooley said.

I shook my head. "The show must go on. That sort of thing. I'd like to come out the end of this with my career intact."

"*I'd* like to come out the end of this not spending the rest of my life in Cedar Junction," Dooley said hotly.

Joey tapped the ash of his cigarette into an ashtray held to the table by a magnet. "I wouldn't mind coming out of this still owning this boat." He took a drag. "Let's see if I have this straight." He pointed at Dooley. "You're wanted for a murder you didn't commit."

Dooley looked at me. "More or less."

Joey pointed at me. "You're involved somehow."

"Yes." That was the absolute truth.

Joey stubbed out the cigarette. "Knowing David here, I bet his little witch girl is in it, too."

"How do you figure?" asked Dooley.

"Old Guillermo was always talking about David's concerts, how he was playing in, say, Philadelphia this week and Charleston the next and how he was living with a Boston cop. Even second hand, I could recognize trouble when I heard about it. When it's quiet out there on the water you talk about anything or you don't talk at all. Not much in between."

"My dad talked about my concerts?" I didn't know why I was surprised but it came as a shock.

Joey looked pained. "Jesus, David. Get a clue. 'Son of Portuguese fisherman takes musical world by storm.' Why the hell *wouldn't* he talk about you or your tiny girlfriend? Hell, he had your schedule posted on the galley wall."

"I never saw it."

"You were never on the boat!"

Dooley interrupted. "So David can probably bluff his way back to his house, by himself. Just remember you don't have to answer *anything* to a policeman. You can't *lie* to him but you are not required to *help* him incriminate you. If they get nasty, call a lawyer." Dooley grinned at me. "You know how to do that, don't you? Pucker up and give them a lot of money."

I stared at him blankly. "I don't understand."

"A perfectly good classical movie reference is wasted on you."

Joey watched us. "The smart thing would be to turn the two of you in."

The grin disappeared from Dooley's face. "Yes, it would."

"Guillermo wouldn't want me to be that smart." Joey laughed shortly.

"If I can get to my house, I can also get to Eli," I said, thinking out loud.

Dooley shook his head. "No way. I need to *be* there. I have some questions of my own. They'll have him staked out both at McLean and in Salem." He thought a moment. "Will he be at your concert?"

I shrugged. "I don't know."

"Would he go if you invited him?"

"Maybe."

"You invite him." Dooley looked thoughtful. "We can hook up there."

I shook my head. "Not going to work. Too many people in the concert, back stage."

"That'll cover us."

"There are parties after the concert."

Dooley fixed me with a glare. "Boo fucking hoo."

"Plus," I continued, "that's two days you need to keep low. I have an alternative. The rehearsal is tomorrow—Saturday. I can invite him to that. Fewer people. No obligations."

Dooley chewed his lip. "No people to cover you."

"There'll be people enough. Lots of people come to the rehearsals. It won't be a zoo but it will be crowded."

Dooley thought for a moment. "Okay. You're taken care of. But *I* need a place to hide." He thought for a moment. "Do you have a lot of set-up for these events?" Dooley asked Joey slowly. "Do you feed the guests? Put out wine? Things like that?"

"Sure," Joey said. "Cater it myself, mostly. Sometimes I hire a cook, but this year I wasn't planning to."

"Tell you what. I'm a fair cook and I look good in a suit. You let me stay on this boat until Saturday night and I'll take care of your guests."

"Katelin might figure this out," I pointed out. "She knew Dad had a boat."

"Does she know it was sold?" Dooley asked.

"I don't know."

Dooley chewed his lip. "I bet she does. I'm sure she knows your father died. She kept track of you."

"Really?" I felt obscurely pleased.

"Don't get too excited. People track melanomas, too."

Joey watched us. "This is starting to sound like fun. Okay, Mr. Dooley. I'll take you on for a couple of days."

"How will we meet up?" Dooley said. "I can't meet you at Symphony Hall."

I looked at Joey. "Where are you picking up clients?"

Joey watched us both. "New England Aquarium."

I turned back to Dooley. "I'll get Eli out of Symphony Hall and bring him to the boat."

"Well, then," Dooley said, nodding. "What do you know? We have a ridiculously complicated plan foredoomed to failure!"

oOo

Gloucester at three in the morning is a quiet place. Nothing but the far-off sound of Route 128 and the wash of the harbor. My house was up and over the hill from the harbor. Close enough Dad could reach the boat by walking but far enough away to be protected from winter storms.

It was an old cape with a wrap-around veranda. Sure enough, there was a car with two men in it across the street. I managed to make it up the steps to the porch before they reached me.

"David Sabado?" said one.

I turned and faced them. I didn't recognize them.

"Yes?"

"I'm Officer Raymond and this is Officer Ditko of the Gloucester Police Department. Would you come with us, please?"

I looked at them and decided to trust what Dooley had said. "No."

"You have to come with us."

"Am I under arrest?"

"No."

"Then I'm staying here."

They looked at one another. "Just a moment," said Raymond.

They convened back at the car. I went on up the steps and let myself in the house, careful to lock the door after me. I called Frieda on my cell.

"Hello?" she said groggily.

"I need you to find me a lawyer."

"This is about that business in Boston?" She sounded instantly awake.

"What do you know?"

"I know Plante was murdered. He was one of my clients. Now you're calling out of the blue for a lawyer. Forgive me for putting two and two together."

"Got it. Yeah. I think it's about the Plante murder. Find me a lawyer."

"How quick?"

"It's three o'clock now. Be nice not to be behind bars by four."

"Got it. Are you at home?"

"Yes."

"I know somebody in Salem. I'll make the call. Don't say anything to anybody." She hung up.

I made my way to the kitchen and managed to make a cup of coffee and pull out a pastry from the refrigerator before I heard a rap on the door.

I carried the coffee and pastry to the front door. "Yes?" I said as I opened it.

Hoffman and Rush were outside. "Mr. Sabado," said Rush easily. "Can we come in?"

I stepped through the door and closed it behind me. "Not unless you have a warrant."

They looked at me for a moment. Hoffman reached into his jacket pocket and pulled out a folded paper. "As a matter of fact, we do."

I looked at the warrant. From what I could tell it looked fine. How would I know the difference? I checked their badges just to be an asshole. Raymond and Ditko again. Then, I opened the door and let them in.

It was a cool, clear night. I put on a sweater, grabbed a cup of coffee and a Danish from the kitchen and stepped outside. I sat on the veranda's wicker seat. I could see some flickering lights over Salem. Witches flying around doing some last-minute practices or just flying for the sheer fun of it. I remembered Katelin when we were first together back in Missouri—remembered that walk back from Easely. We'd walked back as much as five or six miles before Katelin decided she had things to do and flew off. I hitchhiked back after that. I used to love to watch Katelin fly. Such single-minded determination to be undistracted by constant joy. I had tried more than once to channel that idea into my playing, sitting and working my way through a Bach or Liszt piece while trying to visualize Katelin's flying. Sometimes I succeeded. More often I didn't. But I was always able to take away something I could use, a phrase or a tricky bit of timing. Her joy had faded after we moved to Boston. I probably had something to do with that.

The coffee was warm in my hands. I put it down and nibbled at the pastry. The wind was light and I could hear the rattle and click of the dead leaves still left on the branches. I could see first one window light up, then another, as the policemen worked their way through the house.

Maybe it was stupid of me not to watch everything they did. They could plant evidence. Steal valuables. Break china. Do all the things I'd seen on television. They could do anything. But I couldn't watch them pawing through my house. Through my parents' house. I didn't do drugs. I didn't have any child pornography. They already knew everything I had watched on *Where's Katelin* so there would be no news there. What the hell else were they going to do to me beyond what they were already prepared to do?

Katelin eased down onto the front yard.

I froze, coffee in one hand, pastry next to my mouth, crumbs on my lips.

She gave me a pure Misty smile. "Hey, lover." She came up the steps and practically danced across the veranda. "You didn't know what you had with this girl. Such a body. Such a *talent*."

"You don't look so good." Even in the dim light on the veranda I could tell she was thin even for Katelin.

"I feel *great*."

"What are you doing here?"

"Looking for you, of course. I came as soon as I heard. Did you miss me?"

I knew Katelin's features; every spot and wrinkle from her tiny nose to the birthmark on her inner thigh. But Misty, in Katelin's body, didn't look anything like her. Katelin's smiles were cautious, tiny. Misty's were broad and careless. Katelin looked at people directly or she didn't look at them at all. Misty was always watching slyly out of the corner of her eye.

"No," I said truthfully.

"But you miss *her*, don't you?"

I didn't have anything to say to that.

"I can bring her back to you. I'm *her*, after all." She leaned forward, cupped her breasts and made a pout. "Come on, baby."

I put down the pastry and the coffee carefully. I stood up, brushing the crumbs off my lap, thinking I'd go inside.

She slipped up against me, grabbed the back of my neck and brought my face down into a hard kiss.

I remembered Katelin's mouth and tongue, the feel of her against me. I held her close for a long minute, feeling her melt against me and savoring it.

Then, it was as if a drain had opened up and some pulsing essential part of me was slipping away. A sort of purple smoke whirled through me, something I could see without my eyes. I remembered flying out to Missouri after her, not seeing her, not *allowed* to see her, returning and emptying the apartment of my things in a cold fury.

That fury came to me now. I put my hands on her shoulders and lifted her up, pulled her away from me and set her down on the porch.

She stared at me, mouth open, then stumbled away, began to run. She pulled her stick off her shoulder and jumped off the veranda, catching herself on the stick in mid-air and flying off into the night.

Rush came out to the porch. "Mr. Sabado? Are you all right?"

I sat down in the chair, shaking. "I'm fine. I'm fucking fine."

oOo

Rush went back inside and a moment later he and Hoffman came back out on the porch.

"Find anything?" I felt suddenly bitter and self-destructive. If only I smoked.

"We're looking for Abraham Dooley," Rush said soothingly.

"Did you expect to find him here?"

"Actually," said Hoffman, chuckling, fully embracing his inner grandfather, "we did. But he hasn't been here. Do you know where he is?"

I looked at him.

"You are required to cooperate with the police," suggested Rush gently.

I waved towards the front door. "You're crawling through my house. I think that's being cooperative enough."

"We'd like to question you further."

"Are you arresting me?"

Hoffman and Rush looked at one another. "We could," said Rush. "Accessory after the fact. You helped Dooley escape."

"Do you have a warrant for *him*?"

They looked at one another again.

"They don't have to tell you that," came a voice from the sidewalk.

A dark man came up the walk. He was so short he would have to stare up to see five feet. Spanish? Portuguese? He was wearing thick glasses. He put one hand in his pocket and pulled his glasses off with the other, gesturing with them. "But if they have a warrant for you, they need to show it." He walked up the stairs with a pronounced limp. "Roger Pujol," he said, holding out his hand to Hoffman and Rush. "I'm, ah, *advising* Mr. Sabado."

Rush took it and introduced the two of them.

Hoffman looked down at me. "All lawyered up, now. Eh? When did you call him?"

Pujol spoke up. "He doesn't have to say anything, now does he?"

"He needs to come down with us," Hoffman growled.

"'Down', meaning Boston? Or 'down', meaning Gloucester?"

Hoffman didn't answer.

"May I see the warrant?"

Hoffman sourly gave it to him.

"Ah," said Pujol. "Perfectly legal. Are you through?"

Hoffman looked at me, then at Pujol. "Yeah. We're done." Hoffman went to the front door and called inside. A moment later the troupe of policemen came outside. Hoffman came over to us. "Sorry about the mess."

"Did you find anything?" asked Pujol pleasantly.

"We don't have to tell you that," said Hoffman in a nasty voice.

The two of them walked off the porch. My contingent of the Boston Police Department got in their cars and drove off.

Pujol sat down. "Son of a bitch," he said. He pulled off his glasses and rubbed his face. "I really didn't know if that would work."

"Let me guess," I said. "You're not used to this."

"I only passed the bar a *week* ago."

"Are you a lawyer?"

He waggled his hand. "Barely. Legally."

"You sounded good."

"Yeah," he said in a shaky voice. "I majored in drama at Connecticut College before I went to Suffolk. Fortunately for you I only get flop-sweat *after* a performance. Used to be a basket case at the cast parties. I owed Frieda a favor."

"Does rum help flop-sweat?"

"It is the finest cure."

"Come on. I've got some I brought back from Puerto Rico."

oOo

I got the Ron del Barrilito from the cabinet and a glass. I poured a glass for him and topped off my coffee. We sat at the table.

"Who's Abraham Dooley?" Pujol asked after he'd drank half the glass.

"Did you overhear that?"

"Yes," he admitted.

"You read the warrant quickly."

He tapped the side of his head. "Eidetic memory. Got me through law school. The drama major didn't help much."

"I think Dooley's someone they're looking for. They think I know where he is."

"Do you?"

I didn't say anything.

Pujol took a long pull of rum. "Okay," he said presently. "It's interesting the warrant didn't mention Dooley at all—it only mentions Oscar Plante and Tim Rabbitt. Even if they found this Dooley character, his arrest might be problematic because the reasons for the arrest did not derive from the search. Of course, they may have other warrants. While the law compels us to tell the truth to policemen, it does not compel them to tell the truth to us." He drank again. "The sourcing of warrants is, at best, a questionable defense. One of these days the Supreme Judicial Court is going to rule on it. As soon as they can get an Essex County judge they're going to come up here with the full cooperation of the Gloucester Police Department and a warrant for your arrest. That's not the time to have a drama major lawyer wannabe to represent you. This is the guy I clerk for." He turned over the card and wrote on it. "This is my cell. When they come back, you call me. I will call my boss and let him know we're going to have to represent you. Then, we'll see what happens. Say nothing until you talk to us."

"That must be some favor you owe Frieda."

He drained his glass. "It is."

I looked at the card: *Emilio Pujol*. I turned the card over and read the number on the back.

"Is Emilio your father?"

"Uncle. You know *Pujol Fish?* That's my dad. I worked there until I went off to college."

I didn't say anything for a moment. "Your dad knew my dad."

"Yeah," Roger said dryly. "He knew Guillermo Sabado. So did I. Talk to you soon."

It was like there was an entire world hidden from my view only now becoming visible.

oOo

Katelin had woken up in the middle of the night like she did sometimes. She snuggled up to me. Licked my nipple. Moved further down.

"Hey," I murmured.

"Shh," she said. "Don't wake up."

"Okay." I was agreeable.

I lay on my back and Katelin straddled me, eased me inside her. Slow. A long tease until she broke loose.

I shuddered and held on to her hips as she moved. It didn't take long.

At the big moment, when we both seemed to explode, Misty looked down at me with a wicked smile and it wasn't Katelin at all.

I stared at her.

"No," I said. I pushed her off of me. I stood up, shaking with anger.

Misty grinned at me from the bed, naked. "Pretty fine, lover. Was it ever that good without me?"

I had abandoned Misty for Katelin. Katelin had then abandoned me. That all welled up. I turned and slapped her.

Katelin fell back against the bed. She lay there, shocked, sat up and shook her head. Stared at me.

I raised my hand in a fist. I wanted to hurt her. Hurt her badly, Katelin and Misty both. But I stared at her big eyes and her tiny face. I was suddenly struck by how small Katelin was. How small she had always been.

I felt sick. Slowly, I lowered my fist, unclenched it. I stared at my hand, then looked back at her.

"Get out of my house," I said.

She didn't move.

I leaned down until my face was an inch from hers. "*Go!*"

Katelin/Misty grabbed her clothes and ran out of the room. I heard her down the stairs. A moment of silence. Then, I heard the front door slam.

I felt dirty. Ashamed both of the sex and striking Katelin. I badly wanted a shower.

oOo

Dawn had broken some time ago. There was no possibility of resuming sleep. I sat at the kitchen, poured a cup of cold coffee into a cup and put it in the nuke. When it was ready, I touched it up with a little Barrilito and sat at the table. I hadn't known how angry I was. Hadn't known what I was capable of. Again, I wished that I smoked or had some other equally self-destructive habit. Instead, I stared at the bottle of

281

Barrilito and wondered if I should just finish it off and go to the rehearsal drunk. That would put a nice little coda to my career.

I heard pounding on the door. Pujol's card was still on the table. I turned the card over and called the number on the back.

"Roger Pujol."

"Somebody's knocking on the door."

"It's me. Let me in."

Pujol slipped in past me. I looked on the porch. Uncle Emilio was nowhere to be found.

"Where's your boss?" I asked.

"Not coming," Pujol said shortly. "He says I can do all the leg work until it's a court case."

"He must have a lot of faith in you."

"Yeah," he said shortly. "Much faith. Boat loads." He looked at me. "What did your dad do to Emilio to piss him off?"

"What?"

Pujol paced in the hallway. "I go to Uncle Emilio this morning for help and he says, and I quote, 'It'll be a cold day in hell when I help Guillermo Sabado's son.' Unquote." Pujol shook his head. "I called Dad and he was as surprised as I was."

"So you can't help me?"

"We'll see. I can't practice in front of a court of law but I can advise you. Got any coffee?"

oOo

That morning, we expected two of Boston's finest to show up along with a platoon of Gloucester's best. We expected to be handcuffed, carefully folded into the back of a BPD cruiser and escorted by the GPD all the way to route 128 where the Gloucester entourage would drop away as we roared south towards the city.

Instead, Albert Hoffman stood on the porch alone looking like he hadn't slept in a week.

Pujol opened the door.

"I need to speak with Sabado."

Pujol shook his head. "Do you have a warrant for his arrest? Otherwise, you cannot see him."

Hoffman didn't say anything for a long moment. "I'm here on my own. I *know* Sabado helped Dooley and I'm glad he did. Now, I need to help Dooley, too."

"You're not here in your official capacity?"

"No."

Pujol arched an eyebrow. "You do realize that means nothing? You cannot be other than an officer of the court."

Hoffman rubbed his hand over his face. He looked gray. "I swear to you, anything you say to me now I won't tell a soul."

Pujol's face was like flint.

"Come *on!*" Hoffman pleaded. "Tom Dooley is like my family, for Christ's sake!"

I came up behind Pujol. "Just a moment."

Pujol turned a disapproving eye on me. "I don't advise this, Mr. Sabado."

"I know." I turned back to Hoffman. "You know Tom Dooley?"

"I grew up on Winter Hill. Who do you think babysat little Abe when Tom went to ground?"

"Officer Dooley never said anything about you."

Hoffman shrugged. "That's the way he is. Keeps to himself. Come on. He's going to Walpole for the rest of his life if he doesn't get help."

I watched him for a moment. It could be Hoffman was a good actor—I remembered his performance interrogating me. "Do you have a warrant for my arrest?"

"There's not going to be any fucking warrant. The only thing you could help with is *finding* him. The warrant's a threat to make you talk. Arresting you would only prevent you from leading us to him. Instead, we'll just stake you out and watch. We arrest you *after* we find him." Hoffman looked around the porch. "Let me in. They're not here yet but they're going to be."

"Okay."

"Mr. Sabado—" began Pujol.

"I know. I know." I waved him away. "I'm probably going to regret this."

I brought Hoffman into the kitchen and sat him down. I sat across from him. "Talk."

"Christ," said Hoffman. "They got everything they need. The first couple of murders didn't have anything—no DNA. No fingerprints. No fibers. Very clean. But the Rabbitt scene is lousy with clues. And Dooley's fiber, hair and fingerprints are all over everything at the Gifford scene. Even Rabbitt's keys with Rabbitt's blood and Dooley's fingerprints on them— tying him neatly to the Rabbitt murder along with Gifford's murder. In addition, we have a witness—"

"Katelin Loquess."

Hoffman stopped a moment and looked at me. "Yeah," he said slowly. "Have you been talking to Loquess?"

"No."

"Dooley then?"

I didn't say anything. "What do you want from me?"

"Everything says Dooley is the mastermind for it and the actual killer in two of the murders. They are going to put him *away."* Hoffman took a deep breath. "You spent time with him—don't try to deny it. I know. Did he kill them?"

"No." I thought a moment. "Not exactly. He's not responsible for their deaths."

"Tell me."

"I can't," I said. "Not yet. I don't know enough."

"Okay." Hoffman didn't say anything for a minute. "Can you prove he didn't do it?"

"Maybe. Probably not." I shook my head. "Hell, I'm a pianist. I'm not sure I know what 'proof' means in something like this."

Hoffman nodded. It seemed like the wind came out of him and he shrank like some ancient, flesh-colored balloon. "Shit."

I had an idea. "There might be a way you can help me."

Pujol had been watching us with baleful eyes all this time. "Mr. Sabado?"

I looked up. "Yes."

"A word." Pujol dragged me into the living room. "Are you out of your mind? He's an *officer of the court!* He can't *not* be. Everything you say to him is evidence. Everything you show him is evidence. Right here, in this room, he is a walking, talking videocam that can be used in a court of law."

"I know." I sighed. "I think I need him."

"For God's sake, what for?"

"If I know anything about attorney/client privilege, it's something you'd be happier not knowing."

"Shit." Pujol ran his hand through his hair. "You know where Dooley is, don't you?"

"Not exactly."

"You know that he killed two people?"

"He didn't. Not exactly."

"You're a great fucking comfort. Do you know that?"

I smiled wanly. "Yeah."

"Fuck it. In for a penny; in for a pound." He followed me back to the kitchen.

"Okay, Hoffman," I said as I sat down.

"Wait," said Pujol. He looked at Hoffman. "Give me your gun."

Hoffman jerked back as if stung. "Why would you want that?"

"It's insurance. It's our word against yours if anything goes south. But if I have your gun, I can say you gave it to me as proof as good faith."

"I'll just report it stolen."

"Right," Pujol said sarcastically. "That'll look good on your record. You'll do what any other cop would do. You'll pick up a gun from a friend or on the street or borrow one from the firing range. We'll keep the gun and when this is all through you get your gun back, free and clear."

Hoffman hesitated.

"Come on," said Pujol. "How much of a friend to Dooley are you, anyway?"

"No cop would ever do that."

"Sounds like Dooley is pretty close to family. Which is it? Loyalty to the blue or loyalty to family?"

"If I didn't owe Tom Dooley pretty much everything..." Hoffman swore, pulled out his weapon, unloaded it and gave the gun to Pujol.

Pujol took it, cracked it open and checked the mechanism in some mysterious way that seemed to look like he knew what he was doing—Hoffman seemed to relax, anyway. "What do you owe Tom Dooley?"

"None of your fucking business."

"Fair enough." Pujol looked at me. "Okay, David. Your move."

"I have a concert on Sunday at Symphony Hall. Rehearsal is tomorrow. I need to see someone after the rehearsal privately. So I need to get away with him without being followed."

Hoffman chewed his lip. "Who is it?"

"Eli Boor."

"The shrink?"

I nodded, wincing.

Hoffman thought for a moment. "He's in Dooley's report. He and Loquess looked him up as part of the Wallace investigation. What's he got to do with this?"

"I can't tell you."

"This will clear Dooley?"

I shrugged. "It might. Boor knows more about this sort of thing than any man alive."

"What 'sort of thing'?"

"I can't tell you that, either."

"Oh, yeah. This is easy. This is like shooting fish in a barrel," Hoffman said bitterly. "At midnight, blindfolded and without a gun. I can't do this."

"I just need to talk to him. An hour. No more, I'm sure."

"No," said Hoffman. "Give me something."

Dooley is innocent because he was possessed by a malevolent spirit that used to be part of my multiple personality disorder. I thought about telling him. I really did.

"Dooley killed Gifford," I said. "But he wasn't in his right mind. I know it. Eli can prove it."

"Ah, Christ. Oh, Christ." Hoffman covered his face with his hands. "This'll kill Tom."

"Dooley won't come in until he's talked with Eli."

Hoffman lowered his hands. "*Dooley* wants to talk with Boor?"

I nodded. "He'll turn himself in if you let him."

"That's a promise?"

"Yes."

"What do you know? You only met him yesterday!"

I stared at Hoffman. "We share a common affliction. That's all I can say."

"Okay." Hoffman looked at Pujol. "You know that if this goes south, both of us go down."

"Yeah," said Pujol, sighing. "Yeah. I know that."

Hoffman was silent for a moment. "You can't dodge a debt. I'm in."

"Yay," I said, channeling Dooley. "The next step in an incredibly complex plan doomed to failure."

oOo

A car rolled up at the end of the block while we were talking. Hoffman looked out the window.

"Yeah. That's the stakeout. Mixed group, too: a guy from BPD and a guy from Gloucester. Rush isn't leaving anything to chance."

"What did you tell Rush?"

Hoffman looked as if he were eating something sour. "I told him I got drunk with Tom last night. About Abe. Today I was hung over."

"What did he say?"

"He asked if I'd talked to my sponsor." Hoffman snorted. "Lies on lies—I haven't had a drop since my third wife left."

"You can tell him the truth after this is all over."

"Yeah. We'll see how *that* goes down." Hoffman took a deep breath and turned away from the window. "When you finish the rehearsal I'll be in the back. Look at me and I'll give you a high sign left or right as to which side you should exit."

"How will Eli know where to go?"

"I'll send him. You can exit out the back from the side I indicate. I can give you a corridor to that exit and just outside. After that you're on your own."

I shook his hand. "Thanks."

"Screw that," he said sourly. "If you can get Dooley to come in without me having to shoot him, we'll call it square."

Hoffman had parked a few blocks away. He'd already planned to escape out the back door and through the back neighbor's yard.

"They have a dog," I said.

"I have a gun."

Pujol spoke up. "No, you don't."

Hoffman looked venomously at Pujol. "Shows what you know. I'll manage." With that, he left.

Pujol and I looked at one another.

"With no arrest," he said, "what do you need me here for?"

"Want to go to breakfast with me? You can tell me how Guillermo Sabado knew your family and we can speculate endlessly about why your uncle hates my dad."

oOo

Pujol left before eight. I slept a couple of hours. Then, it was time to get to work.

I had three pieces I was playing with the Boston Symphony: the Brandenburg Concerto Number 6 and a new work by a composer named Ross. They were also doing the orchestral version of the Liszt Hungarian Rhapsody Number 2—which I loved to play as a solo piece. I had been exposed as a kid to an old video tape of *Rhapsody in Rivets*—a bunch of animals build a skyscraper with all the sound effects being the music. A grand romp, and that was the way I played it. But not yet with the BSO.

Ross had been commissioned to write yet another work for Conclave. He had chosen a piano tone poem about, predictably, witches and the Salem witch trials. For the last several years, I had seen several such commemorative pieces. "Isn't it terrible what we did to those poor, poor, misunderstood witches back before even our immigrant parents got here?" You can guess the drill. Like most commemorative pieces, they were uninspired. Big, grandiose works in G major without a dissonant note or minor key among them.

The Ross piece had the small benefit that it was more memorial than commemorative and at least contained a mournful tone that I liked. It was something to work with.

I only needed to freshen up on the Liszt and the Brandenburg. I hadn't played them in a few months but I still knew them pretty well. The Ross needed some attention.

I worked through the piece all afternoon, broke for dinner and then hit it again hard that night. I had it pretty well cowed by ten o'clock. Then, I knocked off. You work a piece too hard and it can get stale. I was going to go over it enough times at the rehearsal.

I called Eli. If it was too late he'd let the machine pick it up. Otherwise, he'd answer it or not, depending on his whim.

"Hello, David," he said when he picked up. "How are you doing?"

"Not so bad. What are you doing tomorrow?"

He paused for a moment. "Nothing terribly important, I suppose. Why?"

"I'm giving a concert on Sunday. Tomorrow's the rehearsal. I'd like you to come."

"A rehearsal?" He chuckled. "David, I can afford a real concert."

"I know. But I think you'd like what I've planned. Besides, it'll give us a chance to talk. There's no chance after a concert."

"True." Another pause. "I think that's a good idea. I've been meaning to call you. We have a lot to talk about."

I didn't ask him what about. I was afraid I knew

"Good." I gave him the time and then begged off further conversation, pleading a need for sleep.

I went out on the porch with the last of the Barrilito and sat on the wicker chair. The night was cool and clear but warm for October. The only lights I saw were coming into Logan so the witches were either not flying or flying in the dark.

I knew how that went.

I had watched Katelin for the last year. She'd been miserable. I admitted to myself I took pleasure in that. A sort of *look how well you do without me. See how important I am?* I saw now the truth of the matter. Maybe I had been important to Katelin. Maybe it had been me that messed her up. Not so much "how well you do without me" as "look what I've done to you." I looked hard at myself and didn't like what I saw.

I took the bottle back inside and put it up in the cupboard. I needed to get to sleep if I could.

Tomorrow I was going to have to figure out what to do.

Chapter 3.4: Saturday Morning, October 30

I woke up at seven without interruption. Katelin hadn't mysteriously appeared to wake me with forbidden sex and the police failed to pound on my door. I figured it might be a good day.

I made breakfast: coffee and a roll.

I put on shorts and my shoes for a run and went out on the porch. I stretched for a moment, then took off. Down the hill to the causeway and over to Stage Fort Park, followed all the while by a GPD cruiser. I ignored them.

I like running. I can't manage to think when I run. When I walk I'm always thinking about the music, what I'm going to do the rest of the day, how interesting the trees look and the state of the harbor. But when I run all I can think about is how to breathe, where to avoid the potholes and the cars.

I didn't stop until I'd passed through the park and was starting the return. That was a little over a mile. I slowed down for a minute, thinking about what was coming.

I didn't know how the conversation with Eli was going to go. But I had an idea it wasn't going to be what I expected.

oOo

I like to nail everything down the day *before* a rehearsal. That way I'm free to take advantage of interesting things that happen during the rehearsal itself. I already have my point of view on the piece so I'm free to look at other people's. Other musicians have different methods. That is mine.

I'd been reading a biography of Mozart but I was too antsy for that today with everything that was going on. But I needed to do *something*.

Music binds time. The time between the notes is as important, if not *more* important, than the notes themselves. I knew a painter when I was in France who liked to work up his initial studies from shadows. "The shadows," Mark had said, "are more important than the light. The absence of light defines where light can be." Maybe it's something like that.

I didn't want to fill the silence with brooding.

My parents had immigrated to America from Portugal. They had married late, not expecting children. Then, I had come along.

Like a lot of Portuguese and Italian immigrants, they wanted to grow a piece of home on their property. Olive trees don't make it through the New England winter but grapes do. Over the driveway and before the tiny detached garage, my father had built a grape arbor of pipe and wire. They had been growing there since long before I was born.

This variety had already lost its leaves and needed to be pruned. I went outside with the shears in hand.

The arbor was that small—perhaps twelve feet square. I hadn't pruned it since Dad had died so the vines had, naturally, knit themselves together in a blanket of thick woody stems. I started tracing out the branching.

Guillermo had taught me how to do this. It was one of the few places where our lives touched. I always wanted to be home from the hospital when the vines were to be cared for— Eli had never really appreciated it. From when I was tiny and just carried the tools, handing them Dad, to the point where we were working on trimming together, tracing out a particularly recalcitrant branch to determine if it was a keeper or just a leader that needed to be removed.

At the end of the job, we always had a monstrous collection of ropy branches lying in the driveway. At that point, Dad and I sat on chairs and quickly wound them together—almost braided them, actually. I never knew where Dad had picked this up. The final result was a bundle. Dad had built a small fire pit in the back yard. We put the bundle in the fire pit and lit it—usually at night. He and Mom would sit and drink wine. Our backs would be freezing in the cold fall air but our faces and hands would be warm from the burning branches.

When I finished I had the obligatory pile of branches on the driveway and the grape vines were in straight rows across the arbor. I knew how to bundle them up but without Mom or Dad, it seemed pointless. I stuffed them into garbage bags and put them out by the curb, then went inside, intending to shower and make an early lunch.

There was (inevitably) a knock on the door. I peeked through the window on the door and Pujol was waiting patiently outside holding a paper bag.

"What are you doing here?" I asked as I opened the door.

"Trying to repair Sabado/Pujol relations."

I chuckled. "Can't fix what you don't understand." I opened the door the rest of the way and gestured him in. "I'm getting in the habit of cooking for you."

"Yeah," he said dryly. "About that." He passed me on the way to the kitchen and sat the bag on the table. Out of it he brought bagels, lox, cream cheese, white fish and orange juice.

"Wow." I stared at the feast.

"I don't know what pianists have to eat before a concert."

"Not much. Usually just coffee and a roll."

"So you're not going to eat?"

"I didn't say *that*."

"Then, consider me an overachiever." He pointed to the chair. "Let's eat."

Pujol laid out the bagels and lox and everything else on the table. In a few minutes there was a pot of coffee on the stove that didn't smell like I'd made it.

We didn't talk much. We were too busy stuffing our faces.

Finally, I sat back. "The white fish was good. Lox, too."

"Direct from Pujol Fish."

"My compliments to your dad."

"I'll be sure and tell my uncle." He fell silent for a moment. "Okay. What's going to happen at the rehearsal?"

"I'm going to drag Eli away from Symphony Hall and meet Dooley. We're going to talk. Then, Dooley's going to turn himself in."

Pujol stared at me levelly. "It's not going to be just an hour like you told Hoffman."

"Likely not." I sipped my coffee. "But I think it will be all right. You're going to have to make nice to Hoffman. You're my lawyer, after all."

"I was thinking of letting you go as a client."

"Where would *that* put Sabado/Pujol relations?"

"Yeah." He drummed his fingers on the table. "You have a destination in mind for your rendezvous with destiny?"

I leaned forward. "I know the *Nonantum* is going to be at Aquarium Wharf about dinner time. I plan on sneaking Eli out the back door and downtown. If Hoffman can keep the police off us for an hour we'll be in the harbor."

"You're going to *escape?*"

I shook my head. "But the harbor is a good place to have a conversation without interruption. I hope, anyway."

Pujol drummed harder. "You're not going to be able to manage this without my help."

"I'll manage."

"No. You need me to keep Hoffman focused on our deal. So I'll be coming to the rehearsal as well."

"Suit yourself."

He pointed at me. "You have no idea what you're doing, do you?"

"Not a clue."

oOo

We put the leftover food in the refrigerator and then I booted Pujol out. I ran through some light drills to warm up. I worked through the Ross piece—just the highlights to refresh myself on the ideas I'd had last night. Then, I walked around Gloucester. Sure enough, a GPD cruise car followed me. I didn't mind.

The day had warmed and the crowds were out again. There were no flyers out this morning save those working through practicing the final events. I watched as a set of colorful flying flags shot overhead—the Czech team, I think— working out the kinks of the z-sprint. I half expected to see Katelin.

When I was a kid they demolished the crumbling docks surrounding Captain Jacobs Park and built the event piers.

The piers were big enough for a crowd of a few thousand—much smaller than the Garden or the stadium down in Foxboro. They had been built for the overflow from the Salem Gardens, built over the water in the eighties when Conclave had outgrown the high school. Boston, Foxboro—even Providence and Portland had tried to lure Conclave away from Salem. But Salem held onto it with steel fingers. They reluctantly shared event space with Gloucester only when they were utterly forced to the wall by lack of space.

I walked down to the Gloucester House and along the waterfront. I could only get within a couple of blocks of the piers without a ticket but it was close enough to see athletes coming and going. Some of the contestants waved at the crowd. We waved back.

I walked down Washington Street and made it to the station just as the inbound train was pulling in. Punctuality on the commuter rail isn't a virtue; it's a miracle. I took it as an omen things could conceivably turn out well.

oOo

Rehearsals at Symphony Hall are open to the public. They're a gift from the largess of previous generations. Years ago the elite thought listening to classical music might improve the riff-raff. Of course, they didn't want the people intruding into the actual concerts. Opening the rehearsals to the public allowed them to uplift the common people without associating with them.

All good ideas are diluted by time.

The ticket prices to the Boston Symphony Orchestra are malignantly expensive. The tickets to the rehearsals are merely damned expensive. Thus, uplifting the poor became uplifting the middle class. As far as the arts were concerned, the poor were on their own. Let them eat blues.

I shook hands with Levine and got to work.

The Liszt and the Bach didn't take more than a couple of hours or so to figure out. Levine and I saw the pieces pretty much eye-to-eye. We'd worked on them together. It was just a matter of running through the pieces and getting the kinks out. Then we played both of them through pretty much letter perfect.

The Ross piece was much more problematic.

It was a three-movement concerto form—allegro, adagio and allegro, all in D. But the sections were blended into each other. The first allegro started in D major but ended on a low E-flat minor chord that led into the adagio. The adagio had a slow blues progression that *begged* for some electric backup. But since Ross was a purist, all we had was the entire BSO. The adagio wandered in the fields for a bit before ending in E-flat major. That set the stage for a lively, if derivative, dance tune back in D major. I think his intentions were first movement: the new world. Bright future. Open vistas. All that sort of thing—Dvorak's New World Symphony revisited. Second movement, mourning what had happened to the witches and how that soiled the purity of the ideal—not that the Puritans believed in the American Dream or anything. Historical fact doesn't mean much to composers. Third movement was some kind of Hope Dance, a kind of *Triumph of the Will* in music but without the added complexity of the Third Reich.

I suggested to Levine that we weren't going to score any points just playing the piece. It wasn't good enough. So I figured we'd push a real performance down its throat. Sort of like seventies rock bands: the music wasn't that interesting but my-oh-my couldn't those guys *sing?* The thing was, the BSO had really good musicians and there were some fun, if not very challenging, parts for them to play. I wanted them to milk it along with me.

It's not easy to get a First Violin that's been playing the equivalent of lead guitar in the biggest conceivable rock band to actually act the part. Not that they don't have egos—we *all* have egos. When the FV stands up and plays out the long solo at the end of the Brandenburg's third movement, there's no shortage of strutting and posturing as he plays. But compared to the bumping and grinding of even a mediocre garage band, that FV looks lame.

But Levine and the BSO were willing to try.

We went through the highlights and then started at the beginning.

And it clicked.

The beginning was more or less straightforward. A quick theme in D major. Nothing interesting until the orchestra hands it off to me. That's when the piano introduces the blues riff.

I pounded it in place. Big, thick chords like blocks hammering down the keyboard. I saw the First Violin snap to as he figured out what I was going to do. I handed it off to the orchestra and they picked it up with enthusiasm. I just sat back rippling the keys while they shaped it back and forth and handed it off to the FV.

The FV lit into the theme like he was playing at Shea Stadium. He surprised me with an almost bluegrass feel. Bluegrass blues. Flatt and Scruggs plays James Johnson.

He handed it back to me.

This was the way of the whole first movement right up to that mournful E-flat.

I started out the second movement with the low, soft theme—like a lullaby, I thought as I played. A lullaby for the dead. I felt better for Ross.

It came to me halfway through the second movement, after I had given the theme to the orchestra, that the music applied to me and Katelin. The hopeful beginning. I'd never been that happy before, playing for Katelin in that cramped little apartment in Columbia. There had been a creek nearby. We'd had to cross an ancient bridge to get into the parking lot. A couple of times that winter we'd stayed home, preferring to snuggle in rather than chance a crossing.

If the first movement was our irrational joy, what was the second? The descent into the Valley of the Shadow of Death? That long decline into obsession for me and the drinking and misery of her? There had been hope for us—I realized that now. We had squandered whatever we had. It was gone forever.

The orchestra handed the theme back to me. I turned it inside out and began the third movement.

Right at the heart of the third movement was the only real inspiration in the piece, a blend of the blues riff in the first movement and the minor mourn in the second. It was a duet of a strong and simple theme reminiscent of a hymn or a folk tune backed up by a harmony that Ross had to have heard from some deep Southern gospel choir. The result was simultaneously lively and poignant, like a child singing a workchant amidst the dancing rhythms of textile machinery. I was convinced Ross had discovered this tiny theme and that had been the germ for the rest of the piece.

As I was playing, I thought of everything that had happened in the last forty-eight hours. To follow the metaphor to the ground—and if I was going to follow this piece down the rabbit hole there was no holding back—this movement had to represent unreasonable hope. Not the hope that we would ever get back together. That couldn't happen— I'd seen that in Katelin's eyes at the police station. This was the hope that something could be salvaged, that redemption was possible.

I handed it to the BSO. The BSO handed it to the First Violin. The FV took it and held on to it, half dancing himself as he fiddled it down. Then, we took it together, first me on the theme and him on the harmony, then me on the harmony and him on the theme. I stood up and brought it together with this long run up and down the keyboard as he held this high, high note impossibly long.

It came to me. I was going to save her. Our being together was no longer important. My obsession with her was no longer important. Who we had been to each other and my obsession had been of the past. The past was gone. I was going to save her *now*.

The BSO picked up the high note as I brought up the run from deep down in the bowels of the piano and we all came together in a great dissonant crash—which the FV almost immediately resolved. And I backed him up as the orchestra rearranged the chaos into that final major chord. We held it, faded on it and stopped.

There was *dead* silence in the theater.

Then, down in the audience applause erupted. People stood and whistled. Called out.

The FV, red and sweaty, smiled and waved at them. Levine leaned against the podium wearily. I looked out. I saw Hoffman, now. And Eli. In the back I could see Rush and he had some men with him.

Oh, yeah, I thought, suddenly depressed.

No. Stand up straight. Don't forget. You're going to save her.

oOo

Hoffman indicated stage left.

I shook Levine's hand, shook the hand of the First Violin. Smiled. Chatted. Tried to look at ease but at the same time tense. I confided privately to Levine that I needed to find the rest room. He nodded.

I exited stage left.

Eli was waiting for me there, confused.

"Come on." I grabbed his arm and we walked past the dressing rooms and prop areas, down the back stairs and out the alley door onto Saint Stephens Avenue.

I flagged down a fortuitous cab and bundled us in. We turned onto Mass Ave just as Hoffman and Rush were turning the corner. Rush looked furious, Hoffman dejected. Rush looked around and I dragged Eli down.

"Where to?" asked the driver.

"New England Aquarium," I said.

The cab turned onto Huntington and I chanced a look back. Rush was scanning the traffic but didn't seem interested in this particular cab.

Eli sat up slowly. "What was that all about?"

"The police are trying to keep an eye on me."

He smiled uncertainly. "This must have something to do with Katelin and that Officer Dooley that came to see me a few days ago."

"You could say that."

"Tell me more."

I was about to but then I remembered Dooley saying he wanted to be in on the conversation. "It'll have to wait."

"Until we get away," Eli said. He laughed. "I think I've waited my whole life for something this exciting. If I could yell 'follow that car!' my life would be complete."

I allowed myself a smile. "We'll see what we can do."

"What car?" said the driver in confusion.

"Never mind," I said. I pointed ahead. "New England Aquarium."

oOo

The New England Aquarium building housed one of the biggest captive animal collections on the Atlantic coast. But that wasn't what interested us. Next door were the Aquarium Docks from which whale watch, harbor tourist and night watch trips departed. It was near dark, now. The *Nonantum* would be boarding. Joey needed to get out of the harbor proper and up into Salem Sound and Nahant Bay before actual night fell. He would have to anchor and put up an identifying light to prevent collisions. Which meant leaving the docks very, very soon.

The cab reached the front of the Aquarium. I paid him and dragged Eli across the plaza and down the ramp. Sure enough, the *Nonantum* was boarding at the end of the dock. I waved.

Joey was wearing a suit—which I had somehow never expected.

"You know, I was hoping you'd show up," he said as we came on board. "I needed some entertainment on the trip out there."

"Beg pardon?" I stared at him.

Joey pointed towards the bow with his chin as he disconnected the gangplank. I looked in that direction and saw my electric piano set up.

He put his hand on my shoulder—a reach but he managed. "You have no idea how I filled up the boat when I announced you were coming."

"You didn't advertise, did you?" Suddenly nervous.

He shook his head. "Of course not. Word of mouth. Now you have an excuse to be here."

Joey moved forward. "Ready with the ropes," he called.

Dooley, in a tuxedo, moved smoothly past me, undid the stern rope and then moved forward to the bow.

"The police wanted to prevent *this*?" asked Eli.

"They're purists," I said. "They only want me to play the classics. No sense of adventure."

Chapter 3.5: Saturday Evening, October 30

Eli circulated while I played. Blues, mostly. A little Couperin and Saint-Saen. A Debussy or two. But I kept coming back to the blues. I wished I had a singer. Blues begs for a voice.

Once we were anchored in the bay Joey dimmed the lights to almost nothing—just a few faint lights around the deck to keep people from falling into the water and to help them find the snacks. Then, he put up a single dim green light and hushed us.

A moment later we were buzzed by a dim shape in the night—a laugh. A cry of pure delight. Then, there were two. Then, perhaps a dozen.

I watched the shapes—some carried faint lights. One woman—I *think* it was a woman—had painted her face and hands with glowing paint and liked nothing more than to hover over us and look down. Those that flew into the light had painted their faces as well: devil masks, skulls, blood.

This was Halloween and the witches were in flight.

Joey stood next to me.

"I never thought they would play with the boat," I said softly. "I thought we'd just be spectators out here. Not—participants."

"What's theater without an audience?" Joey said with a chuckle. "You should know that."

I looked at him. He was watching the witches flying with a big grin. "Just wait."

The witches were done with us for a moment. They chased each other in elaborate swirls—figure eights, circles, spirals.

A long bright filament trailed out behind one flyer, neon orange. Two others rolled out different colors. They spun around each other leaving an elaborate glowing braid hundreds of feet long across the water. They separated, doubled back on each other and rose vertically. The flyers were invisible; only the filaments could be seen.

The filaments started to pulse so that the light moved behind them. The flyers synchronized their speeds to the movement of the filament so that the light didn't appear to move so much as be created at one end and disappear at the other end. The circles and curves were now so tight that the only mark of the flyer was a break between the beginning of the filament and the end.

They came down to the water and looped horizontally. Then, the flyers rose, bringing the light with them in spring-shaped spirals. They interleaved, a complex triple helix reaching from the water high in the air, narrowing, nearly touching. Then, the light at one end seemed to stop. The remaining light was drawn up into the darkness, a diminishing thread until with a bright flash, it disappeared.

On the boat we breathed out in a collective sigh and applauded.

Then, high in the air, a star seemed to fall. It grew brighter as it fell until just before it struck the water, a flash and the concussion of an explosion.

I looked at Joey, confused.

"Flyers teamed with pyrogens and levitators," he said next to me. "A bunch of pairs—these guys have been practicing for this all year long."

Imagine intelligent fireworks: rockets that burned and sputtered, dancing together before the inevitable explosion, the sparks swirling together into patterns: mandalas, rivers, an occasional pixellated face or landscape. Once, perhaps a dozen flyers circled the boat, vertical fountains of sparks erupting behind them, reflecting in the water: *Nonantum* floated in an ocean of fire.

"These were the athletes that failed out of competition?" I said to Joey. "What could the winners do?"

Joey put his hand on my shoulder. "I think there's a lot of talent that comes that doesn't participate in the events. They come for this."

"I never knew."

"From shore it just looks like elaborate fireworks. You can't see the detail. They're not doing it for us. They do it for each other—we just happen to be convenient props they can have fun with."

I wondered if Katelin knew about this. Surely, she must. How could something like this not be known throughout the flyer community? On the other hand, how could something like this not be publicized across the world?

Joey seemed to read my mind. "It's not legal. If it were a real public event the FAA would have to step in. It only exists as long as it's under the covers." He sighed. "It'll get squashed some day. But hopefully not soon."

We passed perhaps an hour there. We paid no attention to anything but the flyers and their partners. Then, the fireworks tailed off and the remaining flyers were painted as figures: pterodactyls, bats, birds. From dramatic to subtle. *Fortissimo* to *pianissimo*.

He gave me a quick glance, then watched his clients. "This is going to fade over the next hour. You go on downstairs with Dooley and that guy you brought. I can manage things up here."

With that he stepped behind a big woman leaning too far back in her heels. He steadied her effortlessly. "Careful there, Mrs. Carstairs."

The woman murmured a rapt "thank you", never tearing her eyes away from the sky.

I snagged Eli and made my way to the cabin door. Dooley was waiting for me.

oOo

Dooley led us through a maze of provisions towards the galley.

"They eat all this?" I asked.

"This is for the whole weekend. Joey said he'd have to stock up again on Monday."

"Then they *do* eat all this?"

"The upper crust eats well."

Eli laughed, bringing up the rear. "Not that well," he said. "I never had dinner."

"Should have eaten the snacks out there," Dooley growled. "I worked on them hard enough."

We made it to the galley. Eli sat down and scooted over to the far end of the table.

I looked around. I knew how much work had gone on. This galley was *clean*. I had never seen it so clean.

Dooley caught my glance. "Joey's a slave driver."

"I can see that."

"Is there coffee?" asked Eli hopefully.

Dooley filled mugs for all three of us from the big coffee maker on the counter. "Okay," he said as he sat down and passed us our mugs. "Let's talk."

"I'll go first," I said. "Eli: I always thought the different personalities in my head were just in my head. Gerald, Amanda, Donald—they weren't real."

"I'm not surprised," said Eli.

"But they *were* real."

"You're not being precise enough, David." Eli sipped his coffee. "Personalities in a case of MPD case are very real."

"You're hiding things." Dooley measured his words, each word a tap on the table with his finger. "Don't. Be. Coy."

"Fair enough." Eli nodded. "You mean you were convinced the personalities of Amanda, Gerald and Donald were *limited* by your mind. For the longest time, David, so were we."

"Go on," I said. I leaned forward.

"Bohr brought the paranormal out of the closet and carefully placed it in the middle of the physical world. He didn't figure out how it *worked*, you understand, any more than chemists understood ionic bonds back in the time of Lavoisier. But Lavoisier didn't need to know about them to determine the constancy of mass, and Bohr didn't need a physical model to demonstrate the paranormal. He had his mother."

Eli leaned forward. "We don't know a lot more even today. Imagine Galileo having to demonstrate the principles of falling bodies but limited to chickens as his laboratory materials. Imagine Newton trying to formulate force equations limited to experimenting with goats. That's the position of paranormal physicists. If it wasn't for Bosch's work we wouldn't even have any of the tests."

"You have my sympathy," said Dooley sarcastically.

"I'm not complaining. I'm trying to provide context. The preliminary test is very good at spotting something we don't understand in people who have no idea what they've got. When we discovered David," he nodded at me, "we knew he was special. First, his tests results were variable, from sub-normal to off the charts. Often in the same day."

"I don't remember being tested that much."

"Remember the games we played? Word games? Games with pictures? Story games? They were all child versions of the secondary screening tests."

"Oh." It's an odd feeling to realize most of what you knew about your past was wrong.

Eli continued: "So we knew we had *something*. But we had no idea what it was. You see, there are two unique aspects of the paranormal. One is that it exists at all. How do you cause force to be applied to an object without an intervening medium? All other energy transfers require a medium—a lever, a wheel, steam, something—but not paranormal actions. It's all 'spooky action at a distance' under human control. The second is the way it consumes energy."

"That's why Katelin was always eating," I said.

"That's part of it. Certainly, paranormal activity consumes energy. Conservation of energy and conservation of momentum must be observed—that seems to be required of everything, even witches. And it's very true that paranormal energy transfer—*however* it's going on—seems to require that.

This is not a perpetual motion machine. But it doesn't all come from the witch."

"But Katelin's always eating—"

Eli waved it away. "I know it requires energy from the witch, but the witch can't supply enough. An Olympic bicycling athlete burns up more than half a horsepower in the time trials in a controlled environment and low speeds. That's the equivalent of a big ice cream sundae—two, really, since digestion is only about 50% efficient. Katelin expends that much energy flying ten minutes at forty miles an hour. Witchflying is more efficient than bicycling but not *that* much more efficient. And while Katelin needs more energy than most human beings, she doesn't need to eat the equivalent of a dozen sundaes a day. Not to mention other lower energy paranormal activities also require considerable food consumption by the witch. Martin believes that the energy required from the witch is to enable the energy transfer but does not execute the energy transfer itself."

"Where does the energy come from?" I swirled the coffee in my cup and tried to get my head around this.

Eli shrugged. "We're not sure. If you can effect an energy sink without an effecter it means you can probably effect an energy source the same way. It could be anywhere. I mean we *looked*. There's some evidence that the temperature drops in the local area of the event. Some geographical areas appear to be have more available energy than others, suggesting there is some sort of locality—"

"Bring us back to David," Dooley said quietly.

Eli stopped, startled. "Yes. Of course. We couldn't figure out if David had Multiple Personality Disorder or if he was housing parasitic paranormal intelligences."

"Excuse me?" I said.

"Intelligences that are composed of the same physical phenomena that comprise paranormal phenomena but require a human brain as a host." Eli looked at me crossly. "I can't put it much simpler than that."

"You weren't sure if Gerald, Amanda and Donald were real or not."

Eli nodded. "Right. On the 'real' side: when they were active your paranormal tests results dropped to normal or below. That doesn't happen with MPDs. On the 'not-so-real' side, you weren't manifesting an ounce of paranormal activity *other* than the personalities."

"Which is why you brought him to McLean," said Dooley.

"Exactly. Then, one day all three of them were gone. There was no evidence of any extra personalities whatsoever." Eli gave me an accusatory glance. "You just said you got rid of them."

Dooley turned to me. "There was a fourth personality: Misty."

"Yes." I had finished my coffee and found myself fiddling with the cup. "Misty came to me after I'd been in McLean a couple of years. She showed me how to play the piano."

"And how to get rid of the others," Dooley said gently.

"Yes."

"Eventually, you got rid of her, too." Dooley kept looking at me.

"Yes."

"Wait," interrupted Eli. "There was a fourth personality?"

"Right," I said. "And it's possessed Katelin."

Eli looked bewildered. "Against her will? That's impossible."

"Why not?" An edge crept into Dooley's voice. "Who's to say it can't happen?"

"I mean—"

"You had special knowledge about David, didn't you?" Dooley leaned forward, suddenly looking every inch a cop. "You knew there was something special about David long before you ran a test. A little bird told you."

"I don't know what you mean."

"Yes. You do. It's the horizontal whisky problem. If you weren't looking for David you would never have found him." Dooley stared at him for a long time. "Dr. Boor, it's time I met Martin Miegle."

Something happened to Eli's face. The expression, the set of the jaw, the skin around his eyes.

"Officer Dooley," said Martin Miegle. "How can I help you?"

oOo

It was the voice I'd heard on the phone a score of times. I'd never met him in person, but there was no doubt who I was looking at.

"Creepy. But not in a bad way," Dooley said with a low chuckle.

I looked at him questioningly.

"Something Loquess said about him."

Miegle didn't respond. He just watched us.

"You're like Misty?" I didn't know what to think.

Miegle shook his head. "No. I'm more like Gerald, Amanda and Donald. Misty is different from all of us."

"But you knew about Misty, didn't you?" asked Dooley.

Miegle nodded. "As part of my nature I could detect all four of them."

"So you released David knowing he had something like that in him?"

"No. After Misty helped David remove the other intelligences she managed to make herself undetectable. We accepted David's statement that he had removed them all. After that, he improved markedly. There was no reason not to release him."

"You didn't tell Eli about Misty?" I asked.

"No. He knows now, of course."

"Why not?" Dooley said idly, as if he were finishing off a list of questions on a checklist.

"It wasn't germane."

"Martin?"

He turned to me, his face quizzical and without any real feeling at all. "Yes?"

"What is Misty?"

"Like all of us, she is a self-organizing assembly of quantum Toffoli Gates in an unknown configuration."

There was a deep and sudden silence.

Dooley said, "I was sure you were going to say 'black lectroids escaped from the eighth dimension.'"

Martin said, "I don't understand." I just stared at Dooley.

"Come on! Another perfectly good movie reference just wasted on you guys." Dooley threw up his hands.

We continued to stare at him.

"All right," he grumbled. "Dr. Miegle—"

"Just Martin. I don't have any advanced degrees."

"—Martin, then. Here's what we know." Dooley walked Miegle through the entire set of murders, Dooley's own possession, Katelin's escape.

I added my own embarrassing history.

"What do you see that we don't?" Dooley finished.

"Interesting," said Miegle. "All of the subjects—Officer Dooley included—have high paranormal potential. That is

316

probably why they were chosen as subjects. I have never forcibly entered a host. Nor have I ever entered a child, so my experience here is limited. However, it is clear each murder served at least two purposes."

"Which are?" I prompted.

"The first is clear: to cover the tracks of what is happening. Clearly, Misty didn't want her activities traced before she was ready. She needed time to prepare the next vessel for entry. Both religion and tragedy can make a subject open to suggestion. In the case of Wallace and Rabbitt, the preparation appeared to be largely religious. The murder of Sean Gifford is what prepared Loquess. Are you religious, Officer Dooley?"

Dooley looked uncomfortable. "A bit."

Miegle nodded. "But not in the same vein as Wallace and Rabbitt. Any recent tragedies?"

"No."

"Interesting. I don't know Misty's constraints. Perhaps she didn't need to occupy you for long and that made it easier. Or you might have an easier accessibility than some others and require less energy. Or by that point she had become strong enough to force herself on you. But I knew Katelin, and she was emphatically not religious nor particularly susceptible to suggestion. Hence, the use of the murder of Sean Gifford as a tool, a shock, to open Loquess sufficiently for Misty to gain entry."

"She tried to force herself into me," I said.

Dooley looked at me. "What happened?"

"I didn't let her."

"Neat trick," said Dooley. "Wish I knew it."

"If I knew how I'd tell you," I said. To Miegle: "Why the hell is all of this happening?"

"For you, David," Miegle said mildly. "She wants to get back inside of you."

"What's special about *me*?"

Martin looked at me for a moment without speaking. "Isn't it obvious? You created her. You created all four of them."

oOo

I stared at him. "You're kidding."

Martin stared back. "I don't do that sort of thing. I never learned the knack."

"I *created* all four of them?"

"I think so, yes. My model of these entities is of self-organizing Toffoli Gates, as I mentioned before. But the energetics are incorrect. Once the gates are organized they can stay organized—and grow or change. But the model denies the possibility of that organization coming spontaneously into existence. For a long time I thought the flaw was in the model. I couldn't recall my own creation so I had no empirical evidence of how initial self-assembly occurred. Then, we met David." He nodded towards me. "Few can contain more than one parasitic intelligence, much less four. I concluded my model was correct but incomplete—it described the existence of the intelligences, either hosted or free living, but it could not in and of itself describe initial conditions and assembly. I've been working on extending the model for the last ten years—with some success."

I stared at him. I didn't know what to say.

He continued in his dry voice, showing what for him passed as excitement. "Consider these facts. The mere occupation of a vessel requires energy on the part of the vessel." Miegle gestured to himself. "Eli Boor is fairly well adapted to being inhabited by me. Even so, it causes

318

significant stress. He requires heart medication, a strict diet and at the same time a significant food uptake. Look what it did to Tim Rabbitt. Officer Dooley said it had a similar effect on him after barely a day. David, however, managed to house four intelligences at the same time without significantly increasing his energy expenditure. Looking at Wallace's scores, he may have had an even better ability to house an intelligence but created none. It also happened to make him psychotic—though it's possible Misty did that for her own purposes. David was never crazy even sharing his brain with four other people."

"Will I make any more?" I felt numb. If I had inadvertently created Misty, I was responsible for everything that happened. I was the alcohol in a drunk driver. I was the car. I was the enabler.

Martin shrugged. "As far as we can tell, you haven't. Eli has speculated that the creation of intelligences occurs during specific stages in childhood neural development—specifically when the neural pruning occurs around ages three and six. They grow from there."

"I did it to myself." And to Katelin.

Dooley leaned back. "You realize this changes everything."

Martin turned towards him. "How so?"

"Ever since the public first heard about paranormal abilities, they've been constrained to the physical world. Fire. Movement. Energy. That sort of thing." He pointed to Martin and then at me. "But now you've opened the box. Now we have evil spirits—"

"Come now, Officer Dooley!"

"—telepathy." He spread his hands. "Ghosts. What's next? Past lives? Prognostication? Reincarnation? Werewolves? Vampires?"

"We're hardly spirits."

"Disembodied beings with the ability to take control of the living. Sounds like demonic possession to me."

"Hardly scientific—"

Dooley shook his head. "Americans have, at best, an uneasy relationship with science. Until now, they've had an uncomfortable relationship with the paranormal that was enabled only by *science* telling them constantly how normal and explainable the paranormal was. 'Everything is explained by science. It's just that we don't have all the science.'"

"That's true."

"Now we find out that not only was science *wrong*, it *lied* to us. How's that going to play?"

Martin didn't say anything for a long moment.

oOo

"I believe Misty is looking for a permanent host," Martin said suddenly. "A free living... *spirit*—" he nodded towards Dooley "—has a rough life. Misty is quite a powerful entity as we have seen. It's quite possible that only someone with an equal aptitude—such as David—can house her without injury."

"Let's line it up," Dooley began. "David creates these parasites when he's a kid. He gets picked up by the police. Natick Labs is trolling for things like this and realize what's happened. Boor contacts David and manages to get him committed to McLean's instead of Roslindale where he, and the Army, can watch him. But it's not clear if David has MPD or parasites. That's the way of things for a while. David begets Misty—a super parasite. She knows more than the others. One of the things she knows is how to get rid of parasites. This is something she teaches David. David dumps his earlier parasites and keeps Misty. One of the other things Misty knows is how to lay low. She does and Boor and Miegle decide David's a dud and let him go."

"She taught me the piano," I said.

"And she teaches him the piano. In the annals of the miserable earth her efforts are duly enshrined." Dooley looked at us for a moment, then shrugged. "Time passes. David keeps Misty, thinking she's just a personality and he's just sick. He gets famous. Misty just hangs around—what does Misty want, Martin?"

Miegle shrugged. "I have no idea. Long life. Wealth. Happiness. Reproduction."

"These things can *reproduce?*" Dooley said, aghast.

Martin shook his head. "You must comprehend this about our understanding: we were wrong. I can't reproduce. No other intelligence I know can. But Misty is something different. She knows things. She has capabilities. Perhaps reproduction is among them."

"Now that's a nightmare I'd rather not see," Dooley said dryly. "To continue: David meets Katelin and falls in love. He dumps Misty. He gets together with Katelin. They live happily for a while, split up. Katelin becomes a drunk and David a pervert."

"Hey!" I yell. Dooley looked at me and I didn't say anything more.

Dooley went on. "Meanwhile, Misty floats around and hooks up with William Wallace—which drives him over the edge. Or she drives him over the edge on purpose—since religion seems to have some enabling effect. Wallace and Misty move to Boston. They follow Katelin around for years making their plans. They hook up with Rabbitt and convert him to a more intense form of Christianity—religion again.

They start up *Where's Katelin* to drag in David. They milk Rabbitt's church and sock away the money to a place only they know about it. Then, when the time is right, Misty bails on Wallace in a series of murders that are intended to ultimately snare David. Am I right so far?"

Miegle nodded. "I think this is supportable."

"But David's not so snareable. Turns out David has a trick up his sleeve: he *can't* be forced. Misty tries twice and fails twice. What's she going to do now?"

Miegle considered for a moment. "If David can't be a host, she'll have to find another one or perhaps try to make do with Katelin. I expect that won't last long. Katelin's not talented in that area. I would expect being occupied by Misty is taking a great toll on her."

"How long does Katelin have?" I wasn't sure I wanted to know the answer.

Miegle shrugged. "She has a strong talent for the paranormal as expressed in flight. So her ability to channel energy is good. How much of that talent Misty can repurpose to maintaining herself is an unknown. A week? Two weeks? Two years? I have no suppositions."

Dooley glanced at me, looked down at the table, looked back at me. "Wallace lasted two years and looked fine. Rabbitt looked like he'd been ridden hard and put away wet. How did Katelin look when you saw her?"

"Tired," I said. "Thin."

"It's only been two days."

"Two and a half."

"Fair enough." Dooley nodded. "I held her that long. I'm fine."

"It's not the same thing at all," Martin said. "From what you've told me, you, Wallace and Rabbitt just *housed* her. But

Misty is *using* Katelin, not just residing there. She's using Katelin's talent to fly. Whatever the base cost of Misty occupying Katelin it must be considerably less than Misty occupying Katelin, *and* flying her all over the city."

"Yeah," said Dooley, giving Martin a sour look. "Thanks for pointing that out." He thought for a moment. "Wait a minute. Something's not right." He pointed at Martin. "You let David go because you thought he was a dud. But you also said you had modified your model based on what you'd learned from David. You can't have it both ways. Something happened."

The shift in Martin's face happened again and Eli was watching us. He didn't say anything for a moment. Then, he leaned his elbows on the table. "We found Gerald, Amanda and Donald. That's what happened."

"Where are they?" I asked.

Eli grinned and rubbed his hands. "We have them."

"Who is 'we'?" Dooley asked.

Eli looked at him with a smile. "U.S. Army Laboratories in Natick, of course."

oOo

"You *knew* what was going on after all this time?" I half rose. "I thought I was crazy all these years and you knew I wasn't and didn't *tell* me? God *damn* you!"

"It wasn't that simple," Eli conceded. "We figured things out later. Gerald came sniffing around Salem a few years after you left town. You were in France. Once we found him, it wasn't hard to find the other two. They were happy to be found."

"Why didn't you tell me?"

"You seemed well enough. We didn't know about Misty — for all we knew you were happy and whole. Why change things?"

"I don't believe this." I was never crazy. Everything I had *known* about myself was a lie. All those times with Katelin, holding it together, trying to make her feel loved even when she was slipping away from me, trying so hard because I *knew* I was damaged goods. I *knew* that it was only a matter of time before something *else* in my brain would go wrong.

"Would you like to meet them?"

"Let's think on this," Dooley muttered. "Meet the ghosts David created that possessed him as a little kid. How about no?"

I didn't move. I felt like I'd be betraying myself if I did. "I'm surprised you're not blown up, set on fire or killed yourself."

Eli chuckled. "They're better adjusted now."

Dooley turned to me. "You're not considering this, are you?"

"I don't know," I said as honestly as I could. "Maybe they could tell us how to get rid of Misty. If Misty can't get in me, what could they do?"

"Gang up on you for one. Make you do what they want."

I shook my head. "I don't think so. Misty never made me do anything. She just told me what I should do. Like any kid, I did what the adult told me to do. If she couldn't force me to do something I don't think these others stand much chance."

"Like I said: we're in new territory."

I shrugged. "We're taking a risk."

"Do we have to go to Natick?" Dooley demanded of Eli.

"Oh, no," Eli said, rubbing his hands. "They're at my house. I had the Army bring them."

324

Dooley sighed and pointed a lazy finger at Eli. "You do know your house is being watched."

"Not anymore. Being connected to the Army has its perks. If everything went according to plan, my boss spoke to his boss who spoke to *his* boss, who spoke all the way downhill to *your* boss. I expect all of the surveillance has been pulled."

Dooley leaned against the hull and just looked tired. "Had we known *that*, none of this crap would have been necessary."

Eli smiled sweetly. "My heart bleeds for you, Officer Dooley."

Chapter 3.6: Sunday Morning, October 31

The show goes on.

Joey's permit expired at midnight so we hauled up anchor at eleven and steamed over to the Salem docks. Dooley tied us off and together we put down the gangplank.

Joey came down from the wheelhouse and watched as we shepherded the few guests besides ourselves that were disembarking here. Then, he shook my hand.

"Let me know how this turns out," he said, gripping hard with twenty years of handling nets. "And don't be such a stranger. You're a lot more likeable since you grew up."

"You, too." I grinned and gripped back. Twenty years of six hours a day practice made it no contest.

He yelped and pulled back his hand, laughing.

Eli had a car waiting for us. It was, not surprisingly, big and black and driven by someone in uniform.

"I didn't know you were this important," I said as we got in.

"It's for Martin," he said. "He likes the show."

Eli's house was only a few blocks away and we were in the car, down the street and out again too quick to notice. Then, inside the house I'd known so well. In the main foyer—the big staircase in the front, the white banister across the second floor above us, through the hall and in front of the study. The doors were closed. I stood in front of them, unmoving.

"Go on in, David," said Eli gently.

I could hear them muttering—no. Not hear, exactly. Feel them? Smell them?

I opened the door and stepped inside.

Two attendants were playing on the floor with a middle-aged woman, her mouth open and drooling. An old man stood at the window, the right side of his face, his right arm and leg, all slack as he leaned against a chair, watching us enter. A young boy, a grotesque scar on the side of his head, sat on a chair, rocking, his hands clasped tightly around his knees, his eyes screwed tightly shut.

Eli touched me gently on the elbow. "Can you see them?"

And it was like suddenly recognizing a figure in a painting or seeing the design crystallize out of a mosaic.

Gerald was leaning against the chair, his right side slack. Amanda looked up from the game she was playing. Donald was watching me even though the boy's eyes were so tightly shut.

I saw them in spite of the bodies they wore.

"Hey," I said.

"Hey," slurred Gerald. Amanda grunted but Donald clearly said "Hello".

"What happened to them?" Dooley asked.

"Mrs. Burgess was in a persistent vegetative state when we found Amanda. Mr. Shale was in a stroke-induced coma. Billy shot himself playing with a gun. They were all permanently damaged. Brain dead, as it were." He glanced at me. "You didn't think we'd use real, living people, did you?"

I shook my head. "I didn't know what to expect."

"Well, not *Night of the Living Dead*," said Dooley softly. "That's for sure."

Eli ignored him.

We communicated as we had when I was little, with never a spoken word.

You're a son-of-a-bitch, snarled Donald. *Casting us out like that!*

It was my home, I said in return. *Not yours.*

We belonged there. You said we could stay, Gerald said reproachfully.

What does a five-year-old know about commitments to disembodied voices?

Point taken, laughed Amanda.

I have a proposition, I said.

They gave me their attention.

I'm going after Misty. I'm taking her back inside whether she wants to or not and I'm going to hold her here. Will you help me? I can't do it alone.

That bitch! Donald shook his head.

Donald, please. It's monotonous. Gerald looked at me. *How much chance do you have with our help?*

I have no idea. She's stronger than she was. I'm hoping I am, too.

Amanda watched me quietly. *And we'll have a place with you?*

For better or for worse. In sickness and in health. As long as I live.

I reached out my hand. Gerald tottered over and took it. Donald grasped it without looking up. Amanda gave a bubbly laugh and reached up from the floor.

I took their hands and reached across, drawing them inside.

The boy and the woman on the floor collapsed. The old man seemed awake for a moment. Then, he clutched his chest and fell. His breathing rattled a moment and then stopped.

I turned to Eli and Dooley.

"What did you do?" Eli stared at the bodies on the floor, then at me. "What did you do?"

"I brought them home."

A horn honked outside. I looked outside. Pujol was standing beside an amazing sports car. I'd never seen the like.

Dooley was standing next to me. "1978 Lotus Europa, like I said."

I turned to him and he looked at me sheepishly.

"Hoffman told me who to call," he said and shrugged. "If it's my last night as a free man…"

The car was powder blue and low slung to the ground. It looked like a big cat waiting to run.

"Sweet," I said.

"What are you going to do?" Eli screeched at us.

"We're going hunting."

oOo

Eli didn't like it but fuck him. Pujol didn't like it either but he could only advise me, so fuck him, too. I told him where my important papers were. For his part, Dooley told Pujol, "Ask Pop. Hoffman knows where to find him."

Then, it was a screaming run down 128, then I-95, left on I-93. Some traffic—even at two in the morning, there's always some traffic in Boston. In the wee hours of Halloween on the last day of Conclave there might have been a bit more. There might have been cops on the road that had been told to watch for us; there might not have been. There weren't any cops that could have *caught* us.

"Where are we going?" Dooley yelled over the roar of the engine.

Where to? I asked.

Not sure, said Gerald. *South?*

You're guessing, said Donald.

Can't you feel her? said Amanda. *Go where the other flyers are—that's where she is. She loves to fly.*

"Chinatown," I said, my teeth clenched. Dooley's driving was going to kill us all. "The party always moves down into Chinatown.

"Figures," Dooley said. "I even know a place to park."

Dooley pulled out red light with a magnet and, at ninety miles an hour, slipped it onto the roof. It took hold with a clang.

"Damn it!" he yelled. "I just had her painted."

The traffic was thickening as we crossed the river but the lights cleared the way.

"Good thing," he said in my ear. "I don't have a siren in this thing."

I didn't have breath to reply.

oOo

Dooley found an alleyway I had no idea existed. The Lotus fit just behind the dumpster and couldn't be seen from the street.

"How did you find this place?"

"I didn't. Misty did."

It took me a moment: Katelin. Sean Gifford.

Dooley saw it on my face. He grimaced. "Yeah." He popped the hood and pulled something round with dangling wires. "At least nobody's going to hotwire it," he said as he put it in his pocket. "Where now?"

We weren't sure.

Outside and around the corner, Kneeland Street was jumping. Every store was open—a grocery store, its windows papered with huge and indecipherable Chinese symbols, each symbol given unintelligible emphasis by a string of exclamation marks. The grocery was flanked by a butcher shop, naked chickens hanging lewdly from stainless hooks. The bakery had a line out the door and I saw stacks of almond cookies shaped like witches on brooms.

That made me think of Katelin and I looked up.

A woman was hanging from a long wooden pole perhaps fifteen feet in the air. She spun around the free-floating high bar doing giant loops, streamers tied to her feet, a continuous human spiral. Jugglers were everywhere. Anything could be juggled—I saw one man, bent and sweating, ponderously maintaining three cinder blocks in a simple fountain. I gave him a wide berth. He didn't notice.

And the *noise!*

Gongs. Bells. Firecrackers. Whistles. Long plastic horns. Drums. There were at least a dozen people singing different songs and across the crowd I could hear, but not place, the thin voice of an oboe.

The merchants had set up tables in the street. Next to the usual T-shirt hawkers and souvenir sellers, there were Chinese herbalists. Next to *them* were hucksters selling every possible way to increase your paranormal talent: magic words, crystals, wire rings, complex electronic machinery, rays, beams, glowing water, juices, oils, sexual methods, methods of sexual abstinence.

Dooley saw her first. She was standing in the shadow of a billboard advertising some Broadway show. I could barely make her out—I couldn't believe Dooley saw her.

But she leaned out and the spotlights and lasers against the building across the street lit her face. Thin. Green in the reflected light. Then red. Then orange. She looked haunted.

It was Katelin looking down at me. Not Misty. For that moment, whether Misty was busy or whether the two of them were united in some shared misery, I saw Katelin's face as if I was using a telescope. And I remembered her lying next to me at night, her sharp features softened in sleep, but still able to open me up and lay me bare. I could never hide from her. I remembered at that moment why I had needed her, why I had felt lost when I left.

Why I felt lost still.

She saw me and stepped back in the shadows.

We reached for her, all four of us, but I heard Misty laugh. I saw her now—she looked *nothing* like Katelin. A narrow, cruel face, a mocking smile.

"Oh, lover. *Now* you want me."

She shot off the roof like a rocket.

"Crap," said Dooley. "Now what?"

oOo

We couldn't catch her, I said.

Are you so surprised? Amanda said. *You were only able to cast us out or house us. You were never able to force us to do anything. Nor could we force you.*

It came to me that maybe I couldn't hold her. Not for long. *Where is she?* I asked.

No one answered. Then, Amanda repeated: *she loves to fly.*

"Exchange Place," I said to Dooley.

"Is that where she is?"

"If she isn't there now, she will be." I looked up. "Katelin's favorite building."

"You have a plan?"

"I have a plan. I'm going to need you."

Dooley grinned at me. "It's good to be needed."

Congress Street was only a few blocks away. We forced our way out of the crowd and ran between the buildings. There was nothing unique about Boston's financial district; they look the same the world over.

We stopped at the night entrance.

"Get us in," I said to Dooley.

He looked back at me. "How?"

"You're a cop. You should know these things."

"How should I know—"

"A *detective* would figure it out."

He gave me a nasty look and walked up and rang the afterhours bell. When a voice came through the grill he looked around and found the camera. "Hey there," he yelled. He held up his badge. "We need immediate entrance to this facility."

"This is after hours—"

"There is a felony happening in this building at this very moment and this is hot pursuit. Check my badge and let us in."

"Hold on a second."

A minute passed and a harried-looking middle-aged black man came to the door. "What the hell do you want here at four in the morning?"

"Crime never sleeps," I said.

"And who the hell is he?"

"This is my associate, Mr. Sabado. He is assisting me in this apprehension. Now let us in."

"He better have a goddamned badge before he gets the hell in—"

The door was glass. Dooley tapped it carefully, pulled out his gun and shot through it.

The guard cried out and hit the floor.

"Don't kill him!" I yelled.

"Of course not!" He hauled the guard up. "You okay?"

The guard had his eyes tightly closed. He felt his chest, stomach and groin, then opened his eyes. "I'm not dead?"

"Not yet."

"You better be damned glad I got a good heart!"

"We are." Dooley looked at me. "Where are we going?"

"The roof. Where else?"

"Yeah," said Dooley. "Where else, indeed. Come on." He pushed the guard to the elevators and we went up. Elevator music had never been so disturbing.

"This," Dooley declared, "is starting to get weird."

"That's for damned sure," said the guard.

On the top floor, the guard led us to the door to the roof. Dooley took his keys. "You go on downstairs and call Boston Police Department. Get Albert Hoffman and John Rush. Got that?"

The guard nodded, swore under his breath and started back to the elevator.

"Let's go," Dooley said.

"Give me the gun," I said.

"Hell, no. You can't hit anything with it."

"I know she won't get shot if I'm holding the gun."

"What if she shoots *you*? Did you think of that?"

"No," I said slowly. "But it doesn't make any difference. Give me the gun and we'll put this whole thing to bed."

Dooley looked at me with agony on his face—the same pain that I'd seen on Hoffman's. What is it about cops and their guns?

Finally, he gave it to me. I put it in my jacket pocket. "Do you have any others?"

Sourly, he pulled out a smaller gun and a knife

I stared at them. "There ought to be a movie reference here somewhere."

"There are," he said. "Hundreds."

"Okay. Let's go up."

oOo

The roof of Exchange Place was broad and flat, studded with misshapen pipes and machines and no edge to speak of. We stepped out on it. The gravel ground together and pressed into the asphalt top. It smelled of rain and chemicals. The wind, nonexistent on the street, was stiff up here—not enough to pick a fight but burly enough to push you around. The roof was lit with blinking aircraft lights and the dim lamps from adjacent buildings.

"What now?" Dooley whispered.

"We wait. She'll be here."

The wind was cold and we stood near heater exhausts to keep warm.

"Are you sure she's going to show?" Dooley said, rubbing his hands.

"She'll show."

In the distance we heard sirens.

"She better do it quick." Dooley gestured towards the sound. "They're coming for us."

"She knows that."

"Knows what, lover?" Katelin said twenty feet above us.

"Hi, Misty." I looked up.

I couldn't see Katelin clearly when it was dim, but she was lit clearly every few seconds in garish green and red by the aircraft lights. She was thinner. Her wrists looked bony and her face was hollow. In the red light she looked like some ancient crone. All she needed was a broom.

"You didn't know what you had here, lover," she said, twisting in a slow circle. "This one's special."

"I know that."

"I may just keep her."

"You can't," I said, trying to keep the edge out of my voice. "Not for long."

"True." She sighed. "But what a ride. Why are *you* here?"

"What do you want?"

"You know what I want."

"Yeah. I do." I took a deep breath. "You never asked me. You tried force and you tried seduction. But you never actually asked."

She didn't say anything for a moment. "You threw me out."

"So?"

"You didn't want me!"

"You don't know what I want. We spent twenty years together, closer than anybody. You don't just quit wanting someone because you throw them out."

She banked away and came back, a cat not sure of its welcome. "This is a trick."

"In a way. If I have you, no one else is going to die. That's got to stop."

"Do you hate me?"

"No." Astonishingly, it was true. For all she had done—done to her victims, done to Katelin, done to me—I didn't hate Misty. It was like having a crazy sister or brother or wife. They might do terrible things but they *are* crazy, and no matter what, they remain your sister, brother or wife.

She drifted down to me. "We can live well. I stashed Rabbitt's money in an island account. I know the numbers—all we would have to do is claim it."

"That's a relief," I said. "This is going to cost me my career. It's nice to know I won't starve."

"You won't starve. It'll be great. Better—*much* better—than before. *I'll* be better."

I held out my hand.

Tentatively, she reached for me.

"I knew you would forgive me," she said.

I tried to grab her hand but missed.

She pulled back. "It's a trick. I should have known." She backed away, rising slowly. "Take a good look, David. You'll never see her again."

Misty started to take off.

I ran after her, reached the edge of the building and jumped, caught her.

She cried out and tried to right the stick, holding us both in the air.

All four of us grabbed *her* and yanked her inside. Misty screamed.

"Come on, Katelin. Wake up!" I yelled in her ear. Then, I let her go.

I held the four of them now. Both hands. Arms. Nothing now between me and the ground below.

It felt like I was flying.

oOo

Time slowed down—I wondered if Katelin ever experienced this. I don't think I'd realized my plan until the moment I did it—though I must have conceived of it, came up with it and executed it. Surely on some level I must have known I was going to do this. I thought over what had brought me here. Falling was the inevitable conclusion from where I started.

Inside, they were all screaming at me: Donald, Amanda, Gerald and, of course, Misty. I closed my eyes and stopped listening to them.

Then I was jerked suddenly. I opened my eyes.

Katelin had grabbed me by the collar of my coat and was trying desperately to slow me down. I looked down, looked at the building rushing by.

It's not going to be enough, I heard Donald say.

I had a sudden vision of all of us lying there on the ground, broken for my mistake.

Okay, then.

I pushed out everybody but Misty—Gerald, Amanda, and Donald cried out as they left. Then, I spread my arms wide and raised them. I slipped through the coat like a rocket. Katelin went tumbling above. Misty screamed at me.

Okay, then.

I held on to Misty. Hard. With everything I had. Whatever happened was going to happen to both of us.

I was never letting go.

Epilogue: Katelin, Christmas, 1999

My father stared at me from across the restaurant Formica.

He played with his cup of coffee. I looked around the room.

As I promised, I'd brought Sandy home to her folks in Sedalia. After that I came directly here. Mattie had been right. There were many bridges to rebuild and the first one had to be to my family.

My father and I were meeting in what could only be called a neutral venue: Ernie's Restaurant in Columbia. Ernie's wasn't in Jeff City and I didn't live in Columbia anymore. For better or worse, I was now a Boston girl.

"What happened then?" Dad leaned forward from his side of the booth.

I toyed with my soda—no more alcohol for me. "I tumbled against the building, broke my shoulder and collar bone, fell about forty or fifty feet before I managed to get some kind of lift. David hit the ground from at least twenty stories—that's how high we were when he slipped away. I managed to bring myself down beside him. He was still breathing, barely. I had no idea what to do—how do you give CPR to a broken doll? Then, he stopped. As carefully as I could I started breathing for him—I kept doing it, too, until the EMTs got there. We did it in shifts—me, Hoffman, Rush and Dooley. The EMTs took over. Shocked him. Injected his heart. But it was no use."

"Do you think he planned it as a suicide?"

"Suicide? David?" I shook my head. "I'll never really know, of course. Dooley said he was as surprised as I was. I think it was pure impulse—he was trying to save me and that's the only way he saw to do it."

"Did any of them live?"

"Eli said they found Gerald and Amanda. Donald is still missing as far as we know—even Gerald and Amanda don't know what happened to him. Maybe he didn't survive. Maybe he thought hanging around was a bad deal. Martin tells me he could detect no sign of Misty."

"He couldn't before when she wanted to disappear."

"True enough."

"What about David?"

"What do you mean?"

Dad pushed the spoon through his coffee a couple of times. "I mean if *they* could live, why not David?"

I nodded. "Yeah. I wondered about that, too. Martin said he couldn't detect him either. But like you said, Martin never knew Misty was there before. Maybe he wouldn't be able to detect David. Maybe both of them were flitting around." I shook my head. "But I don't think either of them survived."

"Why not?"

"David created all four of them and cast them out without ever knowing what he was doing. When he was falling, he was able to release Gerald and the rest and hold onto Misty. That's what Gerald told me, anyway. At that point, he knew who he was and what he was capable of. I think he held on to Misty until the very end. Martin says that would be the end of her. Martin says as far as he knows the 'intelligence', as he calls it, disintegrates along with the death of the host. David was lot of things and stubborn was one of them. So if she survived, I believe he did, too. And if *he* survived, I don't think much of Misty's chances."

"How would Martin know?"

"He's been through it before. The first was with Niels Bohr's mother in 1930. Then, with Herbert Bosch in 1970. Now he's with Eli." I sipped my soda. "That's why he's never stuck with a host until the end."

"Martin was wrong before."

"I know."

We didn't say anything for a bit.

"I was worried about you when I heard about all that business in Boston."

I looked at him. Peter Loquess looked old—brown hair now gray. Lips thin and pale. Wrinkles around his eyes. I thought for a moment and realized he had passed sixty—I never thought about him getting old. I never thought about him losing his strength. I never thought about him worrying about me.

I put my hand out on his hand. "I'm okay, Dad."

The moment stretched, and then we pulled our hands back at the same time, noticed it. Both of us chuckled.

"Martin wanted to clone David," I said.

"No! What did Eli say?"

"Eli asked me to have David cremated. Just to make sure."

Dad laughed. Then stopped. "I'm sorry."

I smiled at him. "Don't be. It's funny. I've come to the conclusion that a lot of my life is funny."

Dad thought about that but didn't seem to come to any conclusion he liked. "What was all that stuff I saw in the news? 'David Sabado implicated in serial killings. Officer Katelin Loquess questioned.' It doesn't fit the story you just told me."

I ticked off what happened on my fingers. "Natick Labs didn't want any of the research they'd been doing or anything at all about paranormal 'sprits' to get out. So they didn't want anything about Misty published. BPD didn't want anything to get out either—after all, one of their own had been possessed and committed murder. That left David."

"That's where the 'person of interest' came from?"

"Can't prosecute the dead. They can't in all fairness attribute the murders to him either, since there could be no case. Consequently, they just said he was a POI and that the murders were over. They let the reporters make up the rest."

"You didn't correct them."

I watched him levelly. "No. I did not."

"How come? David is going to be remembered as another Jack the Ripper."

"Yeah." I held my hands around my soda. "I thought about that. But David has no family left. Those close to him—me, Joey, Dooley, Roger—know the truth. I thought about what David would want. Would he want Dooley to face an investigation for a murder committed by his hands but not by him? Would he want Joey go to jail as an accessory after the fact in that murder or Roger be disbarred before he even has a chance to practice? Would he want me to be looked on as the penultimate repository of a killer spirit?" I shook my head. "No. I don't think he would. He saved me. I think he would have saved all of them, Misty included, if he could have."

"There could be thousands of these things out there."

"I think there probably are. Most of them are just little bits of shed impulses and ideas floating around that latch onto us. A few are like Martin, Gerald and the others. Martin had never even conceived of something like Misty. He thinks that for every Misty there must be a David. They can't find the Mistys so they look for the Davids."

"Have they found any?"

I shook my head. "Not so far. They tested David for years. They knew his signature on the preliminary and secondary tests to the decimal point. But so far they haven't found a match."

Dad nodded. "You know why I asked you to come home, don't you?"

"Sure. We can go with *asked*." I smiled at him. "You think I'm crazy living in that house."

"It's the house of your dead ex-lover. It's the house of your dead ex-lover who was possessed by the evil spirit that possessed you and killed three people including both your lovers. The public only knows you moved into the house of your dead ex who happens to be the Person of Interest in a string of serial murders. You can pick your story." Dad pointed at me. "People are going to think you're strange."

I laughed. "I know it looks that way. David left it to me. Along with a fair amount of money. But you know? I like the house and now I'm going to need it."

"I don't understand."

I pointed to my belly.

Dad looked confused for a moment. "Oh, my god."

"Possessed women forget to use birth control," I said. I patted my stomach. "Nine weeks and counting."

"I don't know what to say."

"Say: Congratulations."

"You're keeping the baby?"

"Why not?"

"Martin wanted to clone David. You're going to have David's baby." Dad spread his hands, unwilling to complete the thoughts.

I shook my head. "It's my baby and I'm keeping it. I'll deal with the consequences of that." I leaned my elbows on the table and ran my fingers over the Formica. "I was broken. So was David. It messed up what we had. I destroyed whatever I had with Sean on my own. But I don't feel broken any more. I feel like David gave me a gift and I can't turn it down." I looked out the window. "Besides, I think it would break Dooley's heart. He wants to be the godfather."

"Boy or girl?"

I shrugged. "I'm going to be surprised."

"Ah." He fiddled with his coffee. "Can you still do police work?"

I shrugged again. "I'm still flying. I'm still doing surveillance. I'm not doing pursuit work, but Sniezek has flown with me a few times. He's not bad once you get past the asshole part. I should be able to keep that up until spring. At some point I'll go on maternity leave. I'm not sure I'll come back to the department after that full time—or at all, for that matter. Sniezek was right about me in one way: police work will never be the number one priority for me like it is for him. Eli said Natick Labs would love to work with me, and they have terrific child care benefits." I smiled. "He said he made them up on the spot."

"You'd work with them after all this?"

I didn't say anything for a moment. "As you said, I don't *know* Misty's not out there. And this is David's child, and David created four personalities before he was six. Who knows what our child could do?" I paused. "There's something else. It's an awful big coincidence that Misty had sex with David *once* and became pregnant. It's not like it couldn't happen—I wasn't using birth control after Sean left and my body works just fine. But still—" I leaned forward on the table. "What if she planned to get pregnant?"

Dad leaned back and blanched. "To... what? Create a new nest, a new host to live in?"

"Yeah. Whatever I'm carrying, Eli's group has techniques and equipment to look for such things. It's a deal with the devil, but the devil has something I want." I shook my head. "But I'm trying to be optimistic. I'm going to keep thinking of it as David's baby unless I find out otherwise."

Dad didn't say anything for a moment. "You did cremate him?"

"Absolutely." I laughed again. "Oh, you should have been at the funeral. It was a circus. There were all these fans of David that showed up and all of these people who were protesting that he shouldn't be buried in a proper church graveyard. Tim Rabbitt's sister Bonnie showed up—"

"*Bonnie* Rabbitt?"

"Makes you a little ill, doesn't it?"

Dad nodded. "Oh, yes."

"And there were these grifters trying to figure out how to get Rabbitt's church money. They figured me or Bonnie still had some of it—sorry fellas. BPD's financial forensics group finally found it and gave it all back. But some of them needed convincing. Dooley helped."

"Have you picked out a name?"

"Not a one. Believe me, if he or she takes after either one of us I'll find out pretty quickly what to call her."

Dad looked out the window for a moment. "You make it sound like a happy ending."

"Five people dead, two of them people I loved? Hardly." I sipped my soda. A root beer. How was I going to get through the next year without coffee? "Dad, David *saved* me. For all the crap he put me through, for all the crap I put him through, for all the amazing *shit* that crazy stalking ghost-bitch did to *both* of us, he didn't let me down. He came after me and he gave his life for me. I can't ignore something like that. I won't *let* myself be miserable. It's not allowed."

Dad fiddled with his coffee. "Pretty cold comfort."

I gave him a completely feral grin. "Welcome to Witchlandia."

Acknowledgements

No work by any author is accomplished alone. There are thousands of hands that help to stir that soup. Far too many for this page. Still, there are a few that deserve special consideration.

First and foremost are my wife and son, Wendy and Ben. Nothing would have happened but for them. This book's for you.

Second is the Cambridge SF Workshop who made sure I stayed on an even course. All deviations are my own, of course. The workshop gave me the stars to steer by even if I wasn't always smart enough to follow them. Thanks to Heather Albano, Brett Cox, Alex Jablokow, James Cambias, Jim Kelly, Ken Schneyer and Sarah Smith. Madeleine Robins belongs here, too, for starting me down the tracks.

Third is Vonda N. McIntyre. If it wasn't for her, this metaphorical book would not be in your not-so-metaphorical hands. Thanks be to Vonda.

Credits

Welcome to Witchlandia
Steven Popkes

Book View Café 2019
ISBN: 978-1-61138-821-3
Copyright © 2019 Steven Popkes

Cover illustration © 2019 by Wendy Zimmerman

Production Team:

Cover Design: vikncharlie & Wendy Zimmerman

Copy Editor: Shannon Page

Proofreader: Shannon Page & Madeleine Robins

Formatter: Steven Popkes

About the Author

Steven Popkes lives in Massachusetts on two acres of land where he and his wife garden, grow bananas and breed turtles. His day job consists of writing support software for space and ballistic systems. He insists he is not a rocket scientist. He is a rocket engineer.

About Book View Café

Book View Café Publishing Cooperative (BVC) is an author-owned cooperative of over fifty professional writers, publishing in a variety of genres such as fantasy, romance, mystery, and science fiction.

BVC authors include New York Times and USA Today bestsellers; Nebula, Hugo, and Philip K. Dick Award winners; World Fantasy Award, Campbell Award, and RITA Award nominees; and winners and nominees of many other publishing awards.

Since its debut in 2008, BVC has gained a reputation for producing high-quality ebooks, and is now bringing that same quality to its print editions.

www.bookviewcafe.com
Book View Café Publishing Cooperative
P.O. Box 1624, Cedar Crest, NM 87008-1624

www.ingramcontent.com/pod-product-compliance
Lightning Source LLC
Chambersburg PA
CBHW032134190626
46814CB00005BA/1688